Toward the Dawn

Books by Mary Conneały

THE KINCAID BRIDES

Out of Control

In Too Deep

Over the Edge

TROUBLE IN TEXAS

Swept Away

Fired Up

Stuck Together

WILD AT HEART

Tried and True

Now and Forever

Fire and Ice

THE CIMARRON LEGACY

No Way Up

Long Time Gone

Too Far Down

HIGH SIERRA SWEETHEARTS

The Accidental Guardian

The Reluctant Warrior

The Unexpected Champion

BRIDES OF HOPE MOUNTAIN

Aiming for Love

Woman of Sunlight

Her Secret Song

BROTHERS IN ARMS

Braced for Love

A Man with a Past

Love on the Range

THE LUMBER BARON'S DAUGHTERS

The Element of Love

Inventions of the Heart

A Model of Devotion

WYOMING SUNRISE

Forged in Love

The Laws of Attraction

Marshaling Her Heart

A WESTERN LIGHT

Chasing the Horizon

Toward the Dawn

The Boden Birthright: A CIMARRON LEGACY *Novella* (All for Love *Collection*)

Meeting Her Match: A MATCH MADE IN TEXAS *Novella*

Runaway Bride: A KINCAID BRIDES *and* TROUBLE IN TEXAS *Novella* (With This Ring? *Collection*)

The Tangled Ties That Bind: A KINCAID BRIDES *Novella* (Hearts Entwined *Collection*)

A Western Light ⋆ 2

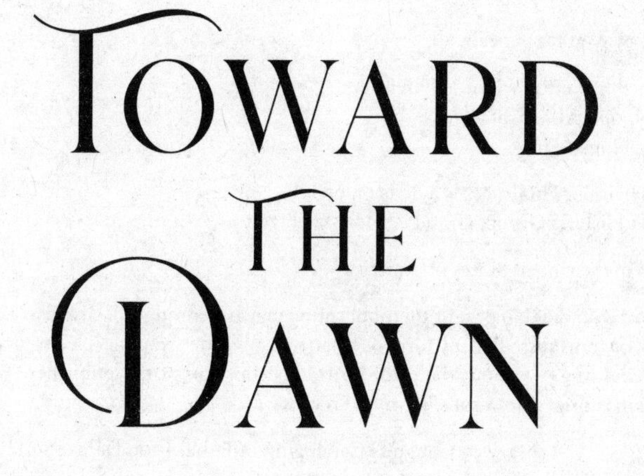

Mary Connealy

a division of Baker Publishing Group
Minneapolis, Minnesota

Published by Bethany House Publishers
Minneapolis, Minnesota
BethanyHouse.com

Bethany House Publishers is a division of
Baker Publishing Group, Grand Rapids, Michigan

Printed in the United States of America

Library of Congress Cataloging-in-Publication Data
Names: Connealy, Mary, author.
Title: Toward the dawn / Mary Connealy.
Description: Minneapolis, Minnesota : Bethany House, a division of Baker Publishing Group, 2024. | Series: A western light ; 2
Identifiers: LCCN 2023050004 | ISBN 9780764242663 (paperback) | ISBN 9780764243127 (casebound) | ISBN 9781493446513 (ebook)
Subjects: LCGFT: Christian fiction. | Romance fiction. | Western fiction. | Novels.
Classification: LCC PS3603.O544 T69 2024 | DDC 813/.6—dc23/eng/20231025
LC record available at https://lccn.loc.gov/2023050004

Scripture quotations are from the King James Version of the Bible.

This is a work of fiction. Names, characters, incidents, and dialogues are products of the author's imagination and are not to be construed as real. Any resemblance to actual events or persons, living or dead, is entirely coincidental.

Cover design and photography by Dan Thornberg, Design Source Creative Services
Cover images from Shutterstock

Baker Publishing Group publications use paper produced from sustainable forestry practices and postconsumer waste whenever possible.

24 25 26 27 28 29 30 7 6 5 4 3 2 1

I dedicate this book to
my very own romantic cowboy hero.
Forty-seven years together and counting.
Whatever I know about cowboys,
I learned from you
(well, maybe John Wayne and
Louis L'Amour helped a little).

1

MAY 1870

"I'm going to tear this canyon entrance open with my bare hands." Sebastian Jones had endured. He'd lasted the whole winter trapped in here. He hadn't known just how much he'd hate it—a hate that had started strong and kept building—until he found out there was no escape.

"Seb, will you stop? The canyon will melt open when it melts opens."

Seb whirled to face the little woman who had probably saved his life last spring when she and her friends had found him, shot, in an alley in Independence, Missouri.

"Kat, just go away. I'm busy losing my mind." Seb tried to unclench . . . his jaw, his fists, his gut. He'd been doing it for months, deliberately forcing himself to breathe, remain calm, endure.

"When is this ever going to melt?" Arriving at the bitter, dead end of his endurance, he threw his arms wide and exploded at Kat, who had done nothing to deserve this.

She marched straight at him, her own fists clenched, and

he braced himself to take a blow to the chin. Or maybe duck.

Then she marched right past him and plowed a fist into the stupid snowdrift that had blocked this canyon closed since January. "I hate it, too."

That pulled Seb up short, distracted him from the sense of being trapped. A little. "You hate it, too?"

She yanked her fist out of the snow, stared at her knuckles for a long, cold second, then slugged the snowdrift again with her other hand. Her fists left tidy dents. Then she whirled to face him. Fists red and raw and still clenched.

Again, he braced himself.

"Yes!" She threw her arms wide.

"Why didn't you say something?" He jabbed a pointy finger right at her shoulder. "You've been listening to me rant and complain all winter." He poked her again, hard enough that she backed up a step. "Let me behave like some ungrateful, irrational madman." Poke, poke, poke. A poke for each insult he dealt himself. "And while I whined and moaned, you watched me with that tidy little complacent smile on your face." Another poke, but this time she swatted his hand aside. "You did that while you *agreed with me*?" He jabbed her again. "That's just pure mean of you. You could at least have spoken up, divided their attention."

"By 'their,' you mean the people that took us both in? Fed and clothed us? Saved us, transported us across the country, gave us a home and heat and friendship?"

Seb fell silent, watching her. The wind buffeted them. The beautiful canyon stretched out for miles. But the narrow-necked entrance to the hidden canyon stood clogged with snow up to at least twenty feet over their heads. Probably higher, as he couldn't see the top.

She stood glaring. Blond, blue-eyed, delicate, with doctoring skills that had probably saved his life. A hardworking woman who, he just now realized, he knew very little about. She was quiet. She never talked about herself. It hit him that she was almost as secretive about her past as he was about his. Only he was a man who needed to be secretive. An inventor who wanted to earn a living with his work had to get his patents and not share anything until the patent was firmly in his hands. Did she hold something as secretive? What was she hiding? She was with Beth and Eugenia Rutledge when he'd met them. He'd just assumed—

"Us?" She plunked her hands on her hips. "How'd they save you? You were with them from the beginning. You, along with Beth and Ginny, saved me."

More silence. He saw something in her, something bubbling, like a pot with its lid too tight. Pressure building.

"What's the matter? What are you thinking? You're standing there trying not to just flat-out tell me I'm furiously mad."

She swung a fist.

He ducked. Glad he'd been ready for it.

"Hey, why'd you do that?" Maybe for all the poking, but it could be for anything. "Now *you're* acting like a lunatic."

"I did it . . ." She threw her arms wide as she shouted at the top of her lungs. "I did it because . . ." Tears almost spurted from her eyes.

Seb hated it when women cried. No, not hated. Feared.

He always felt helpless and stupid, like a reckless and clumsy bull turned loose in a glass factory.

And still she yelled. Crying, yelling, arms moving like pistons on a speeding locomotive.

"I did it because I *am* a lunatic. I am *not* a friend of this family, or I wasn't at the beginning."

Seb shook his head. "I'd been shot and was on the verge of death when I met you. I don't know what brought you to this locked jail cell of a canyon. I don't know anything because you've never *said* anything."

She looked as though she was fighting not to speak. Then she exploded. "I escaped from the same asylum as Ginny!"

Seb froze. He felt his eyes go wide. He clamped his mouth shut so he wouldn't say another thing. Just in case it led to more yelling, more tears, more agitation.

Her eyes narrowed, and she glared hard enough to burn the flesh from his bones.

"You agree, don't you? You believe I'm a madwoman just like my wretched uncle did when he locked me away and took all the money I inherited."

He didn't have a choice now of keeping his mouth shut. Her accusation called for a response. Silence might seem like he agreed with her wretched uncle. "Really, you escaped from a lunatic asylum?"

She swung again. Open hand this time. But he was ready, and she missed.

"Cut that out." He braced himself to duck again.

"You should let me hit you."

"No, I shouldn't. Why would I do something that stupid?"

"You just seem like a coward is all. Ducking like that.

Stay in there and take it." She shrugged, and some of the white-hot fury seemed to ebb. She swiped the sleeve of her blue gingham dress across her eyes, then pulled a handkerchief out of one sleeve, turned aside, blew her nose, mopped her eyes a bit more, and turned back.

He said, "So, tell me about the asylum."

Kat shook her head and turned back to the snowdrift. A hundred yards long and twenty or thirty feet high. She stepped up to the place she'd punched and studied the holes she'd left. "Do you remember last September when we came in here?"

An annoying question when he'd already asked one and had been ignored. "Of course I remember it. It's the last time I was in the world outside of this paradise."

Kat glanced over her shoulder at him, her mouth in a grim line. "Me too. Well, last September when we drove the wagons through here, there was snow on the ground. Not snow like a recent storm, but old, melting ice tucked into the nooks and crannies along the edges of this canyon."

Seb remembered. "You think it was still melting in September?" He was shouting by the time he finished saying it. Horrified. There was no escape. His next invention had better be wings.

"Mountains have snowcaps that never melt. We're not on a mountain peak, but we're high up. Really high up. Yes, I think this will take months yet to melt. If it ever does. You remember this closed up in January?"

"I remember that, too, Kat," he said impatiently. He didn't want to talk about that. "About the asylum—"

"It strikes me that Oscar came out here maybe late

summer before we made the trip on the wagon train. He must've gotten in. He did so much work in here, he couldn't have come in September."

Oscar Collins was the man who'd helped Beth plan Ginny's escape from the Horecroft Insane Asylum. He'd discovered Hidden Canyon a hundred miles from nowhere. He'd bought it. He'd driven in a herd of cattle. He'd built the cabin the women lived in. With Jake Holt now married to Beth, Jake lived in the cabin, too. He'd planted a garden of plants that would reseed themselves or come back from their roots. He'd planted trees. He'd had to work for months to get the canyon ready.

The men, meanwhile, lived in a cave near the cabin with a decent entrance built onto it. The men were warmer in the winter and would probably be cooler in the summer. They had a hot spring in the extensive cave that provided most of the heat, and each of the three men, Oscar, his brother Joseph, and Seb had their own rooms. Plus there was a kitchen area and honestly any other rooms they wanted. The cave stretched back a long way. Seb used one room for a laboratory, although Oscar was threatening to build him his own laboratory because his experiments occasionally created fumes, making breathing difficult.

"I don't know when he came. He said he knew about this canyon from years ago—how it had called out 'home' to him from the first moment he saw it. But his life drew him back to Chicago. Then, when Ginny needed a hiding place, he thought of it. Beth gave him enough money to buy it, and enough to outfit three wagons with enough supplies to last forever. They intended to come here and stay for the rest of their lives. Or at least the rest of

Thaddeus Rutledge's life." As long as Thaddeus, Ginny's husband, was alive, he had rights over her that included locking her away in an asylum based only on Thaddeus's opinion that his wife was insane.

Beth had warned Seb of their plans. She'd offered many times to get him to the railroad and give him enough money to go wherever he wanted. But no, he'd come along instead. It had sounded so safe. And he'd been shot by an unknown gunman. Fear had made a hidden canyon sound perfect.

If only he'd known it would end up feeling like a noose around his neck.

"I wonder if Thaddeus survived those stab wounds last fall?"

"How could we ever know when we're trapped in this stupid canyon?" Seb turned to the mountain of snow and punched it right in its snowy face.

Kat came and studied the fist marks, three of them now, side by side. "I think we can get out. We have a shovel in our cabin."

Seb's head snapped around. "Again with 'we,' like 'us'? Admit it, you want out as badly as I do."

"At least as badly."

He moved up close enough that his nose almost touched hers. He wasn't an overly tall man, five-foot-nine . . . and a half with his boots on. Yet she was a little thing and made him feel tall. He did his best to loom over her.

Then his blue eyes met hers and held.

She was a pretty woman, no doubt about it. He'd noticed that before. But only a fool tried to court a woman with no preacher in sight and a group of men who'd shoot him for anything less honorable than a true courtship.

Her eyes held the same as his. Speaking just above a whisper, he said, "You've never talked about yourself or your past, Kat. But I'd've said I know you because I've seen you work. I've seen you do what's necessary to survive out here and do it with wisdom and patience. Right this minute, I've learned I don't know you at all and that's because you treat life like it started on that wagon train. And I've never even noticed. But what I do know is you're as sensible and sane as any woman—any *person*—alive. Who locked you up? Who's this uncle that wanted you out of the way so he could take your money? Who is he, and where is he? I've a mind to go have a short, hard talk with him."

"No. You don't dare." Her hand snaked out and caught the hand he'd just poked her with.

Well, not *just*. It'd been a few minutes. He'd stopped poking and ranting when he realized what a terrible thing it was for her to be declared anything but the most rational of women.

They stood, locked in combat, her eyes urgent. Her grip was like iron . . . well, very soft, warm iron that he could have freed himself from instantly, except he didn't want to.

"I'm getting out of here. Come with me." The words just popped right out of his mouth, as if his brain was in no way connected to them. He paused for a moment and wondered if how he felt right here, right now fit the definition of insanity.

She let go of his arm as if she had to force her hand to open. Then she shook her head, closed her eyes, and turned back to the snow. "How will you do it?"

Seb's mind went a little wild when he heard something

in her question that she probably didn't mean the way it sounded. How will you do . . . oh, the snow barrier!

"See where you punched your fist in and where I did?" He turned and stared blindly at the snow, anything but look at her, just in case she could read his mind.

"Yes, of course I can see it. It's a foot in front of my face."

"Earlier it was like powder, remember? There was no getting over it. A person would just sink in over his head and flounder." He didn't admit it, but he knew because he'd tried. He'd made it until about March before he tried to climb out the first time. He'd tried again in April. Now it was late May. He hadn't really started wanting out desperately until he'd realized it wasn't possible. "It was impossible to make forward progress, and a horse was out of the question."

He finally started seeing the snow instead of what he'd *seen* when Kat had asked him that question.

He continued, "It's changed. It rained twice in the last few weeks. I think we can climb it now. We can cut a more gradual slope in it, one a horse could walk over."

There was no way to leave, not without a horse. It was just too far a distance for a man to walk. And Seb didn't have a horse. Which was something else he needed to figure out. He had some money. Jake would sell him a horse. He glanced at Kat. Or two horses.

Kat leaned forward, clawed at the snow. "It's crisp and tight and heavy. It's not going to go back to powder. And look." She pointed at the ground right up against the canyon wall. A stream of water flowed like a spring. "It's melting. It'll take a while, but it *will* melt."

Seb didn't think he could wait any longer, not without

losing his mind. He didn't mention losing his mind to the little escapee from the asylum.

Crossing her arms, she studied the stream of water, the wall of snow, the fist dents. "You're right—we can do it. And it's spring now. Granted, it's early spring, but spring nonetheless." She turned to him, her gaze different now. She seemed to be studying him. "It's as wrong as it can be for the two of us to ride off together, to travel together—an unmarried man and woman."

Seb stared right back at her, and he knew exactly what she was thinking. Same thing he was.

They both spoke at once. "We have to take Beth and Jake along for propriety's sake."

"We need to get married."

Kat's eyes widened when she realized what he'd said. She opened and closed her mouth, not unlike a landed trout. She was so shocked, he almost laughed. Except he was a little insulted that his proposal had come as such a shock. No, *a lot* insulted.

She said, "I think we'd better get out of here soon because I'm about a week away—maybe an *hour* away—from needing to be locked up for real."

2

It won't be that long before it melts open," Jake said. He didn't say 'before it melts open, stupid,' but Kat heard it anyway. She'd bet Sebastian heard it, too.

In fact, probably everyone in their small circle heard it as they stood in front of the wall of snow. To the north, the canyon was green, the fruit trees were blooming. They were already eating spring onions and asparagus. Their Angus cattle had added generously to the herd with their silky-black babies. Two of the horses had foaled, the cat had a litter of kittens, and the dog, to everyone's surprise, a litter of puppies. There were piglets, and the hens had hatched out eggs.

The cabin stood, sturdy and warm, down the slope from them. A new barn was close behind it. They'd built a tidy little chicken coop and a pigpen. Oscar had worked with all of them, Kat included, to teach them the skills they'd need to survive in the West.

Kat now knew how to chop down a tree, cut the corners so the logs would latch together. She could build a chimney with a fireplace out of native stones, put a roof on a building and windows and doors.

There was a corral that stretched away from the barn, with three milk cows grazing quietly, each with a baby calf at her side.

It was a glorious, fertile, beautiful Eden-like place.

Kat supposed that made her Eve, dragging Seb-Adam into trouble. Except they were dragging each other, now, weren't they? God had stayed with Adam and Eve after their fall, so Kat expected her heavenly Father would help her along, too.

"We need to get married."

She'd heard Seb say that, hadn't she? Right after they'd sort of paused in their ranting and locked eyes and quit thinking.

"I've decided I no longer want to live in this canyon, cut off from the world." Sebastian sounded calm, reasonable, like he'd come to a decision after careful consideration.

Kat had yet to speak up that she was going with him. And she most certainly wasn't going to marry him.

Or should she?

She could hardly ride off with him alone. But Beth was very pregnant. She wasn't about to go for a long ride.

Why was Kat feeling so trapped? Was it possible that having been locked up for a year, this was a little too similar? Not that she was mistreated, as she had been in the asylum, but just not being given a choice. No free will. There were some unfortunate similarities.

The Lord worked in mysterious ways. Kat prayed fervently, deep in her heart, that the Lord would help her dig out of the canyon. She knew being shut in wasn't right for her.

Yet her uncle was out there, wandering, controlling her company, spending her money. He'd delight in locking her safely away again. Not safely for her, but for him.

"We need to get married."

If she was married, her uncle wouldn't be able to lock her up. Except, to her understanding, he shouldn't have been able to lock her up anyway. As her uncle, he had no authority over her. It was only wives who could be locked in asylums, with just a husband's word claiming his wife was mad.

What a stupid law.

And she was in no way seriously considering that strange statement about marriage from Seb. He was under great pressure to escape this canyon after all. He couldn't be held responsible for the words that came out of his mouth. Wouldn't stepping into a marriage in such a reckless way be yet another sort of prison?

She wondered if speaking words that sounded like lunacy, suggesting actions like marriage that were lunacy, proposing to dig a hole in a mountain of snow because you felt trapped to the point of lunacy didn't fit the definition of insanity.

But she'd been locked in a madhouse and had seen plenty of poor souls who were very clearly insane. And she wasn't that.

She drew a deep breath, determined to tell them she was going with Sebastian, when Beth clutched her stomach and looked frantically at Jake. "I think the baby is coming."

Sebastian sat on a rock, watching Jake pace back and forth, a wild look in his eyes. He'd tried to stay with Beth, but finally had been ejected from the cabin. "I need to be in there. This is my responsibility." Back and forth. Back and forth. "Saying a father shouldn't be with his wife while his child is born is the most half-witted thing I've ever heard of. How did that tradition get started?"

Oscar leaned out over the spring, watching the waterfall cascade into the canyon, then flow through the entire pasture. "I think they were planning to let you stay until you started threatening Kat."

"She's not a doctor. What is she even doing in there?"

"You heard her say her pa was a doctor," Sebastian said, "and that she helped him a lot, including delivering babies. She's a lot closer to a doctor than you are. You shouldn't have grabbed Kat and shook her."

The sun was low in the sky. The labor had started midmorning. How long would this take?

"I didn't shake her *hard*. I just wanted her to pay attention to Beth." Back and forth, hands clasped behind his back. A look of stark terror on his face. "What if something goes wrong?"

"Then Ginny dragged you away from Kat, who, praise the Lord, you had the sense *not* to shake Ginny." Oscar shook his head as he watched a trout glide by. The man was calm as the clear Idaho sky. As steady as the Sawtooth peaks. As focused on fish as a hungry eagle ready to go into a killing dive.

Oh. Seb saw it now. Oscar wasn't all that calm. Beth, the woman he treated more like a daughter than her own father did, had him worried down to his toenails. He was just a lot better at hiding it than Jake.

Sebastian had brought a knife and a piece of walnut

and was trying his hand at whittling. He'd about cut his finger off three times now . . . and the stick of wood looked nothing like the dog he'd hoped to create.

At that, their dog came running up with six puppies tumbling and scrambling behind her. Six dogs. Seven counting the mama. What were they going to do with seven dogs in this canyon?

"And Ginny, your mother-in-law, who loves you as much as if you were her own son, kicked you out and threw the latch so you couldn't get back in. Which you tried to do, front door and back."

"Ma's got a mean streak I've never noticed before." Jake glared at the house.

Joseph sat cross-legged on the grass, reading his Bible, though Seb couldn't think when he'd last turned a page. He set the book down, dropped his face into both hands, and rubbed.

"You know, your child is going to have the blood of Thaddeus Rutledge flowing in his veins. He'll also be heir to the Rutledge empire back in Chicago." Sebastian found a strange pleasure in torturing the usually calm and capable man who'd helped lead their wagon train west and never seemed unsettled. Now Jake couldn't stop pacing, looking up at the cabin, then pacing again.

"No son of mine is going to grow up to be like Thaddeus Rutledge."

Seb sure hoped not. Though Seb had never met Thaddeus, he'd heard plenty. The man was awful. But where was the fun in admitting that?

Oscar, who'd worked in the Rutledge stables before he'd helped Ginny and Beth escape, knew Thaddeus Rutledge as well as anyone. "He owns property in Chicago, miles of it. Much of it is covered with apartments overcrowded with poor folk who have nowhere else to go. I heard tell of one tenement building where they'd gone in and taken rooms with ten-foot ceilings and cut them down to being five-foot high and forced folks to live like that. And he owns factories with children working at dangerous jobs. Carpet mills with looms and metalworks with molten iron splashing around, filled with workers making no more than a penny a day."

Oscar looked away from the fish, his eyes hard on the house. Then he tore them away and turned to Jake. "Blayd and his men went around collecting rents from folks who could barely feed themselves. That's a lot of valuable property Beth will someday own. Beth and your youngsters.

"Blayd, Rutledge's top henchman, did plenty of dirty work for his boss."

"Yep, Blayd was there with Rutledge last fall." Jake quit pacing. "That Pinkerton shot him dead when he was aiming to kill Yvette."

Sebastian had heard all about it. Blayd had died last fall when Rutledge, chasing after Ginny, had caught up with Beth and trouble exploded.

So Blayd had died, and Rutledge was stabbed nearly to death by a fragile woman, who was also from the asylum where Ginny had been locked away, and who had led Rutledge west using remembered information she wouldn't share unless he took her along.

"Neither Beth nor my youngsters will inherit a cent. Surely he'll cut her off for smirking at him last fall and calling him Pa."

"That might be enough," Oscar conceded, sneaking a glance at the cabin. "Although a rumor I heard whispered said Rutledge bought too much, borrowed too heavily, and is badly overextended. If things keep on as they are, he'll end up being one of the richest men in the country. But if we have one of those financial collapses that strike the country now and then, he could be in real trouble. That's why he wants Ginny and Beth back—more than pride, more than just a man who will not be thwarted. They're both heiresses, and Ginny's folks were wise in how they set up trust funds, so that Thaddeus had no access to them."

Joseph huffed a humorless laugh. "So your son might end up inheriting a bankrupt estate from old Grandpappy Rutledge? Hope that bankruptcy happens soon."

"Blayd is dead and buried. I wonder if Rutledge survived his injuries?" Jake asked. It was the first time in a long time he'd thought of anything but his wife and his coming baby.

Seb didn't figure it'd last. But then he thought of a way to extend the distraction. "When I leave, I'll see if I can find any news of Rutledge in the papers. If he died, surely that would get mentioned. If he lived, there's bound to be some mention of some big deal he's a part of."

"And then what?" Jake snapped. "You'll mail us a letter?"

"I could mail one to the O'Tooles. You might call on them from time to time, and just maybe I'll stop by for a visit. I'm not sure where I'm headed." Kat hadn't mentioned her intention to go with him, so he didn't include her. It was her news to tell. "I need a good-sized town with dependable lawmen and access to a train. I might go to Texas, settle near Dallas. But that's a mighty long way from here. Maybe California or even Laramie, Wyoming, or Cheyenne. They might have what I need. My invention is—" He cut off the sentence and looked up. All four men were watching.

"You've never told us just what you're inventing, Seb. We could use a story about now. Good chance the news won't reach the wrong ears from anyone here. Besides, you have our word we won't tell anyone, and that oughta be good enough for you."

Seb looked at them. Jake stopped pacing. Oscar stopped counting trout. Joseph stopped rubbing his face.

Their word *was* good enough for him, so that wasn't the reason he talked about his invention. Instead, he decided to talk about it just because it was keeping their minds off the dramatic event inside the cabin.

"Thank heavens you got him out of here." Beth breathed slowly while Ginny wiped her brow with a cool cloth.

Kat smiled at her courageous friend. The three of them—Ginny, herself, and most especially Beth—had been at the laboring awhile now. There wasn't much to it until the baby was ready to emerge. Kat had boiled water, which she kept off to the side, sterilized and ready, with a string and a pair of scissors in the hot water, also perfectly clean. That water and those supplies were not to be touched until they were ready to be used.

They had a thick pad of blankets under Beth and clean ones ready if they needed to be replaced. Birthing a baby could be messy.

Kat was calm, while Ginny was anxious—holding herself together through sheer endurance.

Beth was exhausted, but there was no way she got to leave, so Kat expended her energy to distract her and keep her as comfortable as possible.

"I had just one child." Ginny leaned down, replaced the cool cloth with a kiss on Beth's damp brow. "One perfect birth. I had no great liking for the process and was glad enough it never happened again."

"And Father didn't try to insist he stay with you through the birth?"

Ginny snorted. "As far as I am aware, he came home from work, late as usual, and if he noticed he had a child now, he made no mention of it."

"Why only one child, Ginny?" Kat knew Ginny had no liking for her husband, but that didn't usually stop the babies from coming.

Ginny shrugged. "I don't know. Beth was born before we'd been married a year. I already knew my marriage was never going to be a happy one. But a wife does her duty. Thaddeus for the most part lost interest in me and Beth. I suppose he went to other women, but I'm not even sure of that. He used my dowry to enrich himself and was so obsessed with work that he was gone before I woke up, and he didn't come home until late at night."

Beth, between labor pains, said, "We rarely saw him." Then with an eye roll, she added, "And when we did, we wished he'd go away."

"I won't say another baby wasn't possible, but he rarely came to me in that way. A man like Thaddeus, well, you'd assume he'd want sons to run his business and just to make him feel like a—" Ginny hesitated, then shrugged—"like a big successful man who could bring sons into the world.

I suppose he thought he could live for all eternity or take the money with him somehow."

Beth choked on a laugh, then giggled helplessly. "I suspect he thought both of those things. The world worked as Father commanded."

Her breath caught. Her hands went to her belly. Kat rested a gentle hand high on her stomach. "They're coming so close, it won't be much longer."

Ginny handed Beth the wooden spoon Kat had found in the kitchen. Beth bit down hard on the spoon, already dented with her teeth marks.

"My pa always said not to fight the contractions. Think of them as your stomach muscles working and just do your best to endure it. It's the hardest work you'll ever do, but it's for the greatest achievement, to bring life into the world, so why shouldn't it be hard?"

Beth's belly turned rock-hard. The contraction went on for so long, Kat gasped and realized she was holding her breath. They all were.

"Breathe, Beth. Keep breathing." She heard a long breath escape Beth's clenched jaw. Ginny breathed with her.

Kat chuckled, and then they all did, even Beth when the contraction finally eased.

Beth said, "That one was different."

Kat had noticed.

"It's time. We'll have a baby soon."

Beth rubbed a hand over her middle. "I never expected to have a baby get so big."

Ginny mopped her brow again. "You're just ready to give birth is all. Your baby is going to be a good-sized boy, I'd say."

Kat thought Beth indeed had a big baby on the way. Her arms and face had remained slender, yet her belly grew much larger than Kat would have expected. She was glad they were getting this child born and hoped Beth was up to delivering without trouble. She'd been involved a few times when there had been trouble, and she prayed now, silently and fervently, that nothing terrible would happen to this woman who had been so kind and generous to Kat.

Another pain began. Barely a minute since the one before ended. It was indeed time. Kat had left Beth covered to preserve her modesty, but the time for that was past.

It was time to add to their little community in the most miraculous way possible.

"I've invented a battery. And I think . . . that is, I *hope* maybe I can power it with the sun."

The men remained motionless. As if their minds were far too busy with their thoughts to notice the world around them. There was a light breeze. An eagle screamed overhead. A black Angus calf gamboled past. Two puppies chewed on Joseph's boot laces.

"Is that possible?" Oscar asked.

"Well, it's all a theory at this point. My first goal is to make a much smaller battery so it's portable. But powered by the sun? Maybe, just maybe I've figured it out. I need time and supplies. And I've got ten patents to get before I work on my sun-power idea. But I've drawn up preliminary plans." Seb looked at the beauty around him and wished he could harness so many things. "Someone must think it's an idea with merit because they tried to kill me to get my plans. I need to find a safe place to work. I would do it here except I can't get the materials I need—materials I hadn't considered before. I must live and work someplace where I'll have access to shipments of odd materials. The ideas are burning in me, like an itch I can't scratch."

"How would that even work?" Jake looked up at the sun. "How do you make that"—he pointed upward—"power anything?"

"A French inventor named Leclanché built a battery and got it patented in 1866. He called it a wet cell battery. The Leclanché battery is a huge breakthrough, but it has some real weaknesses. For one thing it's heavy. That's why my first goal is to make a smaller one. Something portable would be so much more useful. It also needs to be longer lasting, more powerful. As it is now, the power ebbs and surges, but it needs to be steady. So I—"

"Hush up!" Jake slashed a hand at Seb and whirled to face the cabin just as Seb was getting ready to tell them all the really exciting parts.

Seb heard a high, thin cry coming from the house that could only belong to one member of their little family. The newest member.

Jake ran for the door. He almost staggered when he reached it to keep from slamming straight through. But since the door was made of split logs latched shut by dropping a heavy squared-off log into iron bars, all founded on solid rock, that wasn't going to happen.

Seb and the others were just a pace behind, but they all three stayed back out of respect for the father and his moment with his new child.

Then the latch scratched away, the door opened, and Ginny stepped outside, bearing a wiggling, crying cloth-wrapped bundle. "It's a girl, Jake. A little girl."

Ginny's eyes were wet with tears, her cheeks and chin as well. Her smile was so bright, it was blinding.

"How's Beth?"

"Still a bit busy. There's, uh . . ."

A second cry sounded—just as high, just as newborn—from deeper inside the cabin.

Jake's head snapped up so fast he might've hit Ginny in the chin, but she was looking away. Then Kat came out with a second bundle. "This one's a boy, Jake."

"Twins?"

Nodding, Kat grinned at Jake. When Jake went to looking between the babies, Kat's eyes locked on Seb's. He'd never seen such a smile on the woman before. A match for Ginny's, as if they'd witnessed a miracle. And as he looked at those two wriggling bundles, he suspected they had.

The moment stretched. He felt the draw of those joyful eyes. He'd seen the wonder and joy on Jake's face and wanted such a thing for himself. For the first time in his life, he wanted something more than he wanted to invent. Machines and chemicals had been a near obsession since childhood. Now he saw the possibility of so much more.

He'd asked Kat to marry him. He wondered if she'd thought about it.

Kat said, "Go on back, Jake. She's fine and wants to see you. We'll bring the babies."

Jake dashed between Kat and Ginny to get to his wife. The two women stepped out of his way, sharing their smiles of a miracle, happy to see how deeply Jake loved his Beth.

Oscar came up beside Ginny and leaned close to look at the little girl. Then his eyes slid to the boy. His smile shone bright enough to power a hundred batteries.

They all stayed out there to give Jake and Beth a quiet moment together. Oscar said, "Kat, you and Ginny take the little ones in to their parents. Give the four of them some time alone. I've got a roast going in the cave, a good cut of beef. I'll go see to it. By the time we get a meal ready, maybe Jake and Beth will want something to eat."

Ginny rested her head on Oscar's shoulder for just a few moments. Everyone was focused on the babies, but Seb noticed the look of tenderness on Oscar's face as Ginny leaned on him. He'd always known Oscar loved Ginny and Beth. But right now, Seb could see it was more than that for Oscar. He was in love with Ginny.

A difficult thing for a man to feel for a married woman.

But Oscar was an honorable man. Seb knew he'd never speak of his tender feelings for Ginny, never do anything but care for her and see that she had everything he could possibly provide in the way of comfort.

Seb thought of the hidden canyon. Oscar had built this cabin, brought in a herd. Bought supplies and trained cattle to pull three wagons across the country. He'd given everything he had to provide safety for Ginny and Beth, safety from Ginny's husband.

But he'd done it as a loyal friend. Even more, he'd acted as a servant and treated Ginny as a fine lady, far above him. Ginny hadn't behaved as if she expected that, but Oscar had maintained an utterly respectful distance. He'd never show that there was anything more. In fact, he'd hidden his feelings so well and so deeply, Seb suspected Oscar didn't recognize those feelings himself.

But in that moment, in that gesture, Seb saw a grandma and grandpa cooing over their grandchildren. Whether they realized it or not.

Seb wondered if they could maintain their current relationship forever, because if they couldn't, things in the canyon might become very difficult.

3

It took Seb a few more months until July to get his head out of the clouds from the happy event and the busy aftermath.

July and the constant sound of babies crying.

Then he started wanting to get away again.

The snow had receded enough that he thought he could get his horse through the canyon's entrance. The days were hot, the sun stayed up for long hours, and still the pass had a pile of snow.

But much less formidable. He figured he could make it.

Everyone, and that meant literally *everyone*, was exhausted from tending the newborn babies. Seb had taken his turns, right along with the Collins brothers. He wasn't much with babies, but Oscar was a good hand and showed him the way of it.

Oscar would go early every morning to make breakfast for all those in the household. As he walked over, they heard the crying. None of the folks in the cabin were getting much sleep, not with two hungry, growing babies around—Jake Jr., who they called Jacob, and Marie, which was Eugenia's middle name. The cabin was small enough that no one could escape the crying.

Oscar would feed them all. Then, with Ginny's help, he'd bring Jacob and Marie to the cave. He and Joseph had built cradles for the babies, a pair of them for the cave and a pair for the house. But the twins rarely slept; they cried instead. One or the other, or often both at a time. The babies would be walked and bounced, talked to and cajoled. If a person did that really well and never stopped, sometimes the crying would fall silent for a bit.

Heaven help the person if they tried to sit down.

After the babies were brought to the cave house, Ginny went back to her cabin while Oscar, Joseph, and Seb would care for the twins most of the morning while the folks in the house slept. There was a midmorning break to feed the little tykes, and then one at a time was taken to the cabin. They were bald and cross-eyed and so cute, Seb couldn't look at either of them without smiling.

When one twin came back, the other went over, until finally they had them both back in the cave house, which meant more sleep for the cabin. Oscar and Joseph would feed everyone a noon meal. By that time, Jake and sometimes Kat would emerge, groggy but rested enough to get by for another day. Seb had seen Beth briefly when he got to carry a baby over to her. But only for a brief moment since the day the babies were born.

This had gone on for nearly two months. Then last night, wonder of wonders, one of the little ones had slept through the night.

Beth had to get up with the other baby only once.

Seb saw the light at the end of the tunnel. An exhausting, noisy tunnel.

Now he had time to check the canyon entrance, and sure enough the snow had shrunk and hardened enough that he was going to be able to ride right over it. He'd need a horse to get to the train, so he'd approached Oscar and offered to buy one of his. Oscar seemed to think there'd be no problem. Except the problem of Seb saying the wrong thing to someone outside the canyon about where they all were.

Kat drew his attention as she walked up the sloping sides of the canyon to stand beside him.

"Is it wrong to go?" She sounded urgent. "I don't think they need my help. But when the babies are awake at night, we're all awake. Still, either Ginny or Jake walks with the one Beth isn't feeding. Sometimes I help—I'm always willing and wide awake—but mostly we're a pair of hands too many."

Seb looked at those blue eyes of hers, thinking about how they'd shone when she'd held little Marie in her arms for the first time. How more and more he'd been thinking about having those eyes fixed on him.

"Have you thought more about marrying me, Kat? I think we'd make a likely pair. We can go wrestle your money from your uncle, or we can just slip away, find a place for my work, and leave all of that behind. As my wife, he can't touch you. And if you've got ownership of something, with me beside you, we can take control of it."

Kat began shaking her head before he'd finished talking.

"Is that a no to the proposal or a no to taking a fight straight to your uncle?"

"It's about the uncle." A smile crept over Kat's face.

Seb's heart sped up. He wanted that smile for himself. He wanted to see how it tasted.

The snow had receded enough for him to draw Kat into the entrance, out of sight of the cabin. He drew her in right close to himself and kissed her. It was nice. More than nice.

With her arms around his neck, she whispered, "I-I'd like to marry you, Sebastian. Leaving here, well, I have just got to get out. I'm not sure anymore why except I can't draw in a deep breath when the entrance is snowed in. But leaving and striking out in the world on my own feels terrifying. I can't stay, and I'm afraid to leave." She glanced at his lips. "Those seem like very selfish reasons to force a man to chain himself to me for life."

"I'm doing the same thing. A man striking out on his own isn't so dangerous as a woman maybe, but I'm dreading it. I've spent most of my life alone. I was a straggler child in my family, and my older sisters and brothers, five in all, were grown and moved away from Independence almost from my first memory. Three of them, both sisters and one brother, married before I was born, and one at a time they headed west on the Oregon Trail. We never heard from them again. Ma always said the West swallowed them up.

"The two brothers closest to me in age, but still twelve and fifteen years older, are the only ones I ever met. They fought in the Civil War for the South, which Pa and Ma didn't approve of. They both died in battle. I lived a quiet life with my aging parents in a modest home. Lots of books. My father was a schoolmaster in Independence and encouraged my inventions. I had four patents by the time

I got done with high school. Then I got five more during college in St. Louis. Ma died while I was away. After college I moved back to Independence and spent my pa's last years caring for him and inventing."

Frowning, he said, "I need to find a way to get the money that is no doubt sitting in my bank account in Independence from those patents." He shook the distracting thought aside and continued, "After my folks died, I stayed at their house alone. I never had much of a family besides those two. I've enjoyed being part of this Rutledge-Collins clan for the last year. I don't relish being on my own again. Having you along sounds good except I might face danger, and you'll be chained to me for life. There are men who want my inventions—the same ones who shot me in Independence, and others. I need to be careful, discreet, set up a lab and work. We can get my money wired to a bank near where we settle, but will there be men who can find out where I am through that?"

Kat shook her head. Though she looked concerned, she was still standing with her arms around his neck.

"What if we get married, then hop on the train and head east?"

Kat gasped. "Not Chicago."

"No, not that far. I was thinking maybe Cheyenne, Wyoming. It's along the train route, big enough for me to get the materials I need. We could homestead around there, out of town far enough that we can see trouble coming. In the city, trouble can sneak up on you."

"Can we build a cabin?"

"Oscar made us help build the barn, but I'm not sure if I can build a cabin by myself."

Kat remembered how Oscar had always pushed them to learn. He left a lot to each of them to handle on their own. He was a wise man and a good leader. "I think I could build one maybe, but I'd need help with heavy things—although Oscar showed me how to use the horse to move logs, use pulleys and such. And you want to invent, not build."

They stared at each other.

Sebastian nodded. "We'll figure it out. Laramie is closer, but Cheyenne is the territorial capital so it might have better law and order. If we moved to a big city like San Francisco, the men searching for me might be better able to find me. Anyway, I'd like to stay close enough we could come here and visit the twins once in a while."

Kat smiled. "Jake said it took five days to ride here in the wagons from where we turned off the Oregon Trail. But it's only a day's horseback ride to the nearest train station. It wouldn't be a hardship to come visit."

"With the train we can reach most anywhere in a day or two. In a week we could be in New York City if you wanted that."

Nodding silently for too long, Kat said, "I am a wealthy woman, and yet I have access to nothing. So that's what I bring to this marriage. But you're saving me because to be married puts me out of the reach of my uncle. At least to the extent he obeys the law."

"You're bringing something." Sebastian met her gaze, then leaned closer.

Kat touched his chest to stop him. A few things needed to be said. "We'll get married in the first town we reach, ride the train to Cheyenne, homestead some land, build a house, get a milk cow and some chickens, plant a garden. I'll keep you fed while you invent. You're right—I am bringing something. And you're right—we will figure it out. I wish now I hadn't kept my past such a secret all through the winter. Ginny felt she had no choice but to admit what had brought her here. She said what I'd been through was my story to tell, and she wouldn't speak of it unless I did. It was easy to keep quiet about such a humiliating experience."

"But now," Sebastian said, as if he understood exactly what she was trying to say, "here we are. More strangers than we should be after a year's acquaintance. Getting married is, I think, a good idea. I can promise to treat you with respect and be faithful to you. Even so, let's take our time getting to know each other better before we . . . well, before we are fully married."

Kat felt a lot of the tension ease from her heart. This was what she wanted to say and didn't do well. "I like that idea, Sebastian." She stopped holding him away from her and leaned toward him to meet his lips with hers. To seal their promises with a kiss.

One of the babies started crying in the cabin. Even across the valley they heard it. Then the second one joined in, a little chorus of bawling.

Kat flinched. The kiss ended. Their eyes met, and they laughed.

4

"I can't believe you're leaving us." Beth burst into tears as they stood at the mouth of Hidden Canyon. She was prone to that lately, so Kat didn't let it upset her overly.

Except it turned out she wanted to burst into tears herself. She hugged Beth as close as she could with Baby Jacob in Beth's arms.

"The only thing that makes me hesitate to leave is how much I've come to love all of you. Most especially these babies. I want to watch them grow up."

"I can tell you're half mad with wanting to leave, though." Beth held her tight.

Ginny came and pulled Kat into her own arms. "We don't use the term *half mad* in this canyon if we can possibly help it."

Kat laughed, which helped stave off the tears. She was grateful to Ginny for lightening the mood.

"Will you two be getting married right away?" Ginny, acting like some kind of chaperone, which got a smile out of Kat.

"We're planning to be married as soon as we reach town, which we hope to do before the end of the day. That's why we're out here just past sunrise. It's why we ate breakfast in the dark." She exchanged a look with Seb, who smiled and gave his chin a firm nod.

He was currently shaking hands with each of the men who'd also been trapped in here, along with Kat and Seb, all winter. None of the rest seemed inclined to escape.

"I spent time last night after supper, scooping." Oscar gestured at the bottlenecked canyon entrance.

Seb slapped him on the back. "It was melted down enough, Oscar. You didn't need to do that."

Oscar shrugged. "I'm going to miss you two. It suited me to throw my upset into hard work."

Kat turned to look at the way out. "You must have worked half the night."

"It was going to be treacherous climbing through that snowdrift. I didn't want your horses breaking a leg or either of you coming to grief wallowing in a sunken drift."

The snow rose nearly to the horses' shoulders to the sides of where the trail had been dug out. They'd planned to walk right out over it, threading their way through on the ground. But even with all of Oscar's work, they'd still be treading on a sheet of sharp, hard ice. It was possible the horses could get hurt—possible but not probable.

Still, Oscar's scooped-out trail would make the crossing both simpler and safer.

Kat went down the line of men, getting a warm squeeze of her arm or hand. The men showed their affection and loyalty by their hard work, not emotion.

"I'll write to you," Kat promised.

"Send the letters care of the O'Tooles, using Jake's name, and let them know your plans," Ginny said cheerfully. "Oscar is eager to see how his brother is doing, so he'll go visit now and then. And leave the gifts we're sending."

Oscar's third brother, Bruce, had stayed with the O'Toole family who'd come west with them, turning aside from the Oregon Trail. He thought they needed more farming skills than they currently possessed, especially after the death of the family's father, Shay, in a drowning accident along the trail. "Don't bother sending the letters directly to town in our names because we're not going."

"We'll ask the O'Tooles to gather any mail that comes addressed with your names on it." Kat understood better than anyone how important it was that no one find Ginny. "We won't speak to anyone about knowing you or knowing of your whereabouts."

Kat gave little Jacob a quick kiss on the forehead, then turned to her horse.

Beth, speaking quickly and quietly, said, "I packed venison in your satchels. Seb said he's got enough money, but I included a bit so you can transport your horses if you want to take them along."

"You already gave us the horses, Beth. No more was needed."

"Take the critters east with you or sell them in Alton and keep the money you earn to buy a new horse in Cheyenne or wherever you settle. Not a bad idea to have a bit of money in case there's trouble. And remember what I said about the laws getting changed concerning insane asylums. There are ways to fight what happened to you."

Kat's gut tightened to think of her uncle. She saw Ginny's eyes go wide and knew she was thinking of her tyrant husband. But Kat didn't argue. She had no courage to face down her wealthy uncle Patrick, yet now wasn't the time to debate that again with Beth.

Beth gave Jake an arch look, and he produced two satchels, both of them squirming. Kat peeked inside one to find two puppies, and the other contained two kittens.

"And these are for the O'Tooles, along with the other supplies we're sending. I ought to send four of the six puppies with you. I'll bet you could sell them, too." Jake hitched them like saddlebags to her horse.

Kat gave a smile while fighting back tears.

Alton was the little railroad town where they'd catch the train. When they'd turned off the Oregon Trail in Idaho and headed north, they'd crossed the rails. But no one had gone into Alton. It didn't suit a one of them to speak to anyone outside their group. Hiding was the point.

Jake had known the town was there and he'd given them careful directions to the O'Toole place, which Kat and Seb would stop at on their way.

Kat hadn't brought anything along on the journey west such as a satchel or trunk. A woman traveled light when she was escaping from an asylum. But the Collins brothers had a lot of such things packed in the wagons, and they had shared generously.

"I also packed some hardtack, and Jake filled two canteens for each of you. I threw in a little wedding present, as well."

"Th-thank you." Kat sniffled and could barely respond as she swung up on horseback. Once in the saddle, she looked at Ginny and Beth. A mirror image of each other. Dark hair and blue eyes. They'd started out the wagon train passing as sisters, and it was believable. Jake, tall and whipcord lean, held his daughter like he'd been doing it all his life. They'd all certainly had enough practice.

The Collins brothers watched with solemn eyes. They were a matched set for each other. Blue-eyed, stocky, and comfortable in their western clothes.

"I'm going to miss you all." She felt her throat closing as tears threatened. "Ginny, you saved me by getting me out of that asylum. Beth, you were there to get us away as fast as could be. Oscar and Joseph, you carried us all the way out here. Jake, thank you for leading our wagon train and being part of all this. You all rescued me. I am going to miss every one of you."

Ginny smiled, but her eyes were suspiciously bright. Ginny had taken Kat under her wing until Kat felt like she had a mother again. "I think we all helped save each other, Kat. With that train zipping across the country, there's no excuse not to come and see us often."

Kat thought of Seb and his saying how the West had swallowed up two of his sisters and one brother he'd never heard from again. She waved, then reined her horse around to follow Sebastian. As the horse's hooves crackled across the pitted ice, she wondered if she'd ever see any of them again.

5

"Are you all right?" They were the first words Sebastian thought to say. After all, there was little to say that wasn't already known.

"Let's just ride for a while. Watch where we're going." Kat had her head down as they escaped the canyon.

The walls overhead were so high, all he could see was a thin line of blue sky.

With the ground under their horses' hooves so uneven and treacherous, Kat was wise to pay strict attention. And besides, he'd seen the tears in her eyes.

Seb kept quiet and guided his surefooted horse through the choke hold of a canyon entrance.

When they emerged, Seb shuddered a little from the weight of finally being free. They paused a moment, and he wondered if this was the right thing to do. He already missed those good men and woman. Even through tears, Kat gave him a brave smile, and his mind was set as he turned his horse.

Seb didn't know much about the West, about trails and

such, but he could tell that the sun was on his left. With it being early morning, the sun in that position meant it was in the east and they were heading south now. They would ride south all the way to the train tracks. The O'Tooles were in this direction, too. Jake had talked about a creek, a two-hour ride. He said they couldn't miss it. The ground here was rocky and broken, nothing that could be called a trail.

Keeping quiet and paying attention made good sense.

He just kept riding. Let Kat get her tears finished as they rode the horses to smoother ground. There'd be plenty of time to talk later. And Seb had to manage a lump in his own throat. So, with his mouth shut, he focused on the ride south. They had their whole lives to talk.

"Let's stop and look back," Kat said some minutes later. "I want to try to find the canyon mouth. It won't be easy—it's so hidden."

They both turned around and peered to the north. Seb looked for landmarks, for boulders or lines in the sheer stone wall that were memorable.

Kat looked at him. "Well? Do you see it?"

"Not really, but I figure I could find that wall of rock and, knowing there's a way in, keep hunting until I found it."

Kat nodded. "That might work. Let's go then."

They turned to the south again and rode until an hour stretched nearly to two. The sun rose steadily. The ground leveled more with every mile. Seb was leading as they rode single file, yet the land wasn't so broken here, and he was about to tell her to ride beside him when he saw something mighty shocking.

"Kat, look at that," he said, pointing.

"It's a trail, coming from the northwest." Kat moved closer, then twisted around to look over her shoulder at the very visible trail. "Was there a trail here last year?"

Seb met her gaze. "I never noticed one. Remember how careful Oscar was to cover our tracks?"

"Yes, he walked behind our five wagons. He and Jake. He talked about covering our back trail, or something like that."

"So where did this come from?" He hesitated, then added, "Do you think we're lost?"

Kat gave a small shrug. "We're lost in that I've got no idea where we are. But we know we're riding south, and that train track cuts all the way across the state. We can't miss it."

She didn't sound all that confident.

Seb tried to sharpen his attention, be more aware of his surroundings. "Men like Jake and Dakota, the wagon-train master, understand the West. I envy them that skill. Only now when my big skill is keeping my left shoulder warm from the sun shining on us do I realize just how little I know."

"Jake said to look for a jagged ridge. We'll reach the O'Tooles' land when we pull even with it."

They stopped and looked to the west and to the north just as they had several times. The landscape was all jagged. They rounded a corner, Seb worrying about where they were headed, when a redheaded girl dashed out of a grove. She saw them and froze, then waved wildly.

"Sebastian! Kat! Hello!" It was Bridget O'Toole. Seb felt his worry melt away, replaced by a smile. The Irish lilt to her voice rang like music through the mountain air.

She was a hundred yards or so down the slope they were riding, and they picked up speed to meet her.

She turned and shouted something. Hard to tell what with her back to them, but within seconds Fiona appeared, stepping from the woods.

"We built their cabin in that grove, remember?" Seb said to Kat, who grinned and nodded.

"I'm glad Bridget saw us. All these groves start to look alike after a while. We might've ridden right by their place."

Conor dashed out, saw them, and lit up. He charged for them so hard, Seb held his reins a bit tighter, afraid his horse might spook and trample the little guy.

"Maybe we should walk from here?" Seb drew his horse to a halt and swung down just as he thought of the puppies and kittens. They'd checked them frequently, and now the satchels that carried them wriggled as if the babies were excited to see who was coming.

Kat unhooked the satchels, came to the front of the horses, and handed one to Seb. They closed the distance with the sprinting child.

Kat said, "We'd better have a care how we let them loose."

"I'd hate to see them turn and run for home."

Conor hit Seb in the legs, and Seb couldn't resist hugging him.

"You came. We were hoping for some company."

They kept moving and reached Bridget, then Fiona. Down lower, they could see the cabin now. Across the stream, Donal was setting aside a bag he must be using to sow oats or corn. Bruce was fiddling with the corner of a large corral. He paused, waved, and went right back to work, but soon finished. Bruce and Donal walked across the stream on flat stones.

Maeve came out of the house, wiping her hands, her red curls pulled back in a bun but flying loose with every step she took.

They were smiling. They'd had time to heal. Yes, they'd always miss Shay, Fiona's husband who'd drowned, but they would survive.

Seb reached Fiona just as a yip sounded from inside his bag. Conor froze.

"What's that?" He sounded too excited to dare to hope.

"Everyone, get ready. We can't let them run off." Seb crouched to the ground, and Kat did the same. They set the satchels down and opened them. The kittens exploded out of the bag, hissing and climbing Kat until they were sitting on her shoulder. Kat squeaked from all the little claws digging in.

Conor howled and clapped his hands.

Fiona said, "Hush now, boyo. They're scared."

Seb placed a hand under the round belly of the little puppy he reached first and handed him to Conor, whose eyes went round.

"Gentle now, son." Fiona tried to sound stern, but the smile blooming on her face ruined any scolding.

Bruce reached for a kitten and peeled it off Kat's shoulder.

Seb handed the second puppy to Bridget, and Bruce handed the kitten he had to Donal. Then he freed the other one from trying to climb Kat's head. This one went to Maeve.

"We've need of a good dog and cat. But two of each?" Fiona shook her head.

"Our cat had a litter of six, and the dog did the same. We had no expectation of that when we got them. You'd be doing us a favor if you'd take them before we're overrun. Jake threatened to send about five dogs and ask you to find homes for them."

"Well, it's time for our morning coffee. You're welcome to join us. I made dinner rolls, along with our loaves of bread. Can you stay awhile?" Maeve's eyes gleamed like a young woman who'd seen no one but her family through a long winter.

"We'll stay for coffee, but Kat and I"—Seb smiled up at her—"we're headed back east. We've found Montana winters don't suit us."

They'd been a married couple on the wagon train, and Seb didn't think the O'Tooles had ever heard different.

"I'm going to miss you."

"With the train, we hope we can come and visit now and again."

Maeve threw her arms around Kat.

"Seb, good to see you." Bruce came up and shook Seb's hand. Donal clapped him on the back.

"Welcome." Fiona took her turn hugging Kat. "How're things going?"

Seb didn't exactly want to tell them everything. He realized he'd adopted Beth's habit of not explaining where exactly they were going. No reason not to, and yet he hesitated.

Kat said, "We've decided to climb on the train and ride a bit. We have no firm plans beyond that."

Fiona slid an arm across Kat's back. "Come inside. We want to hear all about it."

"And we'd love to hear all about your winter." Seb pointed across the stream to a small herd of Angus cattle, five of them—one a bull. Each cow had a calf at her side. There was a brown-and-white-spotted milk cow with a spring baby as black as its Angus daddy and a match for the other calves in the yard. The calf from the milk cow mama was a little bonier, a little taller. Most likely every calf they had would match the bull from now on.

In the corral with the other cows stood seven oxen. They'd started the winter with eight, so Seb was sure they'd eaten the oxen and spared the Angus to grow the herd.

"It's our hope to reach Alton before the sun sets, so we can't stay long." Seb walked behind the women and children, lined up with Bruce and Donal. "The place looks nice. You've made it into a fine home."

Bruce said, "Our wagon train rolled through first last summer, but there were others. Many have turned aside just as we have. When I'm out riding, whether to hunt or scout, I find new homesteaders real regular. This land is going to be plumb crowded in a few years. I might stay out here—outside the canyon, that is. It suits me."

Seb was startled. Seb had seen it as Bruce making a sacrifice to remain behind, but maybe the man had begun to build a life here.

"I had some cash money, so I rode into Alton early in the spring and bought a stretch of land. No need to build a cabin, as it's not a homestead." He swept an arm toward the mountains, not distant in this fertile valley. "My land ends where those hills rise up."

Bruce looked at Donal. "If'n you want your cabin to yourself, son, just say the word and I'll go."

"Maybe at some time, but for now it'd be mighty lonely. I'm used to a big family. Of course, my family is right here at hand. But staying in the cabin alone, especially since we built a separate room on for you, isn't anything I wish for." Donal bumped Bruce with his elbow in such a friendly way, Seb was glad Bruce had stayed and stepped in for Shay.

"If I get to thinking you're ornery, I'll let you know."

Bruce laughed as they all went into the O'Tooles' cabin. "Why are you here so late?"

Seb thought of how desperately he'd wanted to leave months ago. He didn't talk about the snow-clotted canyon entrance; he was leery of telling anything that might give away their location. "We'd planned to leave as soon as the cold weather let up, but before we could do so, Beth had twin babies. A girl and a boy."

The excitement almost burst from each of the O'Tooles as Kat talked about delivering them, and Seb talked about how much the little angels cried.

They settled at a kitchen table big enough for everyone. When the news about the babies finally calmed, Seb looked around. "I like this cabin. Cupboards and a dry sink. A table and chairs. Two rocking chairs. All anyone needs."

"It's been a long winter for a fact. Plenty of time for working on the place." Bruce sipped his coffee.

Seb ran his hand across the tabletop. "Smooth as silk. Who built this?"

Bruce shrugged, and his cheeks might've pinked up a bit. "I've always enjoyed woodworking. And with Donal's help, and Conor's, plus the women keeping everything else running while I fussed a bit, we managed to build a nice table and a few other bits."

Donal slapped Bruce on the back with true kindness. "You taught me so much. I don't know if I could come close to building such fine things as you did. Yet I could build a table and chairs."

"Oscar's got a knack as a teacher, too. He did his best to teach Kat and me how to build the barn and corrals."

"How is everyone?" Fiona nearly burst with the question, wanting to know everything. They spent a pleasant hour together full of news and friendship. They'd brought the puppies and kittens into the house, and Conor and Bridget played on the floor with their new pets. Maeve found them a meaty bone, leaving the four critters to settle into their gnawing while the O'Tooles, Bruce, Kat, and Seb talked.

Seb found himself with yet another place he hated to leave.

They all ate the warm rolls Maeve had cooling on the counter and drank fresh coffee. It was with great reluctance that Seb finally announced it was time for them to go.

Fiona and Maeve begged them to stay for the noon meal or stay for the day or even the night—a few days maybe.

It wasn't easy to resist, but then Seb itched to get on with his life, to set himself up to work. And he had an itch where Kat was concerned, too, and wanted to get on with marrying her. He wished he could tell these good folks that. He could even encourage them to come along to Alton, so that Kat could have friends attend her wedding.

But they were supposed to be married already, so Kat was hugged all around. Seb shook hands and got his back slapped and listened closely to Bruce's directions to Alton. There would be no worry about finding their way.

There was a clear trail. They were trotting south long before midday.

"This trail is no trail. It's a road. And look at that." He nodded westward.

They both looked wide-eyed at the tidy log cabin with horses in a corral behind it and a small barn. There was a clothesline with what were definitely women's clothes among the drying laundry. And the rectangles of white waving in the breeze were probably diapers.

"A family." Seb's hands tightened nervously on the reins until the horse tossed its head with a jingle of iron from the bridle. Seb relaxed his hold but not his gut. "Were they here last fall?"

Kat shook her head. "Do you think the O'Tooles know they've got company a half-hour ride away?"

"Probably. Bruce seems like a knowing man. And he said settlers are flooding in. Oscar might have known about them. Or noticed them at a distance and avoided them. He might have avoided this trail, too."

"Another cabin, and one on past that," Seb said, pointing. "And there's one over there."

"I'm no judge of space, but those cabins look to be built on a bunch of acres. Probably the size of your usual homestead. And they're newly built. Just this spring by the looks of 'em."

"If folks are coming out on the train instead of on wagon trains, they can get into any area the minute it thaws in the spring."

A man stepped out of the nearest cabin and watched them ride past. He raised an arm and waved. "Howdy, folks. You on the way from Boise? Are you settling around here?"

Boise, Idaho, was the capital of the territory. Seb knew that much. Honestly, he hadn't known that before he'd come west. Oscar and his brothers and Jake talked about settling in the West and the Oregon Trail country. He'd heard talk of new territories and a lot about the train.

Kat then said something that made Seb cringe.

"We're headed for the train. Do we follow this trail all the way there?" She asked the man for directions.

"Yep, heads right for Alton. You'll pass through Darius on the way."

"Darius?"

"Yep, a new town. It's laid out and being built up fast. There's talk of a train spur heading up from Alton to Boise. There's a good chance it'll happen, too. The territorial capital should connect to a train." The man shook his head and chewed on what looked like a straw of dried oats or maybe a grass stem. "You folks have got a long day ahead, though."

The cabin, the corral, the barn all looked so new, Seb could tell they hadn't weathered a winter yet. Which meant this man had arrived here recently.

"Did you settle here just this spring?" He drew his horse to a halt, though his impulse was to hurry on. Not speak to anyone. Beth and her family's wariness had rubbed off on him.

"Yep, came out on the train headed for Oregon. Then folks on the train spoke of the Snake River Plain and how fertile it is, and a bunch of us decided to go no farther. Folks are pouring into this country, more every day. It's a rich and beautiful land. You folks want to come inside? Share a meal with us or have coffee?"

"We'd better get on." Kat sounded friendly, and Seb noticed she wasn't offering the stranger much information. "The long ride sounds like we don't dare tarry. But thank you for the invitation."

And on they rode through a land teeming with neighbors.

After they'd passed several dozen homesteads, Seb said, "I feel like we ought to go back and warn Jake and Oscar about all these folks. Probably more will be coming every day. They may think they're isolated out in Hidden Canyon, but they're kidding themselves."

Every time they passed near enough, someone would come to the door of their cabin or their barn or straighten from hoeing their garden. The women often sat outside, doing needlework or working over a steaming washtub, children playing nearby. They'd call out a greeting, and occasionally someone would approach them and talk for a few minutes.

"I almost asked that first man how long it would take us to get to the train, but he likely doesn't know. He might well have climbed off the train, then driven a wagon for days to get here. And it's doubtful he's gone to town since he settled."

The cabins were closer together as they followed the increasingly broad trail south. Seb had let go of any worries he had over getting lost. Not much chance of that on a trail that had turned into a road. He saw a half-grown boy driving a yoke of oxen across a field, pulling a plow. "I guess I'd gotten used to there being only one small group of people in the whole world."

They ate hardtack and jerky as they rode. Their only stops were to water the horses when a stream came into sight. And they gave the horses a chance to graze every couple of hours. Seb was grateful for the break. He hadn't done much riding in his life, especially since they'd moved into the canyon, though Oscar had insisted everyone ride a bit to keep the horses gentled.

They'd trot for a while, but mainly they traveled at a fast, steady walk. The horses probably could have galloped, and that would have shortened their travel time, but there was no sense in being hard on their mounts.

The sun was getting lower in the sky when a town finally came into view. Now their plans to marry came back quick. Seb had thought of it a little on the trail, but he'd had plenty on his mind to keep from focusing on it for very long. And now they were in town, the train tracks visible. Suddenly he found himself nervous, fretting about getting married. They should probably put it off, but he wanted to marry her. It all seemed so rushed. Still, he couldn't just plunk her into a hotel room and get a separate room. It wasn't safe for her to be alone, nor proper. No, they had to get married right away. They'd have to find a preacher and—

"Seb, listen."

The distant clacking of wheels could be heard. The sound was coming from the west.

"Let's try to get on that train. We're going to have to hurry. We can . . . uh, get married when we get off the train, can't we?"

Seb fought a smile. They did *not* have to hurry. In fact, they could let this train go. Talk out whether to sell the horses or take them. Have their stay in Alton be a bit of a honeymoon while they plotted out their future. In truth, she was as nervous as he was. Seeing this helped to steady him.

"Let's hurry then."

When they got to town, Seb said, "Let's sell the horses if we can. We can buy another pair when we disembark, can't we?"

Kat looked at him, then the horses, then pointed to a livery stable near the railroad station. "Let's see if we can do it in time. I'd just as soon travel light."

Riding up to the stable, they dismounted.

A man ambled out, watching them, wiping his hands on a piece of red-checked flannel. "Help you, folks?"

"Do you buy horses and saddles? We want to catch the train and will pay for the horses to ride along if we must, but if you'd—"

"I'll give you fifty dollars for the two of them and another ten for the saddles and bridles."

Seb blinked. He figured he was being cheated, but then he had no idea what things were worth out here. Twenty-five dollars was a fair price for a horse in Independence.

"Deal. We'll unload our satchels and leave the horses with you right now."

The man nodded, as calm as the nearby mountains. He was probably very happy inside, but he was doing a good job of covering it up.

"The train stops here for an hour. Folks'll get off and stretch their legs and eat, usually at that diner right there." He pointed to a tidy little building close to the station, as new and raw as the rest of the town, with the words *Alton Diner* painted over the front door.

"Get in now and you'll beat the crowd that comes in

from the train." He pulled three twenty-dollar gold pieces out of his pocket. Kat and Seb unloaded their supplies, headed for the diner, and were eating roast beef and mashed potatoes when the train pulled into the station.

"Let's get on over there in case the train doesn't stop for as long as that hostler said." Seb sopped up the last of the gravy with a bit of bread.

"I hadn't realized how hungry I was," Kat said. "And how nice it would be to talk to people other than those in the canyon."

She reached for his hand across the table just as the diner's front door opened and folks who must've come from the train straggled inside.

"We did the right thing leaving. But it was hard." She squeezed his hand tight, and he nodded.

"Hard and right—I think that about covers it." They walked straight to the train station and purchased tickets to Cheyenne.

"Do you have a newspaper for sale here?" Seb asked the station agent.

The man shook his head. Then he pointed at a bench near the front door. "There's one that got left by someone earlier. I've read it through twice. Go ahead and take it along. It's a strange paper from back east. Out of Chicago, I think. Nothing in it but crime and worry. Makes a man glad he came west."

"Thank you kindly, sir." Seb picked up the paper, folded it neatly, and tucked it under his arm. Speaking quietly, he said, "I'll be interested to see if there's any news of Thaddeus Rutledge in the paper. He's a powerful man. He might well be in the news—if he's still alive."

They boarded while water was still pouring into the tanker car from the water tower beside the train tracks.

By the time the weary travelers returned, the sun was low in the sky. Seb and Kat had chosen the rearmost passenger car and the seat farthest back. She twisted to look out the window behind him.

"Look at that sunset." Kat silently stared at the sky while the train car filled with passengers. They watched as God painted a glorious red across the horizon, and then the train let out a whistle blast. With a jerk of their car, they started pulling out of the station.

Seb leaned close to whisper, "We probably should have hunted up a preacher and gotten married. There would have been enough time."

She took his hand. Seb looked down at their intertwined hands, just as their lives would soon be. She said, "Nothing improper about sitting together in a train car full of people. Besides, I'd prefer to have the wedding when we aren't in such a rush."

Seb meant it about wishing they'd managed vows. But it was all part of an uncertain new future, rushing at them with the speed of a train. Traveling together made a wedding inevitable now, and he didn't hesitate to accept that. Even so, he was a bit afraid of what the future held.

6

Cheyenne was a bustling railroad town still growing over the heads and under the feet of the people who'd settled there. As the territorial capital, it had been chosen by the Union Pacific Railroad to be the headquarters of the railroad's mountain region. There was also an army fort just a few miles out of town. The future looked bright indeed for the town of Cheyenne.

Kat was overwhelmed by the noise, the people, the motion of it all.

Seb edged closer to her. "I thought the ride from Hidden Canyon to the train was crowded with all those new settlers. Then I thought the train was ridiculously crowded. Now?" He made a broad gesture at the dozens of people on Cheyenne's streets. Their fellow passengers clomping down the steps of the train depot, with new passengers clomping up. Horseback riders trotting past. Newspaper vendors and food vendors hawking their wares. The train hissing and steaming. Voices surrounding them until it was a din. Wagons taking on supplies from the train while other wagons jostled for position to add crates to the boxcars once space opened up.

"I thought two babies made life hectic." She looked at Seb, and they laughed.

She let the crowd press and urge her forward until it was their turn to descend to the street. "Let's look around town and find the church and a parson. We'll have to buy horses, but the town isn't so big that we'll need the horses right away. We'll buy them once we find a homestead."

"Are you ready for a wedding, K-Kat?" He then got a very strange look on his face.

After a long night and most of a day on the train, it was finally time to get married.

"I am ready, and what are you looking at me like that for?"

"I just realized I don't know your name."

A giggle slipped through Kat's lips, but then she lost all traces of humor as she realized what she had to admit. And she'd better do it here and now, not wait for when they were standing before the parson. Seb's reaction needed to come out now. "I'm . . . well, I'm Katherine Wadsworth."

"Wadsworth?" Sebastian's head jerked up. "From Chicago?"

A shudder at his expression surprised her. She'd left the name so completely behind her.

"You've heard the name?"

"So you're part of the famous Wadsworth family?"

"Yes. Um, I'm a widow. I was married to a Wadsworth."

Sebastian tilted his head a little. "You're a widow?"

Kat shook her head. "We really don't know much about each other, do we?"

"No, we don't. Wadsworth is your *married* name then?"

"Yes. I married into the Wadsworth fortune."

"I've noticed you don't talk much about your past, but we've been talking for days now. How come you've never told me this?"

With a shrug, Kat said, "That name was always trouble. It just got the wrong kind of attention whenever it came out. Even back in Chicago, while Jeremy was alive, we both got in the habit of not saying his name very often. Then I was announced to be a Collins on the wagon train, and I never corrected that."

"You were supposed to be married to me even back then. And now you're going to be a Jones. That name doesn't grab much interest."

"His father and uncle controlled it together. When his father died, Jeremy, an only child, and his uncle Patrick became equal partners. But Jeremy was never quite ruthless and greedy enough to suit Uncle Patrick, so Jeremy never *ran* anything. Then Jeremy died, and my owning half of all that money suited Patrick even less. I was suspicious of the events surrounding Jeremy's death. I made a lot of accusations, which made it easy for me to be thought of as hysterical. Next thing I knew, Patrick pronounced me as insane and had me locked up."

"I knew Jeremy Wadsworth."

"You knew Jeremy?" Kat was shocked.

"Yes, he went to George Washington Institute with me. In St. Louis. We weren't well acquainted, but he was good friends with Marcus Coleman, a student I knew well. I knew Jeremy enough to say hello."

"Marcus Coleman, that's the name you wrote on that

packet you tried to get us to mail when you thought you were dying."

"Yes, the two of us, we were both inventors and spent most of our time in a laboratory at the Institute."

"Jeremy did go to St. Louis to college, but that was before I met him. His grandmother lived there, and he stayed with her through his college years. He studied literature and for a time considered going to seminary and becoming a pastor. His father, Douglas, didn't approve. His father was cut from the same cloth as Uncle Patrick. When Jeremy was drawn back to Chicago to learn the family business, he met me. I'm a nobody, plain little Katherine Pendergast. My father was a doctor in a modest neighborhood in Chicago. Ma helped him until she died when I was sixteen. Then I stepped in and did nursing work with him. I brought no family fortune or powerful connections. Jeremy and I met at church, and we loved each other. I'd heard of the Wadsworth name and knew Jeremy was connected to them, but there was nothing wealthy or powerful or ruthless about Jeremy. I didn't know he was an heir to the fortune until after we were married."

"You were married to a man who inherited half the Wadsworth fortune? And now you're marrying me?"

"Yes, and I'll never get that money, nor do I want it. Jeremy hated how greedy and unkind his family was. He was too kind for that world. When he died, I was devastated. I threw around some accusations, challenged Uncle Patrick about it—privately then, and publicly later. It made him furious, and he called me insane. When I was still deep in mourning, I found myself under lock and key at the

Horecroft Asylum, and Uncle Patrick had taken control of the reins of the Wadsworth empire. I think they've built half of the tall buildings in Chicago."

"And that's where you met Ginny? At the asylum?"

"Yes, I found her wandering the halls one night, which I tended to do myself. I realized she was escaping and stuck to her like a burr."

"So you hadn't known them much longer than I had when you scooped me up out of that alley."

"I met Beth about four days before you did."

"And you've been blocked from an inheritance worth a fortune?"

"Now that you know just how much money should be mine, do you still want to marry me, even if I reject that money?"

Sebastian smiled. "I reject it right along with you, and yes, I still want to marry you." Then his smile faded. "That's a powerful family with a dangerous reputation. I can see why you're afraid of your uncle. But you'll be a married woman soon. He'll have no power over you."

"No power beyond that of a man who takes what he wants and is a law unto himself. And he would crush me like a cockroach to keep me away from his wealth."

"Yep, no power beyond that." Seb shuddered. "We'll stay clear of him. Now, let's go see about finding a parson and a homestead."

Because they came upon it first, they headed for the land office, where they picked the homestead closest to town, a fifteen-mile ride away. The area close to town was getting well settled. When the land agent found out they weren't married, he encouraged Kat to claim the parcel next to

Sebastian's. He said women, especially in the equality state of Wyoming, did it all the time, then got married and built their cabin double-sized so it straddled the property line.

Kat had no great aspiration to be large landowners, nor were they sure they'd stay anywhere for more than five years. She also didn't want to tell the man her real name. "One homestead is enough," she said.

The land agent pushed and showed them a piece of land up against some wasteland in the foothills of the Laramie Mountains. The rugged land would likely never be homesteaded, so they'd have the use of a large stretch beyond their claim.

For their nonexistent herd of cattle.

Kat couldn't get too excited about their wasteland or mountain or whatever they were supposed to have the use of. Lots of trees, though, to use for building material, and Cheyenne, there on the grasslands of eastern Wyoming, was a bit sparse of trees.

She gave Seb a pleading look. "I'd prefer just the one homestead." They hadn't discussed it, and if she had to, she would drag him outside and explain that she wanted her name kept off a land record.

"One homestead is plenty," Seb told the man. "Thank you."

"You folks are making a big mistake." The land agent shook his head, as if the younger generation were going downhill fast.

Once they'd left the land office, Kat muttered, "I guess we missed our chance to be land barons."

Seb only laughed and took her hand.

The land agent had also given them directions to his church, telling them the parson lived right next door to the church.

Minutes later, Seb and Kat walked up the two steps to the parsonage. Seb paused and turned to her. "We're going to make a good marriage, Kat. You've told me your father was a doctor. Mine was a schoolmaster. They were both good men, and our mothers were good women. We've come from two fine marriages, haven't we?"

"Yes. We should know how to make a happy home." With a hard little jerk of her chin, she took his hand and said, "Let's get married."

He knocked firmly on the door, and it wasn't long before it swung open.

The parson was a skinny, stoop-shouldered man with wild tufts of white hair and gold wire-rimmed glasses.

"Parson, we would like to get married." Seb sounded quite sure.

Kat worried the parson might want them to take a little more time to think about it. Instead, the man favored them with a beaming smile that eased Kat's heart and made her feel as though she was facing a kind man with a generous faith.

"I'm Parson Roscoe. I'll call my wife, who can act as a witness. You young folks go ahead over to the church." He waved his hand in the general direction, but they'd just walked past it and so knew where it was. "I'll put my suit coat on and get my prayer book. My wife and I will be only a few paces behind you."

They barely beat the parson to the church door.

His wife was as plump as he was skinny, but her smile

was a match for his. "I love weddings. Are you young folks going to stay around Cheyenne?"

"Yes, Kat and I just homesteaded west of town."

"I hope you can join us for church services Sunday morning. We have a prayer service and singing on Wednesday nights, too, and a woman's sewing circle that meets Tuesday mornings. The church is always at the heart of the goings-on in town."

Kat looked around the small church, probably room for thirty people to sit. Forty if they were a very friendly church. "I just realized I don't know what day of the week it is. We've been traveling, and I've lost track."

"It's Monday."

"We're not even sure where our homestead is. I hope it will be possible to attend church. I've missed it. We lived a long way out in a small community through the last year and just had a Bible reading and sang together on Sundays. We will be here if it's possible."

"Fair enough."

Kat and Seb walked down the church's center aisle, Mrs. Roscoe beside Kat, and Parson Roscoe beside Seb. Kat remembered her first wedding and the tidy little march she'd taken while on her father's arm, up to the front to meet her husband. Jeremy's father hadn't approved and hadn't attended. His mother was dead, as was Kat's. It was a quiet ceremony, but she'd had a bouquet of posies and had worn a new dress. Jeremy was in a fine black suit, standing up front waiting for her.

She remembered Beth and Jake getting married in front of the wagon-train members, all of them beside a campfire.

She had to fight a laugh. They certainly did things more casually on the frontier.

They reached the front, and Parson Roscoe eased between everyone to stand up front. Mrs. Roscoe settled on the front pew as if it was her designated place.

"Tell me your names, youngsters."

Kat's smile froze. She'd told no one her real name except Seb. Was she safe out here? She didn't think she had anyone searching for her like Thaddeus Rutledge had searched for Beth and Ginny. But her uncle was a powerful man. If he wanted to find her, she'd have her real name signed in a church register to tell anyone who cared to look that she was married. She'd avoided this at the land office. Now, without much choice and realizing she'd hesitated a bit too long and everyone was staring at her, she said, "Katherine Wadsworth."

Seb might have hesitated for a bit, too, and said, "Sebastian Jones."

It was a firm reminder that someone had shot him. He had no idea who and whether they might try again.

He slid an arm around her waist as if he knew what they'd both just done, what they'd both admitted and put on record. Hiding had been safe. She was only just now realizing what they'd given up by leaving Hidden Canyon.

Then, committed to facing the future—though a bit afraid—she inched closer to Seb and faced Parson Roscoe and his beaming smile.

"Dearly beloved . . ."

The vows were profound, but she made them without a qualm. In fact, she wished he'd spoken them a bit faster.

"I now pronounce you man and wife. What God has

joined together let no man put asunder." Parson Roscoe raised one hand and swept it in an arc that covered them both.

"We have a registry book where marriages and baptisms are recorded." He gestured at a book so crisp and new, she had to wonder how long the church had been here and how long it would last—and who might end up with that book in their clutches.

Kat signed her full name. As Katherine Wadsworth appeared on the page, she wondered if she should have instead said her name was Katherine Pendergast, her maiden name.

It was too late. She wasn't sure the marriage would even be legal with her name written down improperly.

Seb signed after her, and they both gave almost matching sighs, then turned to smile at each other.

"Hello, Mrs. Jones. Thank you for marrying me."

"You are most welcome, Mr. Jones. It is an honor to be your wife. Now we should probably find food and a room for the night."

And that set off a blush. She'd been married before. She knew what it all meant. But they'd decided to wait on marital intimacy. Only just now had she sounded over-eager. Would her overly warm, no doubt pink face make Seb think she had changed her mind about giving their marriage time to grow into a true one?

The tangle in her mind was too much. Kat shoved all her worries aside, took Seb's hand, and strode out of the church, the Roscoes' congratulations ringing in her ears.

All she could do was keep moving forward.

Now here they stood outside the church, a married couple.

"Let's go spend the night at the Drury Hotel." He pointed at the three-story hotel just across the street. "I hope they serve supper."

"It looks expensive."

"We'll call it a honeymoon." Seb swung their hands and smiled at her, then dragged her across the street. Although, honestly, she came along willingly.

"Tomorrow I'll need to find a general store and order some odd things."

"I remember the odd things you ordered and took into the canyon."

"I need more of all that and other things I have thought of since. I suspect they'll have to be shipped to Cheyenne. With the train running, it may not take very long."

"What things do you need?" Kat asked.

"Oh, sheet iron, although I may be able to get that at the blacksmith shop. A forge and bellows so I can bend my own iron. Zinc. Ammonia or the chemicals to make it. Agglomerate blocks. Carbon plates. Maybe some porous pots. I'll need wire and a wire cutting tool. A lot of things."

"I regret asking."

"I could use a lab assistant."

"I assist rather well," Kat said, "if I'm given specific, direct orders I can understand."

Seb chuckled. "I hear some real doubt in your voice."

"Nothing wrong with your hearing, husband. Now let's go eat."

7

"Tomorrow, before we go and look at the homestead, I'm going to talk with the local banker about getting money transferred here from my bank in Independence."

They walked toward the hotel, watching their step because the town was bustling with folks heading in different directions. Kat wasn't sure what Seb was thinking, but she was trying hard not to think about the night ahead.

"I didn't put my name on the homestead," she said, "and I had no choice about signing the church registry book. That's not a very public book, though. But now, wiring your bank in Independence, the town where you were shot, to tell the bank exactly where you are?" Kat shrugged uncertainly. "We are really coming out of hiding."

"I know." Seb glanced at the bank as they walked past it. "What else can we do? I have money in that bank, and it seems foolish not to transfer it here and use it. I'll contact my bank, and I might as well wire my lawyers in Independence about sending new earnings here."

"Lawyers? Plural?"

"Yes, two of them."

"You can afford to hire two lawyers?"

Seb nodded, and Kat thought he looked a little smug. But she couldn't say he was a boastful man since he'd kept all this to himself for over a year.

"I've had some good results with my patents. It's not a fortune, but it's always been enough to buy the supplies I need and to feed myself. I hope they've been investing my earnings wisely while I've been gone. Of course, the patents will run out. I have to get new patents to keep earning money. Still, we can probably afford to have anything we want, as long as we don't want too much."

They exchanged a smile of understanding, then entered the hotel. Seb went to rent themselves a room.

Kat figured he'd had some money when they found him in that alley. He'd offered Beth money to pay for things he wanted to order for his inventions. And heaven knows he'd never spent a cent of it other than for those odd supplies to be shipped to Fort Bridger. She had no idea what they cost, yet it sounded as if he was well off enough that they could afford a meal in the hotel and a room for a few nights. But they couldn't live for long on what Seb had in his pockets.

After a fine meal, they went up to their room. The sun had set, and night had fallen.

"W-would you like me to step out of the room while you change?" Seb had removed his hat and was now strangling the brim. His fretting made hers a bit easier to bear.

Kat, her hand shaking a bit, pointed to the dressing screen. "I'll go back there. You can . . . uh, stay."

She pulled her nightgown out of her satchel, and gold coins went bouncing and rolling across the room. Kat gasped. She and Seb scrambled, chasing after the coins.

"These are twenty-dollar gold pieces," Seb said. Frowning, he dug into his own satchel and came up with a fistful of gold.

Kat pulled out a note. "It's from Beth." She unfolded it and read aloud.

> "I brought most every penny I could gather from my trust fund when I fled Chicago, only to discover that there is no place to spend money here in our canyon. You have both worked hard by our sides. Kat, you were a great comfort to Mama, both in Horecroft and since then. She has told me she believes her escape was successful largely because of you. She views you as a second daughter. Please accept this money as a gift from all of us at Hidden Canyon."

Kat looked up from the note and met Seb's eyes.

"There's no way to return the money," he said, "not without turning around and riding back and handing it over."

"You think we could find that canyon again?"

Seb shrugged. "We studied our back trail as we rode out of there. Remember how much time we spent talking about landmarks and such?"

"I do. I also remember the endless piles of rocks and groves of trees that all started to look alike, and how well hidden the canyon is. Honestly, I'm not sure we could find it."

"I'm not at all confident either. I suppose Bruce could, though."

"We did work hard. I could cook better than Beth and Ginny. I worked at Ma's side while she was alive and ran the household after she died. I grew up working, cooking, and sewing. It all came back while on the wagon train. Still, all the things they taught me, especially Oscar and his brothers and Beth—it was like being trained in how to survive in the West. Beth doesn't owe me a thing."

"I was unconscious or hurt enough to be mighty fragile for a month. And Oscar already had the cabins built. Nope, she shouldn't have done this."

But she had.

Kat looked down at the gold in her hand. "I don't think I'll pack up the coins and mail them to sit in the O'Tooles' cabin for months. And I have no wish to ride back and hand the money to her."

"We'll spend this until my money comes," Seb said. "Maybe we should put it in the bank, too. I wonder if we're more likely to be robbed on the trail or for the bank to be robbed?"

He looked up. Their eyes met.

She'd let the gift of coins distract her from the night ahead. But no longer. She forgot about money and working with Beth and Jake. She forgot about the O'Tooles and mail and bank robberies. Kat stared at her husband, her cheeks heating up, and she whirled away. "The . . . dressing screen." She shoved the money into her satchel and hurried behind the screen, not sure if she'd be so quick to come back out.

"I'll change out here," he said.

Kat squeaked but didn't speak beyond that while she quick changed into her nightgown.

His wife emerged from behind the screen dressed in a white nightgown. It covered her from neck to wrist to toe. Her hair was pulled into a single braid that hung over one shoulder. She couldn't have been more modest if she'd been living in a convent.

And yet he'd never seen anyone more desirable, more beautiful. She stood with her hands clasped together in front of her, her blue eyes wide with nerves.

She said, "We decided we'd get to know each other better before . . . well, before. I'm not sure why I'm feeling so shy."

"I think it's best we wait. Finding out today that you're a widow, and a widow to Jeremy Wadsworth no less—" he hesitated, shook his head—"it's made me realize we don't know each other that well. We have to do better, Kat. We both have to break this habit we have of not talking about ourselves. I understand why you don't like the Wadsworth name bandied about. And I think you understand why I don't talk much about my work. That's still a good idea when we're with others. But now that we're married, we need to trust each other and open up more. And I'm not saying this to goad you in any way. I'm worse than you are with my secretive inventing."

"We've talked about this before, but it seems like we always start planning the future and not talk about the past."

"Let's spend a bit more time tonight just talking—

talking and nothing more. Get to know each other. Then let's get some sleep."

With a bright smile, Kat said, "Thank you." She lifted her hand, which was visibly trembling. "Here I am all shaking and blushing. I'm a widow. I know what goes on between a man and his wife on their wedding night."

"That's probably why you're feeling shy."

"Most likely."

"You know more than I do about married life. I've spent every spare minute of my life in a laboratory mixing chemicals. My best friends were my lawyers and the sweet old lady, Mrs. Gundersen, who lived across the street from my parents. I'm probably more nervous than you are."

She wrinkled her nose and shrugged. "I doubt that."

He took her trembling hand and guided her to the bed, where they sat side by side. "Tell me more about yourself, Kat. What was it like for you in Chicago?"

"Jeremy and I met . . ."

He'd wanted to hear about her childhood, her parents, working at her pa's side. It bothered him to think of her being married to another man. The feeling that burned in him couldn't be jealousy, could it? Why would he care? Probably because she'd loved her first husband, and Seb knew she didn't love him. And maybe never would. Without planning it, he interrupted her before she'd finished her first sentence. "But first, before we talk, can we share a kiss?"

When she nodded, he reached for her and pulled her close.

Then he kissed her, hoping to make the kiss one she'd remember. One she'd prefer to old memories she now seemed willing to share and he no longer cared to hear about. He deepened the kiss and then she kissed him back.

They did get to know each other better that night, but it wasn't in the way they'd planned.

The rattle of a wagon passing by their window two stories below woke Kat from the sweetest dream she'd had in years. Not for one second was she confused about where she was.

Cheyenne, Wyoming. Hotel. Married. Happy.

Her hand rested on Seb's chest. Her head on his shoulder. His arm wrapped around her back.

It was daylight, early still, going by the slant of the sun in their east-facing window.

She moved her head just enough to look up at her husband. His blue eyes met hers. Their children would have blue eyes. The thought made her smile.

"Good morning, Kat. It's a very good morning."

"My only regret is that I didn't marry you ten minutes after we met."

That got a chuckle out of him, which she felt beneath her resting head. "Even when I was bleeding, had broken ribs and a head wound? When I was mostly unconscious?"

"Well, maybe two weeks after." She giggled and yanked the hair on his chest.

He winced, then laid his hand over hers. He pressed a kiss to her forehead. She shifted to reach his lips, and they shared their first good-morning kiss.

"Sebastian, I realize now that I'd gotten in the habit of keeping my thoughts about myself inside. It started even before the asylum when I had people asking me for money or favors when they'd hear my name was Wadsworth. In the asylum I buried my honest feelings and was the calm, sane woman anyone could see should be released. Once I was out, I went to using a fake name and began the fake relationship with you. It became a habit to say nothing for fear I'd say the wrong thing. I wish I'd had more courage after we were on our own in that canyon. I wish I hadn't wasted a year when I could have been getting to know you better. I worked beside everyone in that cabin and never shared much about myself. But I promise to open up more now that we're married."

He kissed her again, then drew back. "I've been in the habit of being secretive, too. Keeping things to myself for fear my inventions will be stolen by someone."

Kat gave him a weak smile. "Like by the man who shot you last year?"

He nodded.

"That was strong evidence that someone was after your inventions."

"Someone, but not you. Not the folks in Hidden Canyon. I was already being secretive, and I suppose getting shot made me even more so."

Kat pulled him close. "I think we both need to try harder to let each other in, especially to let each other into our hearts."

"We'll make it a goal then. To get to know the woman I married is an inspired idea."

As he kissed her once more, he had another inspired idea. No amount of wagon traffic disturbed the rest of their first very good morning.

They were so late to breakfast, the waitress in the hotel restaurant took their order with a smug smile on her face. But nothing could ruin Kat's good mood. Seb was going to be an inventor, and she was going to be a farmer.

She hesitated just a bit when she thought of Uncle Patrick. As a married woman, she was free from him now. But would the law stop him if he came for her to take her away? After all, her name was now listed in that church registry book.

"With you contacting the bank and your lawyers," she said, "I think we have to accept that we're no longer hiding."

The waitress, who was the wife of the hotel owner, and who'd been informed they were a newly married couple, put a plate of eggs and bacon down in front of them with the clink of china on wood. "Enjoy your breakfast, youngsters."

They again talked of the future, not the past, as they ate. They had a lot to accomplish today, so they ate quickly and emerged from the hotel with a long list of things to arrange.

Kat did her best to set aside her fears about Uncle Patrick. She wondered about the laws Beth had spoken of. Though her heart shuddered at the thought of dealing with Patrick Wadsworth, she would study up on the law to learn what she needed to do to make herself safe.

"There's no sense in trying to build the cabin ourselves." Seb looked around the town as if a carpenter might suddenly appear before them. "And I need a separate building for my laboratory."

Kat held his hand, and they wandered the busy streets of the new Wyoming town. "Why a separate building? Can't the laboratory be a room in the house?"

Shaking his head, he led the way to the general store. "I work with chemicals, and sometimes they react with, well, some volatility."

"Volatility? Are you going to blow yourself up, Sebastian?"

"I'm going to try most sincerely not to, but sometimes gases react, and sometimes the fire in the forge kicks up a lot of smoke and fumes. It's best not to bring all that into the house. Oscar once threatened to kick me out of the cave house."

"I believe I heard about that." Kat went back to looking where she was going. "Fine then. We've got Beth's money—let's use it."

"If we must."

"And while we have the builders working, we'll also need a barn and a corral for the horses. Not a barn as big as the one Jake and the Collins brothers built, but just two stalls and maybe one larger one for a couple of milk cows. I want chickens, too, and for that we'll need a coop. It's late in the year, but there's still time to plant a garden with a few vegetables. I'll need seed and a hoe, fabric and supplies for sewing our clothes. I'll need a basin for dishes and a washtub, a skillet, a cook pot, plates, and utensils. I've got a list far less exotic than yours, but possibly more important considering the steady need for food and clothing."

He smiled and swung their arms as they walked hand in hand into the general store.

The proprietor was delighted to help Kat, but completely flummoxed by Seb's list. Yet Seb knew just what he wanted and how to order it and from whom. Between the helpful but slightly confused owner and Seb's careful instructions, they succeeded in ordering his supplies. Including the forge and a bellows, flasks and retorts, and a small crucible, which Kat thought sounded dreadful.

As they were getting ready to leave the general store, with Kat's items on her list to be picked up later, the proprietor gave them the name of a man whom he considered to be a talented builder, and a man eager for the work. The builder had a homestead on the edge of town, and so Kat and Seb walked to his place to meet him.

The builder, Mr. Walther, agreed to ride out with them after his noon meal and get the lay of the land. He learned, too, that they'd never seen their property. They offered Walther a few of their twenty-dollar gold pieces to buy nails and hinges for the doors and a few dollars in advance so he could hire help. He thanked them kindly and said he'd go talk to the land agent to make doubly sure of the property line. He also offered to hitch up his own wagon and haul the supplies from the general store to the building site.

Kat was relieved to have someone guide them to wherever they were planning to live. She'd hate to build her house, only to find out later that they didn't own the land underneath it.

Walther hurried off to get his morning chores done on his own homestead with a promise to meet them in front of the hotel at one o'clock.

Seb's next stop was the bank.

When they finished up there, Kat said, "You have a lot of money."

"It's the same amount I had in the bank a year ago. It's not Wadsworth money, but it'll get a roof over our heads. But the patents will run out after a while, and even before they do, new methods often crop up by other inventors and everything changes. It's the age of progress with new industry steadily replacing the old. I need to keep inventing new things if I want to make a living. And I haven't made much headway in the last year."

Kat nodded. "Jeremy and I had money, but it was all on paper—stocks and trusts and bank accounts he had to have permission to access. Permission he was never granted. It didn't matter really because we didn't spend lavishly. We lived in an apartment in a building his father owned. I found out after Jeremy died that we didn't pay rent. His father hired our cook maid, and she took care of the groceries. We had an account at a clothing store, but neither of us socialized much, so we didn't need fine clothing. Though Jeremy had a trust fund, his father had it tied up somehow. And with Jeremy's father dead, his uncle Patrick held the reins very tightly—"

"Kat." Seb stopped her. They faced each other. "You're opening up about your past."

Her brow rose, and her eyes brightened. "I am, aren't I?"

"It seemed like it was easy for you just now. Maybe we'll both learn better ways. Tell me more."

"Well, Jeremy worked at the Wadsworth company, but he most certainly wasn't in charge of anything. He helped with construction and was decent at it. He had architectural training and assisted the older men Patrick put in charge. Still, I didn't have a need for a mansion or silk dresses. We got by just fine with what he made. Jeremy mentioned a few times that both his father and Uncle Patrick would grumble when he spoke of buying a house."

"You married into the Wadsworth fortune but couldn't afford a house?"

Kat shrugged and went on. "I occasionally still worked with my father up until he died because he needed a nurse, but I also earned a bit of money. Mostly I did it because Jeremy's job was demanding, and he was gone long hours six days a week. He wasn't a good fit for the job. He should have followed God's guiding and gone to Bible college."

"So you married into the Wadsworth fortune and yet had to work to make ends meet?"

"You sound like my father."

Seb, right there on the busy street, growled. Then he kissed her. "I do *not* want to be told I remind you of your father."

Kat kissed him back. "I promise to never say it again."

He jabbed his finger right at her nose. "See that you don't." He said it in a comically stern way that did in fact sound rather fatherly.

But she didn't mention it.

"This is a beautiful piece of land." Seb wasn't interested in being a big landowner, but the homestead—backed up to a mountain that would likely never be claimed because no crops would grow there and the grazing was meager—was soul-stirring.

He and Kat had bought horses. Now they staked them out just as they had so many nights on the Oregon Trail.

Mr. Walther did the same with his horse, then said, "The property line is straight out from this grove of trees. See that creek running there? I'll build the house so you'll have water right out the back door. No need to dig a well. The banks are low, so the horses can drink from the creek without any trouble. I'll build the corral so it straddles the water." Nodding, he began asking Seb and Kat rapid-fire questions to get their thoughts and approval.

At last, Walther said, "I'll be out tomorrow to start chopping trees. I've got two men who work with me, including my brother. We can get a cabin up for you in a week's time with building materials right here on hand. No cost for them except nails and other bits I'll get from the blacksmith. If the weather holds, you can move in by next Tuesday. I'll do the outbuildings next, and you can live in the house while I work. I'll lay a floor in the cabin, which can wait until I get your labora . . . uh, your building up. You sound eager to get on with that."

"My laboratory. Yes, I'm eager to see it get built."

"I'll hope to get that second building up a week later."

Two weeks from today, Seb could get back to his inventing. "Thank you, Mr. Walther." The two men shook hands. "I think we'll stay here and scout around a bit, if you don't mind heading back to town without us."

"Not at all. I need to get back and make the arrangements. I'll build you a nice cabin, folks. I appreciate the work." With that, Walther said goodbye and galloped toward town, a man on a mission.

Seb turned to Kat. "Let's hike beyond the trees and see what it looks like on the mountainside."

"We rode through some big mountains. These ones barely count."

"Barely is good enough." Seb headed for the woods, down the creek bank. The creek was shallow enough that he picked out a couple of rocks to step on and walked across. The musically babbling water was lined with older trees, and the shade was cool and welcoming.

Kat was right behind him. "I think I'll pull out some flat stones and use the horses to drag them to the creek the way the O'Tooles did at their place. We won't need such large stones because the water isn't as deep. Won't take much to have us a sturdy walkway over the creek."

They hiked up a woodland full of rocks and shrubs with the occasional clump of trees. When they reached an open spot, Seb stopped, turned around, and looked back on their property. Kat turned to study the land with him.

"We climbed farther than I thought. It sure looks beautiful from up here." The land swept down before them, then leveled to a pretty grassland. They saw where the supplies Mr. Walther had hauled out were stacked, which was near to where the cabin would be constructed. Their horses stood grazing on the late summer grass.

"Look over there." Seb pointed. "About a mile to the southeast. A cabin. And to the left, you can see smoke curling out of a chimney. That's another cabin. We've got neighbors."

"Should we buy a few head of cattle to graze our land?" Kat asked. "They've planted some crops over there." She was gazing toward their nearest neighbor. "I don't think a big field of corn is necessary. A small herd that lives on the grass might be good, though. Would we need to fence the land?"

Seb turned, a bright look on his face that wasn't a smile; it was bone-deep contentment instead. "There's no rush on the cattle since I don't know how to turn one into a steak. But we can talk about it and decide later. We can be happy here, Kat. We can make a life. We'll decide about cattle and crops and fences as we go along. Right now I'm tempted to buy a tent like the ones we lived in coming west. I'd like to start living on our land straightaway."

"And start cooking outside, hauling wood and water? Mr. Walther hauled the pans out. I know how to cook over a campfire. And I could get a hoe and break up the land for the garden. We'll want to be out here every day anyway. If the weather stays mild like today, we wouldn't even need a tent."

Seb gave a firm nod. "Let's sleep here tonight. If we get hungry for a meal not cooked over a fire, we can ride to town, even sleep in the hotel if we have a rainy day."

And so their married life, on their own land, began.

8

Seb moved into his own home. It was so new that he could smell the raw, newly chopped logs.

"The stove is in." He caught his pretty wife's hand and drew her toward the house. He kept busy working with Mr. Walther. He'd found he had decent skills, thanks to Oscar, but he'd learned more by working with Walther and his two hired men.

Walther told Seb that if he ever needed work, he'd be glad to add him to his building crew. Seb liked the idea, though he doubted he'd have the time. But the skills he'd refined while working on the cabin were important ones to have when living on the frontier.

Kat, meanwhile, had found plenty to do. Seb marveled at how hard she worked. Any job asked of her, she did it well and without complaint. And she thought of plenty that weren't asked of her.

She'd spent days gathering rocks the size of her head and stacking them in a pile to be used for a chimney. The carpenters said they'd do it, but Kat just smiled and said she wanted to have a part in building the cabin. The men seemed to understand, and they'd brought out a handcart like the one that had carried Seb out of Independence, only this one a woman could lift and roll. She worked fast enough so the men would have a good supply of rocks when they were ready to put up the chimney.

And she'd insisted on being taught how to hook up a log chain to a horse, then the log. The men and Seb did all the chopping, while she dragged the logs close to the building site.

Kat did all of this with a smile on her face.

Now that smile made Seb wonder. She'd gone through so much. Losing her husband so young. Being locked away in an asylum. Her ma had died when she was sixteen and her father while she was married, and she hadn't been married long. Could a woman who'd had so little be too content, too easily? Did Kat need to make demands instead of just throwing herself headlong into work to ease the load on others?

As he chipped away at the corners of the logs Kat dragged in, Seb thought of how full of ideas he was for inventions, and he knew he wanted time and quiet to focus his thoughts and work out solutions that he'd need to test and tweak and reimagine. He wasn't as generous and unselfish as his wife. He sincerely hoped the day wouldn't come when she realized she was giving much more than she got.

But at least for today she was getting a cookstove. That would make her life easier. When they'd approached the door with the stove, she gasped and clasped her hands together under her chin. "Oh, Seb. I could have cooked over the fireplace. Heaven knows I've had plenty of practice doing that."

Mr. Walther looked up from where he was connecting the stovepipe to the new potbellied stove Seb had bought as a surprise. Walther smiled and went right back to work. His men were outside even now, chopping down trees for the outbuildings and to lay a floor. He'd built a stone foundation for the fireplace, extending it far enough so the heavy stove could stand on it rather than on the logs they'd use for the floor. The cabin seemed less likely to catch fire that way.

"It's very much like the one my ma had," she said. "I will enjoy cooking on it."

"And look there." Seb pointed to a gap in the chimney above the fireplace.

"What is that?" Kat asked.

"Have you got the door ready, Mr. Walther?"

Their builder straightened away from the stovepipe. "All done here. The stove's ready to be put to work." He lifted a flat, metal rectangle off the floor and held it over the gap.

"There are hinges between the stones and . . ." Kat's eyes narrowed as she studied the little door.

Walther slipped pins in to attach the hinges on the door to those set in the rocks. With a rasp of metal on metal, he secured the hinges on the iron plate to those embedded in the rocks. Then he let the rectangle go. It stayed in place. There was a tidy little hook to hold it closed.

While he tightened the pins in place, Kat said, "It's a baking chamber." She whirled to grin at Seb, and he caught her when she threw herself at him and wrapped her arms around his neck. One quick kiss, then she let him go before he could think clearly enough to catch ahold of her.

She beamed. "That will make baking so much easier."

"Everything's ready now, Mrs. Jones, thanks to all the rocks you gathered," Walther said. "You can tear down your campsite and sleep inside tonight. I knocked together a bedstead, and my brother and partner Paul filled a straw tick for you. You've paid me a fair wage for my work here. Most folks around here are land rich but short on cash money, but you've been generous and paid promptly. I appreciate it. Because of that, I bought you some furniture. That is, the three of us did—Paul, Mike, and I. Our gift to you is a kitchen table and four chairs. These things were bartered for at the general store and have been stashed in rafters and sheds because the store gets more than they can sell. So I got them for a very good price. I also picked up a chest of drawers and two rocking chairs."

"That's very kind of you, Mr. Walther. You've made settling here so much easier than if we'd done the building ourselves."

"Glad to be of help. We said we'd build your building first, Mr. Jones, but we're done in here except for the floor. We'll go ahead and lay that by the end of the day. Logs are all split. Once that's done, we'll haul in the furniture." Walther turned to Kat. "By the way, my wife has a baking oven like this one. If you need to talk to someone about using it, I'm sure she'd be happy to give you some pointers."

Mr. Walther invited them to church to meet his wife. Seb and Kat had missed last week's services because Kat had lost track of the days and only realized it was Sunday when Walther and his brother and friend didn't arrive to work.

Seb helped haul in split logs for the floor while Kat gathered their possessions from around their campsite. They didn't have much. They all worked with great energy, and Kat especially was enjoying this new beginning they were making.

Seb was in his laboratory at last! Two weeks of building, although Walther had yet to erect the barn. He and his men had another job to do, and Seb had been agreeable to let them go work for someone else awhile. Since the horses were their only livestock, now that the corral was finished, they were all set outside.

The laboratory was done, though, so Seb could now get to work on his inventions. The first day he got into his laboratory, Seb started putting his supplies in order. Before long he was bending over chemicals, mixing and refining with the goal of building a dry cell battery. Using the sun to recharge it would be such a new invention, Seb might make himself rich and famous. Seeing the immodesty of such a thought, he told himself he needed to keep inventing just to earn a living. Yet he couldn't pretend he didn't like the idea of being famous for a world-changing invention.

Sebastian Jones, famous . . . a man who'd spent most of his life in hiding so no one would steal his inventions. That was no match for fame. He juggled ideas in his head, trying to sort them into some sort of order, thinking without being hitched to old ideas. A true inventor always thought of the possibilities and looked to find a practical method to make them realities. He thought of his friend Marcus and wished he were here with him. Marcus had a knack for new ideas and going in different directions.

Seb had more materials being shipped to him, but since a few items had already arrived, that gave him plenty to work with.

A hand rested on his shoulder.

Whirling around, holding a wire in one hand that whipped out at her, Kat jumped back and pressed one hand flat against her chest as if to hold her heart steady.

He held up both hands. “Sorry. You startled me.”

Kat’s fear quickly faded, replaced by confusion and at least a little irritation. “You looked like you were going to attack me.”

He smiled and shook his head. “I was long gone into my invention and thinking of how . . .” He felt his face heat up in what had to be a blush.

“Of how . . . what?” She studied him, watching every nuance.

It struck him as wonderful to have someone pay such close attention to him.

He looked down and sheepishly admitted, “Of how famous I might become if I can get my battery built and power it with the sun.”

She arched one very skeptical blond brow. “I’m sure you would be famous since what you’re inventing sounds a bit like *magic*. Very fancy to invent magic.”

That made him smile.

He wanted to launch into an explanation of chemical compounds and the periodic table and magnetic fields crossed with acids and bases. But he'd seen her eyes glaze over before, so he spared her all that. Marcus came to mind again. He'd already contacted his lawyers and his bank. Why not Marcus? He needed someone who had an inventive turn of mind to talk things through with.

"Did you need something? I suppose I've been in here for hours, leaving everything to you."

"It's time for supper. And I've kept it warming on the stove to not interrupt your work. But the sun is setting."

"The days are long," Seb said ruefully. "I've been lost in my work."

"And you started early. It's time to finish up for the day, I'd say."

Which made him think of how hungry he was, and that bedtime was right after the evening meal if they didn't eat until nine o'clock at night. He liked bedtime with his new wife even more than he liked the idea of being famous.

"Let's go. Thank you for being so patient and for figuring out a meal that won't be dried out and awful to eat. And for doing all the work around the homestead by yourself. I apologize. I promise to be more help starting tomorrow. It's just that with getting everything set up and reviewing my notes, this first day I—"

"Don't make promises you can't keep. I'm not doing any real heavy work. If I was, I'd've interrupted you without a qualm. So don't give me too much credit. It's been interesting getting things set up out here, just as your work is interesting. In time we'll find a good balance of the labor around here if we give ourselves a little grace. You're making decent money with your inventions after all. My pa's job took long hours, so I'm used to it. I can run the homestead mostly, and if there's any heavy work I can't do on my own, I'll nag you until you help me."

Seb's money had come into the bank, transported by train. It had arrived fast, just like the chemical supplies he'd ordered. He marveled at the speed of things. Kat had seen the amount and been impressed. Yet he couldn't help but think of the Wadsworth fortune, knowing he was a poor man by comparison.

He shook his head as if to clear his thoughts. "I'm real hungry. Thank you for supper. For everything."

"You haven't eaten it yet. Best to withhold your thanks for now."

It turned out the meal was indeed delicious. And bedtime was blissful.

The next day, as Seb rose from their new, pretty kitchen table to head back to his laboratory, belly full of breakfast, Kat told him she was riding into town.

"Should you do that without me?" He seemed startled.

She considered that her husband was easily startled and wondered if that was a good trait. "Y-you mean you'd go along?"

She could see plainly he didn't want to. His invention called to him. "Well—"

"I'll be fine." She cut him off before he could try to persuade her to wait.

"What do you need that we don't have?"

"I need a few more things for the kitchen, another good knife, more seeds, and a few items Mr. Walther recommended." Walther had come out to the homestead the last day of building, bringing with him a sod-busting plow. He'd broken up the land for her garden, saving her hours of backbreaking toil. "I did some hiking in what that land agent called 'wasteland.' You know the place—where we climbed to look down on our property?"

Seb nodded. "It's a beautiful view."

"I wasn't looking for pretty views; I was looking for grouse and jackrabbits. I saw some deer and found signs of an elk herd up there. Oscar taught me how to fire a gun and follow tracks."

"So you're going hunting?"

"I am indeed, Mr. Inventor. I won't try for an elk until the weather gets cold enough to freeze the meat. It's mid-August, so the wait won't be a long one. I need to find the herd, learn where they bed down at night. Oscar says they're regular in their habits. In the meantime, rabbit and grouse will help keep us fed until I can get some chickens. They're a rarity out here. If I could find us a few hens, we'd have an egg supply. For now, I'll buy eggs and milk in town and hunt for our supper. Milk won't keep—I'd like to ride to town twice a week to resupply."

"It's a wild land, Mrs. Homesteader. Be careful."

She saw affection in Seb's eyes and genuine concern for her safety, and that warmed her heart. Then his eyes strayed to his laboratory, and her heart cooled off fast.

This was her life now. She needed to learn to live with an inventor. And she was afraid Mrs. Homesteader would need to be very self-sufficient. "I'll be careful," Kat promised.

Later, once at the general store, she bought a Springfield rifle and a pair of Colt Peacemakers. She also visited the storage space behind the store and found a few more things they needed and began to wish she'd brought along a packhorse.

She got home in plenty of time to startle Seb again to join her for their noon meal.

9

"Seb, we need to talk," Kat said.

He lowered his forkful of mashed potatoes. She'd had her hands full luring him in to eat the noon meal. After a month of married life, the first two weeks getting a cabin built and a laboratory put up and ready to work in—at which point Seb had vanished into it and rarely came out—she'd begun to realize life with an inventor, at least with *this* inventor, was going to be a lonely one. Or rather, if she didn't want to be lonely, she had to find friends and interests beyond just wanting for Seb to come in from his inventing work.

She watched close to see if his gaze wandered through the walls, out to his laboratory. If he didn't listen to her, she might just clobber him with one of the legs of the grouse she'd hunted, shot, cut up and fried.

Her tone must've been dire because he was paying attention.

"What is it?" He didn't even take the bite of mashed potatoes but instead set it back on his plate.

"Remember Beth saying there are laws now to protect women from being tossed into insane asylums by their husbands or others?"

"Like your uncle Patrick did to you? And Ginny's husband did to her?"

"Yes. Well, my first reaction was fear that I'd somehow end up locked away again. But now, with a husband to protect me and a home to shelter me, and after spending some time thinking and praying about it, I've decided not to start a fight with Uncle Patrick. I'm going to educate myself instead."

"How do you plan to do that?" Seb looked as if he'd lost his appetite.

Kat could hardly blame him. "Well, Cheyenne is the territorial capital. I don't know when the legislative session runs, but surely there's someone in town who is knowledgeable about the law. Beth said the laws are different in each state. Maybe Wyoming, with its laws allowing women the right to vote, has laws on such things as asylums."

"Are there insane asylums in Wyoming?"

Shaking her head, Kat said, "I don't know, but I'm going to find out." She made a fist without really realizing it until she tapped it firmly on the table. "I'll start by asking around to see if there's a lawyer in town who can be trusted to side with women in matters of the law."

Seb reached his hand across the table and took her fist. She relaxed her hand and smiled at him.

He said, "I won't let them take you back to the asylum."

"I won't let them take me back either."

"When you find a lawyer you're willing to talk to, let me know. I'll go with you."

"Thank you. But I won't draw you away from your work unless it's necessary."

"Don't you worry about that, Kat. What matters most is making sure you're safe. I'd love to see you set free from the fear your uncle churns up inside of you."

"And, Seb, I know we've been busy getting settled and you getting to work, but we haven't gone to church since we moved to Cheyenne and we've been here a month. We didn't have a church near us in Hidden Canyon, and maybe when winter comes, we won't be able to attend, but I want us to go together this week."

Seb nodded. "What day is it?"

"It's Wednesday. I think I'll ride into town this afternoon and ask a few questions. I'm not going to tell anyone why I want a lawyer, but I might take the first step."

"Do you want me to come along?"

Kat knew this was him being generous because he didn't want to be away from his laboratory even for the time it took to eat a meal. "I'll go alone this time," she said.

"Can you check to see if I've gotten a letter? I wrote to Marcus to tell him what I was working on. I'm hoping he'll have some ideas. We always worked well together. Even after I moved back to Independence and he stayed in St. Louis, we often corresponded."

"You're so secretive about your inventions, I'm surprised you're telling Marcus about them."

"I can trust him. Check for a letter from my lawyers, too. They might've written."

Kat felt that niggle of fear she always felt when they let their names and locations get out into the world. But if she was going to face up to her uncle, then she'd need to get over that. "I'll check," she told him.

Sebastian let go of her hand, and they both went back to their eating. Kat thought the food tasted a little better now that she'd salted it with courage.

10

The days were getting shorter, the nights colder as the end of September drew near.

Kat had finally decided on the man she wanted to talk to about her troubles. She wasn't interested in gaining Jeremy's inheritance. She thought that would be a good way to bring out the worst in Patrick. But she did want to find out just how safe she was from being mistreated like she'd been before.

She'd read all she could find in the newspapers about the laws in Wyoming, but her well of knowledge was still painfully low.

She had an appointment with him tomorrow. Tomorrow things would change.

Kat had a fresh baking of bread out of the oven. The sun had set. Dinner was ready.

And her husband was in his laboratory. Again. He didn't like being called in this early, but she wanted company.

In her heart, she'd been cradling the hope close that there might be a baby on the way. She'd welcome a new one to love. Today she'd found out there wasn't. That disappointment had helped her work up the nerve to contact Mr. Etherton.

"God, a baby would give me a purpose. Someone to tend. Someone to love." That prayer, uttered as she looked through her kitchen window, gave her pause.

She'd bought glass and hired Mr. Walther to install a window that looked out over her kitchen dry sink so she could see Seb's laboratory. The window had a shutter, which she'd kept closed lately because of the cold wind that seeped through the window's edges. But at mealtimes she opened the shutter wide and gazed out at the laboratory, praying for Seb to come out on his own.

Why didn't he ever remember mealtimes? Why didn't he ever get lonely for her, as she did for him?

Why did she need to have a baby to find love?

Not that she didn't love her husband. She did, and she figured he probably loved her. But she wasn't more important than his work. She thought of how he hadn't known she was a widow. She'd barely known he was an inventor. They'd confessed that they were in the habit of being secretive about themselves. And they'd intended to change that.

But they hadn't, not really. Yes, Seb was fascinated by his work, but had she talked to him? Had she shared more of herself, her thoughts and feelings, with him?

Was it even wise to bring a baby into the world where the child would be largely ignored by their father?

"God, what is the right thing to do? I'm tempted to pick up the rolling pin I bought in the general store and use it to beat my husband. That would get his attention."

No voice from God was necessary to tell her that wasn't the right way to handle things.

She'd learned not to go into the laboratory. He was so engrossed in his work that he startled easily, and she was afraid he might hurt himself with all his wires and chemicals, his glass beakers, and the raging hot crucible.

So she went to the door and knocked. She pounded long and hard because she'd found if she didn't keep at it, he wouldn't come. Later he'd say he meant to, but before he could respond, he'd had one more thing to experiment on or test or write down.

"Behold, I stand at the door and knock: if any man hear my voice, and open the door, I will come in to him and will sup with him, and he with me." The book of Revelation, third chapter. She'd been reading her Bible diligently and had found that Scripture. It suited her life.

The Bible was one of two books they owned. *Pride and Prejudice* by Jane Austen was good, but rereading the novel wasn't as deeply satisfying as rereading the Bible.

She'd had a meager garden because she'd had a late start, and she'd been told that newly turned sod wasn't good for crops the first year.

It all amounted to a lonely life.

Tonight, she wasn't going to wait until nine o'clock. It was past six. Past a reasonable suppertime. Seb had never quit early on his own, and tomorrow he wasn't going to invent. Tomorrow he was going with her to meet with her lawyer.

She knocked again on the laboratory door, this time even harder.

He called out, "Just a minute."

She didn't trust that and so pounded some more. He finally came to the door and swung it open. He looked disheveled, distracted, and mildly irritated—his usual demeanor.

Did he love her?

She had to say no. Or at least not very much. She was no competition for his notebooks and his crucible. "Supper is ready."

"I just need to finish—"

"No!" Her sharp voice made him jump.

Honestly, it made her jump a little as well. Her next words were just as cross. "*Now*. Supper is ready now." She felt like a mother calling her misbehaving child into the house.

His eyes narrowed as if the words in is head didn't bear speaking aloud. Then he nodded and stepped out into the October cold, following her back to the cabin.

Kat had put together a stew from fresh venison with potatoes and onions and carrots. She'd brought down a deer just yesterday, made a venison roast last night and then the stew for supper tonight. Her bread was still warm, and they each had a small glass of milk. She usually bought two quarts of it, and if she was careful, it would last all week.

"Did something happen?" Seb asked.

He was eating her stew. She saw his eyes wander to the clock she kept on the table near the chimney. It said six-thirty.

"It's a bit early for me to quit work. And you seem upset. Tell me what's bothering you."

The things that jumbled in her mind all seemed so wrong.

You work too hard. I'm lonely. You don't love me.

Am I destined to spend all of my life standing at your laboratory door and knocking to try to pull you out of there?

Was that even fair? Why must he be the center of her life?

It seemed right, but her father had worked hard, too. Her mother hadn't complained—it was simply how things were.

Struggling to make sense when she wasn't sure why she couldn't stand him making his work the first priority in his life, she said, "The days are shorter now, and colder. I want us to move suppertime to a more reasonable hour. From now on I'll knock on your door at six o'clock, and I'll expect you to come to the house after you hear my knocking."

Seb watched her as she went back to eating. His jaw tightened, and she saw temper in his eyes. They'd never had a fight before. They'd depended on each other when they left the isolation of the canyon. They'd been alone against the world in some ways until they'd gotten their cabin built.

In fact, they'd gotten along well until Seb's chemicals and equipment had arrived on the train. After that, he'd gone into his laboratory, and she'd stayed out. He experimented, and she did everything else.

A man worked. A woman kept their home. It was the way of the world and yet Kat was deeply dissatisfied and not at all sure she was in the right. Especially because their life apparently suited Seb right down to the ground.

She was left feeling foolish and wrong. Selfish. Trying to be a good wife. A mature woman with common sense, she swallowed her loneliness, determined to handle life as it was, not as she wished it to be. And she had to talk. She had to get past her habit of keeping everything inside. She could start doing that right now.

With her meal finished, she folded her hands in her lap and looked at Seb. "The truth is, I was lonely tonight. I wanted to spend time with you."

Seb watched her. He didn't say it, but she suspected her explanation hadn't fully satisfied him. Nodding, he said, "I'm glad you called me in. Let's spend the evening with Jane Austen, shall we?"

That made her smile. They'd each read the book on their own since leaving the canyon, but they'd never read it out loud.

"I'd like that."

"I'll help you clean up after this delicious meal. Then we'll read for a while, and maybe we can have an early night. I'll be able to get back to work all the earlier in the morning."

"I've got the appointment with that lawyer tomorrow morning. You said you wanted to know about it and that you'd come along."

Seb's gaze sharpened as he looked at her. She suspected he was reading her fear. "I'll come then. I'm glad you're proceeding with this. I want to make sure that lawyer knows you're not alone in the world."

"Thank you. I'll be glad to have the company. Now, tell me how your work is progressing."

He talked of things that made very little sense to her. She knew about medicine as a science, but chemistry was something she had no understanding of.

Seb continued, "I wrote back to Marcus. I've gotten two letters from him now. He's always had a fine mind. He and I weren't exactly partners because we were both working on our own projects, but we worked side by side at college. I'd kept in touch with him until last spring when I was shot. He's always had a knack for helping me think in broader terms. I believe I was able to help him, too. I mentioned I knew Jeremy, remember?"

"Yes. You said you knew him well enough to say hello."

"Well, what little connection I had with him was through Marcus. They were both from wealthy families. The Wadsworths and the Colemans. They lived near each other in big old mansions, Jeremy with his grandparents and Mark with his parents. Beyond our love of chemistry, I had nothing in common with Mark. I have to get my patents registered to support myself. I had a good amount of money saved, but most of the successful patents have expired. Mark didn't have that pressure. He and Jeremy shared family wealth and traditions. That was their bond."

"Tell me more about your college years."

It was a nice evening full of talk, then reading. Their usual closeness at bedtime was wonderful and passionate. Yet somehow, as he fell asleep beside her, the loveliness of the night only made her more fully aware that things weren't good. Or perhaps it was more correct to say that things could be so much better between them.

Turning on her side, she listened to his deep breathing.

Something needed to happen to make their lives better for both of them. Yes, he was content. It sounded like this business of devoting his every waking hour to his experiments went back to college, maybe even earlier, but he needed to balance things out. And it wasn't just for her that things needed to change.

She remembered that flash of irritation in his eyes and thinking that they'd never had a fight before. Was she willing to make their marriage one of strife to make it better? And would it even work? How could things be better if they were at odds with each other? She feared changing him wouldn't be easy or pleasant.

She curled away from him and didn't bother fighting the tears.

Kat had read a poem once about a long, dark night of the soul. She didn't understand it fully, but the message she got after lying awake for hours and weeping as quietly as she could so she wouldn't wake Seb was that it was her job to make herself fulfilled.

She awoke the next morning to the aroma of frying bacon. Startled, because never had such a thing happened before, she tossed aside the blankets, dressed quickly, and rushed out to find Seb in the kitchen. He was busy cooking breakfast.

He smiled when she came in and poured her a cup of coffee. "Good morning, madam. We are going to town this morning, I believe?"

She thought of her night of sadness, her quiet determination to find a fulfilled life, and said, "Yes, we are. You are up early, but you didn't go to work?"

"No. I'm devoting the morning to you. We'll go see your lawyer and then we'll talk about what needs to be done. I can work this afternoon."

Kat enjoyed her breakfast through a glow of contentment.

"Mrs. Jones, welcome. I'm Curtis Etherton." He extended his hand to shake hers in a way Kat really liked. Many men talked around a woman when there was a man involved. But she had made the appointment with him, and she'd told him about the problem that concerned her.

He remembered.

"This is my husband, Sebastian Jones."

Mr. Etherton now offered his hand to Seb. "Please, sit down. Tell me more about what brings you here to see me."

Kat thought of how she'd dreaded Seb writing to his lawyers. How she'd felt a frisson of fear when he'd said he was writing to his old college friend Marcus. Now here she was telling her story to a complete stranger, including details that no one knew but Seb.

"First of all," Seb began, speaking before she could, "we need to be sure that what gets said in this meeting is kept in confidence."

Mr. Etherton's eyes sharpened, but then he nodded. "You have my word. Anything spoken between me and a client is what we call 'privileged.' Nothing said here goes beyond this office without your consent."

Kat turned to meet Seb's gaze. She swallowed hard.

He said, "It's your decision, Kat. You don't need to do this if you're afraid."

Drawing in a deep breath, she turned to face Mr. Etherton. "I-I, well, um . . . I'm an escapee from an insane asylum."

Mr. Etherton's expression didn't change . . . or not

much anyway. He did rub his hand over his mouth, almost as if he were holding in whatever words wanted to come out. "Go on," he finally said.

Kat told him all of it. Once in a while Seb would interject with some detail he remembered. His voice added to hers helped to keep her braced and moving forward, especially when she admitted she was a Wadsworth. Mr. Etherton began listening even more carefully, if that was even possible.

She was careful not to mention Ginny. This was Kat's story, and if Ginny wanted hers told, Ginny would tell it.

When she was finished, Mr. Etherton began asking questions. She realized he was drawing out details she'd never thought to mention, including being curious about the circumstances of Jeremy's death.

When he'd lapsed into silence, Kat added, "You can see why I fear what my uncle might do. My understanding is that a husband protects me. My uncle can no longer stomp in and grab me and have me committed to the asylum on just his word that I'm insane. But he's a powerful man. I'm not one bit sure he thinks the laws apply to him."

Mr. Etherton said, "Let me look into the exact laws as they apply to this situation. I believe you to be an utterly sane young woman. Spending this last hour with you satisfies me that you were locked away without any justification, although you probably made your uncle feel threatened with your accusations concerning your husband's death—especially if he had a hand in it."

"I didn't accuse him of killing Jeremy," Kat said. "I only demanded he look into it." She paused. "I may have demanded with some rather wild insistence. But he might have taken it that way and had me locked up to protect himself."

"He'll make the case that you were hysterical, and that grief had driven you mad. I can have you tested by a doctor, and he and I can draft documents saying you've been proven to be sane. What I'd like to know, though, is if you want me to pursue your inheritance."

Kat gasped and shook her head. "If we do that, it will bring Uncle Patrick down on me like an avalanche, sweeping everyone aside who gets in his way."

"I'm sure he's a wealthy and powerful man, Mrs. Jones, but he won't sweep me aside, or your husband, not from just this one meeting. This is Wyoming. You have rights here, and I'll stand between you and any avalanche your uncle cares to set in motion."

Kat looked at Seb. "Will you mind if I don't pursue the money? I trust you, and you, Mr. Etherton." She turned to her lawyer. "But Seb supports us both very well. We have no need of the inheritance money. And I'd just as soon not draw the wrath of Uncle Patrick if I can help it."

Mr. Etherton nodded. "You can always change your mind later. Let me work on this. I'll find what is most effective in protecting you from your uncle, then I'll get back to you."

Kat stood as if there were a spring under her backside. Eager to be done with this.

Mr. Etherton stretched his hand out to shake hers. She lifted her hand and saw it was trembling.

"You're frightened, Mrs. Jones."

"I think it's my talking about something I'd kept hidden. I feel like the snow has begun rolling down the mountainside, and there's nothing to stop the avalanche I might have begun today."

Mr. Etherton clasped her hand in both of his. "Leave it to me. I'll tread carefully, and no harm will come to you."

Kat Jones, creeping along in the rugged land to the west of her home, searched for the elk herd she'd come to think of as hers and planned her whole life with considerably more optimism than she'd had when she went to bed last night.

She'd taken the first steps toward facing the troubles she'd been hiding from for too long. And now she set that aside to study what just might be a faint trail left by a small herd of elk that would keep them in fresh meat all winter.

Where did they sleep? How far and wide did they travel? Kat did her best to sharpen her hunting and tracking skills and felt better about spotting a grouse hiding in a clump of grass. The land around her was turning brown as the winter weather approached, though things were still lovely. Autumn in Wyoming, at least near Cheyenne, was a big improvement over the Sawtooth Mountains in Idaho.

Of course, she'd yet to see what January held in store, but it'd be hard for the snow to clog up this wide-open space. Though she suspected Wyoming blizzards could be fierce, facing them would be part of the life she and Seb had chosen. The life she was determined to make into a happy one.

And as she rose up to peer over the scrub brush in front

of her, she saw an elk. It wasn't just one either. It was the herd, not just their tracks. Twice she'd seen a single elk from a distance. But when she'd tried to approach it, the critter had taken flight long before she was within shooting distance.

It didn't matter, as it was too early to hunt elk. But when the time came, she wanted to know their ways. She'd been closing in on them for weeks now. And today, finally, the herd was in her sights.

Delighted that they hadn't noticed her, she hunkered low and moved closer to the dozen or more elk. She studied them from behind a pine tree. They were grazing on grass, brown and dried into hay on the stem.

She wasn't ready to take an elk. It was October, and the temperature wasn't below freezing yet. But she made note of where she stood, saw grass lying on its side in multiple little bowls. Their beds. Kat, the not-so-great tracker, suspected the elk slept right here in this meadow with a stand of pines breaking the wind from the north.

She remembered how Oscar and Jake had slipped silently through the woods and knew there was so much more for her to learn, but she was getting better. She pulled her Springfield rifle off her shoulder, lowered the muzzle, and looked down the length of the gun. Judged the distance, looked around for a better spot to shoot from, then decided this was the best place. She shouldered the rifle again.

Satisfied, she eased away as silently as she could. Once she'd put a hundred feet or so between her and the elk herd, she straightened to walk home more quickly. It was time to get out of the cold.

A hand clamped over her mouth, and an arm came around her waist, pinning both her arms. "Don't make a sound."

The man yanked the Springfield rifle off her shoulder and tossed it to the right into some bushes. Then the hard metal of a pistol pressed against her temple. Kat froze, afraid one wrong move and the gun would fire.

"Now, Mrs. Jones, take me to your husband."

She didn't move. The man laughed quietly, and she felt his hot breath ruffle the hair that had slipped from her wool bonnet.

"You think I need your cooperation?"

She should have fought. It had taken her too long to think of it. She'd always been weak. Always been such a good little daughter, good little wife, good little second wife. She'd watched her ma work herself to death, then just stepped in and took over. She'd watched her first husband be cheated and mistreated by his father and his uncle and had seen her job as that of comforter.

She was always such a quiet and polite captive when at the asylum. Always a patient and understanding wife . . . and now she was an easy-to-capture victim.

The man let go of her mouth and shoved her forward. "I know where you live. I've been watching you for days. I've been stalking you just as you stalked those elk. Waiting for my chance. Today when your fool of a husband shut himself into that shed and left you on your own, and then you headed off into the wilderness, I knew it was time."

Before she could scream a warning to Seb, the man shoved a kerchief into her mouth to silence her. He wrapped an arm brutally hard around her waist again, clamping her arms to her sides while continuing to shove her forward, straight toward the cabin. It was a long distance, so she fought her terror and tried to think what to do.

How could she warn Seb? Was this man here to rob them? Maybe he would tie them up, steal their horses, and go. Did he know about the money Beth had given them? It was hidden in the cabin behind a stone they'd added at the base of the fireplace. She was prepared to give it to him in the hopes he'd take it and leave.

As they approached the cabin, her heart pounding, her throat struggling not to choke on the gag, she remembered the pistol she had with her. She'd sewn a pocket into her dress in which to carry it. It was low enough that he hadn't noticed it when he'd grabbed her. The pocket was near where her right hand now dangled.

Her pounding heart resumed a steadier beat as a plan formed in her mind. She was disgusted with herself for not thinking of it until now. She needed to be *thinking* in a crisis. But late or not, she was thinking now.

As they moved, the gun pulled away from her temple, and she calmed down a bit more, all while knowing whatever was going to happen would happen soon. The laboratory came into sight.

There was a window on this side. Maybe Seb would look up, notice her, but she'd watched him work a few times. She knew he closed out the rest of the world when he worked, the big idiot.

He had the matched pair to her Colt Peacemaker in the laboratory. She knew because she'd put it there, forcing him to look at the spot where she'd set it.

If only he'd notice her and take that gun in hand. Come out prepared to fight.

Please, God, let him sense something is wrong.

If this man was here for her, why would he force her to go to Seb? Maybe simply to silence them both when he stole their money to give himself more time to run?

If he was here for Seb, why follow her into the wilderness, grab her, then force her back to the cabin?

Please, God, warn Seb. Protect us. Tell me what to do. Give me an idea.

Of course, she'd already thought of the pistol. Could she draw the weapon and aim it backward in time? The man would be distracted for just a second or two when he opened the laboratory door. She braced herself to draw her pistol, aim it, and fire.

She tried to see it happen in her head. She'd lift the gun, flip it backward. He was looking over her right shoulder. She could feel his hot breath. Aim right there at his face. Pull the trigger.

No, her hand wouldn't raise enough but would point back at hip level. The bullet would hit him in the leg. Still, it would be enough to knock him away from her.

Shoot through the fabric of her dress maybe? Just grab it, don't try to draw, and fire. If she pointed it down and back, she'd injure him enough to make him let go, enough to—

"You be mighty quiet, Mrs. Jones." The man's voice was barely above a whisper. "I'm going to aim right at your husband. Any fight out of you and I'll kill him dead."

His arm tightened around her waist until she could barely breathe. They moved toward the laboratory.

Please, God, protect us.

All she could think of was the gun. Would God do that? Would He guide her thoughts toward shooting someone? Because there would be no doubt she'd have to shoot this man. There would be no time to draw the gun, step clear, aim it at him, and demand that he drop his weapon.

She remembered the time in the asylum when Yvette had attacked an attendant who'd touched her. With Yvette clinging to her back, the attendant had jabbed an elbow backward and knocked Yvette away. Yvette had collapsed, arms around her belly. She'd had to fight for air, even while she was being dragged away.

Now *that* was a memory that had come to her, she had to believe, through her prayers. This man was solid, strong. But if she grabbed the gun and jammed it backward into his gut . . .

As her arm pressed hard against her side, she felt the weight of the gun, felt for the slit of the pocket.

Her assailant pushed her toward the door. Into her ear he hissed, "Open it."

With her hand shaking, she reached for the door with her left hand. Gripped the knob. As the door swung open, she thrust her hand deep into her pocket, pulled the gun, and slammed it backward butt first as hard as she could. The gun fired. The bullet hit the doorframe and ricocheted. She felt the impact and fell, then jerked the kerchief out of her mouth and screamed.

The man roared and collapsed backward. His own gun went flying. Kat dashed for his gun, nearly stumbling over the writhing man.

She got his gun and turned, ready to fight just as Seb came running outside.

"Kat, what—?"

He fell silent when he saw her holding two guns, both aimed at the man on the ground. They watched as he bled from his stomach. Horrified, Kat threw the guns to the ground behind her and rushed to the man's side. She dropped to her knees and pressed both hands over the wound, blood quickly coating them.

The man stopped thrashing around and looked hard into her eyes. He lifted one hand, and Seb came to his other side and caught hold of it to prevent him from striking out.

The man looked at Seb, then back at Kat. "This doesn't end with me," he managed to say. Then his hand went slack in Seb's grasp. His whole body shuddered and became still.

The intruder's eyes stared straight up without seeing the sky.

He was dead, and she'd killed him. Her stomach twisted as she jerked her hands away, turned aside, and crawled forward around the corner of the laboratory where she vomited into the bushes.

"Thou shalt not kill."

One of the commandments. Four words. It couldn't be more stark. By killing a man, she'd shut herself away from God.

Rising to her knees, she clutched the side of the building and turned so she could see the dead man. She saw blood smeared on the laboratory wall, then stared at the already drying blood on her hands. For a long moment the horror of what she'd done locked her in place.

Then the lock broke. With a cry of fear and grief and shame, she staggered to her feet and ran around the man she'd killed, weeping, and threw herself into Seb's arms.

Beth grabbed Jake's arm.

His head came up. He looked at her, then followed her line of vision. He said, "It's Yvette."

"She stabbed my father. Maybe to death." Beth felt her heart speed up as she watched Yvette slipping along through the woods. Far enough away, Beth wasn't absolutely sure it was her. But it had to be. She wore the same dress, though it was tattered and faded now. Had the same white-blond hair, now a snarled mess.

Beth shook her head. "Looks like she's been wearing that dress since we saw her last September. What is she doing here? John McCall was going to find her and take her away."

Jake tugged at Beth's arm. "Let's ease back. I'd say she's been here a long time. How did she survive the winter? Whether she was here or outside the canyon, lost in the wilderness, it's impossible. A woman alone? No food, no rifle, no shelter, no blankets?"

"It's not impossible because there she is."

Nodding silently, they slipped back behind a line of head-high shrubs. "We need to stay away from her."

"We need to help her."

They both fell silent as they watched her.

Beth thought Yvette swayed, even danced to a music only she could hear. Then Yvette disappeared into the trees.

Jake and Beth exchanged looks.

"Does she still have the knife she used to stab Father?" Beth glanced back at the spot where Yvette had faded into the woods.

"We need to talk to Oscar and Ginny." Jake tugged on Beth's arm again.

Beth decided, since she had no idea what to do, she might as well follow his lead.

11

I-I . . . Oh, Sebastian, I'm a killer." Her voice broke. She sobbed into his shirt.

He pulled her into the laboratory, carefully avoiding the man lying dead in the doorway. Drawing his nearly hysterical wife toward the basin of warm water he kept handy, he washed her hands, still unsure if she'd been hurt. Had that man done more than just shove her along?

As she wept, because speech seemed beyond her, he washed the blood from her hands and wrists. She had bloodstains on her face, too, as if she'd pressed her palms to her cheeks. He carefully bathed her face until it was clean.

There was no other blood. No sign she was bleeding, no cuts or rising bruises. Seb heaved a sigh of relief at the same time he was horrified. "Who was that man?"

Shaking her head frantically, she said, "I don't know."

He studied her face. She was still distraught, frightened. "Can you tell me what happened?"

He listened to the whole tale, holding back from asking questions until she'd spilled everything. "I'll go see if he's carrying anything that will tell us who he is," Seb said, "but he's not dressed like a western man. His suit says he's from the city—it's made of fine material with hardly any wear on it. His boots are machine-made with barely a scuff. It all speaks of someone who's well-to-do."

"I didn't think of what he was wearing. I didn't get a good look at him until he was collapsed on the ground. He grabbed me from behind, put his hand over my mouth." Kat's voice rose in distress. "He was watching me. He said he'd been watching me for days. He followed me from the cabin and picked his moment."

Seb, slightly sickened to touch the man, knelt beside him and flipped back the front of his black suit coat, a fine wool that was well tailored. His inner pocket bulged with something. Seb saw a pistol tucked into a holster under the dead man's left arm, and an empty holster hung under his right arm.

"Men wear guns like this to conceal them. And he had two hidden. After his first one went flying, he could have still gotten to the second weapon." Seb didn't know much about guns, though Oscar and Jake had liked talking about them and Seb had listened. And Kat had bought that set of Colt six-guns and left one loaded in the laboratory. He'd seen it, but he'd never so much as picked it up. He'd certainly never fired it.

As a man who'd been shot at, a man who'd recently come out of hiding because of an attempted murder, he probably ought to learn.

He pulled papers out of the man's pocket and a single envelope. Flicking it open, he stared at a stack of hundred-dollar bills. There was a small book along with the money. Seb opened it and saw it was blank, brand-new. It contained one line only, which was written at the top of the first page in a tidy-looking script:

Sebastian and Katherine Wadsworth? Jones. Cheyenne, Wyoming. $500.

The exact amount of money in the envelope.

He turned to Kat. "Does this mean he was sent to find both of us?"

Kat's face, already pale, went bone-white. Her voice trembled. "Or sent to kill both of us?"

Seb moved fast in case she collapsed. Her whole body was racked with shudders. He pulled her close, then got to his feet, bringing her along with him, holding her until she stopped shaking. That was when he noticed some of the tremors were his.

They stood there holding each other for a long time.

"We need to ride to town and get the sheriff."

Gasping, Kat said, "They'll arrest me. I'll hang."

"No, of course you won't. This was an accident, and beyond that, he attacked you. You were fighting to get away from him. The gun going off was his own fault."

"What if they don't believe me?" She clutched his shirt.

He watched her terror and understood it. He remembered how she'd run from the asylum. Then how they'd both run across the country. Maybe they'd done too much running. On the other hand, they were both good at it. And they'd only been met with danger when they stopped running.

"What do you want to do?" he asked.

She let go of his shirt slowly, forcing one finger at a time to release, then rested her head against his chest. She was so pretty, so delicate. So smart and tough. Seb had gotten himself a fine wife.

Against his shirtfront, she said, “Do you think he was sent by my uncle? Or by the men who want to steal your invention badly enough to shoot you?”

Shaking his head, Seb answered, “Hmm, I hadn’t considered that.”

“And what do you think he meant by saying ‘This doesn’t end with me’?”

“Sounds to me like whoever sent him will send someone else to finish the job once they learn he failed and is now dead.”

Kat leaned harder. “Why the question mark after my name Wadsworth?” She lifted her head and met his eyes. “Should we run? Head back to Hidden Canyon? Maybe we need to hide out as much as Beth and her mother need to.”

Seb looked at the small notebook in his hand, then at the dead man at their feet. “I told only one person your full name. Lloyd Sterne, my lawyer. He said I had to because I asked him to put my earnings in both our names. He said he needed your maiden name. But why? Why wasn’t the name Kat Jones good enough? I wired the information to him by telegraph. I should have refused. But we were facing our troubles, so I decided part of that was admitting where we were.”

“He just wanted to know it?”

“Yes, and maybe he was just curious, but—” Seb narrowed his eyes, trying to remember—“he made me believe it was necessary. And whether he intended to do anything wrong when he asked, he’d’ve recognized the name Wadsworth. He might have mentioned you when talking to someone, or he might've been excited about my connection to such an illustrious name. He might've blathered on about it far and wide, even wired Chicago." Seb glanced back at the dead man.

Kat nodded. "I think we should run. Maybe we'd tolerate life in that canyon better knowing killers with our names written in their notebooks were roaming around outside the canyon." Then, despite the pallor, despite the tears and shaking, a glint of anger flashed in her eyes. "Or we could go have a hard talk with that lawyer of yours. Who else knew outside of a few folks in Cheyenne? And why would they want to trouble us?"

"Sterne and Morris. Of Independence, Missouri. I told Marcus I'd gotten married, but I didn't mention your last name to him." Seb thought of those two and felt his heart harden. He'd trusted them. They made decent money tending to his affairs. But did they see a chance to improve their income? "Back east, before I was shot, they knew about my invention work, too."

"If they didn't send that man, they almost certainly mentioned our marriage, including my name, to someone who did."

"Whichever it was, those men need to tell me what's going on. And I'm very much afraid they won't unless I'm standing right in front of them. They might not tell me then."

"So should we hide? Or fight? If we leave and don't get back fast enough, we might lose the homestead. We have to live here six months out of the year."

"I feel worse about losing the material in my lab. But I can get more. We can't stay here, though, not unless we're prepared to fight armed gunmen at any time of the day or night."

Kat pulled her hands down in front of her. Seb saw blood under a couple of fingernails, and her hands still shook.

Both of them looked up at each other.

Kat said, "Fight."

Seb jerked his chin down and up. "Fight."

"Let's go find the sheriff," Kat said, "and I need to talk to Mr. Etherton again. Then we go to Independence. We take the fight to your lawyers' doorstep. Let's take the train. We'll tell the sheriff what happened when we go through Cheyenne. If they want to hang me, they're going to have to wait until I get back."

Thaddeus Rutledge was viciously shamed by bending his knee.

To sit with his valet, helping him dress because he was too badly injured to dress himself, made him furious. The pain he lived with made him furious.

The scars on his body made him furious.

Not much in life had any effect on him besides white-hot fury.

And he was a man who prided himself on his icy control of things.

He stood and walked. He'd walk without a limp one of these days, but for now he was glad to walk at all.

He'd had his life saved by a doctor, who gulped a dram of whiskey between every wound he stitched closed. Thaddeus, weakened by the loss of blood, just lay there like a lump while the fool worked on him. Somehow, though, he'd found the strength to order his men to wire down the line and find out when a train was expected. Two days.

The wait was interminable, and frightening because he was so sick. Only laudanum made the pain bearable. He relied on it still.

The Pinkerton agents hadn't helped him get back. Instead, they'd gone hunting for that furiously mad Yvette. Thaddeus would have left her for the wolves.

He hadn't seen the Pinkertons by the time the locomotive arrived. They hitched the eastbound engine to his private cars, carried him on a stretcher to the bedroom in his car, where he'd lain there so weak it was frightening as the train chugged its way across most of the vast, wretched continent.

He'd been urged to see a doctor in Cheyenne, but he'd been sure Cheyenne would have the same kind of Wild West drunkard that Alton, Idaho, had, and so Thaddeus had demanded that they move on. He'd considered Omaha; he was sure he'd make it that far. But if he was going to survive, he wanted the top man he could find to patch him back together.

Omaha was ridiculous with the rail line ending. Why couldn't they get a bridge built? He'd found the private car he used in Omaha and abandoned it there. He was ferried across the Missouri River where his own car was waiting for him. Someone had thought to wire ahead and have it cleaned and stocked with water and ready to be hitched to an engine. He'd gone on to Chicago, where a doctor who possessed a functioning brain could help him.

It had irritated him when the top man in Chicago marveled at the number of stitches and how perfectly they'd been sewn. Thaddeus's life had been spared, that fool doctor had assured him, by the Idaho drunk.

Still, the Chicago doctor had worked on a few things, including fretting about a nearly severed Achilles tendon. He'd opened that sewn-up wound and worked carefully over Thaddeus's leg, which ended with Thaddeus in a cast through most of last winter. He'd removed the stitches and arranged for an attendant with special training to aid in Thaddeus regaining the use of his right leg.

Thaddeus had worked with the attendant all winter and on through the spring. He was still at it, and he might well be at it for the rest of his life.

But that hadn't stopped him from going to work. He was infuriated about the state of his company after being gone west for a mere two weeks or three . . . maybe four. He'd spent a part of that time more dead than alive.

He'd hired a man named Gerald Sykes to replace Hemler Blayd. The man wasn't working out well, and Thaddeus probably needed to fire him and find a more ruthless assistant, but he'd had his hands full getting his company running efficiently again after being gone, then healing, and so hadn't found a replacement as yet. Sykes had his uses, though. Collecting rent wasn't one of them. Blayd had been huge and menacing. Sykes was lethal, but not so good at bullying people before he did something drastic.

Thaddeus didn't have time to show him the finer points of terrifying hungry people into handing over money they needed to feed their children. Sykes seemed to have no middle ground between calm and deadly. And the dead didn't pay.

In the meantime, Thaddeus's finances were taking a hard beating because people weren't paying their rent on time.

One thing he had found the time to do was to set about ruining Dr. Maynard Horecroft, the man running Horecroft Insane Asylum. The man who'd let Eugenia escape.

Thaddeus began with more investigators and had come up with the information that another woman was missing from the asylum. When he'd found a name, Thaddeus nearly salivated with the pleasure of learning about Patrick Wadsworth's niece-in-law.

Patrick hadn't known she was gone, and Thaddeus had enjoyed informing him. Yes, Horecroft needed to be ruined, and Thaddeus would enjoy doing the ruination. In fact, he'd seriously mulled over whether to just send Sykes on a midnight visit to end Dr. Horecroft, but Thaddeus liked the idea of bringing the man low first. Wadsworth would be a good ally in that venture.

Today he had a meeting with Wadsworth, and it would be the next step in finding Eugenia and bringing about Horecroft's demise.

Striding as best he could out of his house, he climbed awkwardly into his carriage and headed for the meeting room at Patrick Wadsworth's office building. Wadsworth knew better than to ask Thaddeus to walk up a flight of stairs.

Stepping into the newest, most luxurious office building in the best part of Chicago annoyed Thaddeus. His office was in a fine setting, too, but nothing like what Wadsworth had managed. The Wadsworth fortune put Thaddeus in the shade, and nothing bothered him more.

Wadsworth was there, waiting, and Thaddeus liked the idea of being waited on.

"I've found her." Wadsworth announced it before Thaddeus could even take a seat at the vast oak table. There were two dozen chairs surrounding it, but he and Wadsworth were the only ones in the room.

Thaddeus stopped short thinking of Ginny. "Who?"

"My nephew's widow. I heard from a man in Missouri. I got a wire from there a few days ago saying her name came up in another matter. The wire doesn't say where she's at. He didn't know. But he's going to find out."

"When will you get her back here? I have some questions to ask her. Did she hear where Eugenia was going? I know my daughter didn't stay in Independence. I saw her in Idaho of all places last summer, but maybe your niece knows exactly where she was going. Can she tell us?"

"As I said, I haven't gotten ahold of her yet. And I've got questions, too. Most of them for Horecroft." Patrick Wadsworth wasn't a cool, calculating man like Thaddeus. Horecroft had never told him Katherine Wadsworth had escaped the asylum. Wadsworth had dutifully paid the fee for her room and board monthly, but now it appeared Katherine had been gone for over a year.

Wadsworth wasn't a man who liked being cheated. If there was cheating to be done, he preferred to do it himself.

Wadsworth was tall and thin to a painful degree, as often happened to men in perpetual motion. He dressed in fine wool and silks. His silver hair looked like a glowing crown on his head.

Wadsworth owned much of the land under their feet here in Chicago, but Thaddeus owned most of the tenements and slums. He made a fortune on the crumbling buildings, the only homes most of the scum in Chicago could afford. Thaddeus also owned a lot of the factories the scum worked at, or he owned shares in the factories.

Wadsworth's holdings were different. He owned shiny buildings, some so grand that they'd rival cathedrals, all in the richer sections of town. His renters were prosperous men who liked to show off where they lived and worked. They paid on time and without much urging.

Wadsworth owned shares in many of the same factories as Thaddeus, and both men had their hands in the railroads and shipping lines.

Thaddeus liked to sit and calculate, while Patrick preferred to pace the room with his arms swinging. He had fire in his soul, while Thaddeus had ice in his veins. But the end results were the same, for they were both men to be reckoned with in Chicago.

"I'm waiting to hear back from Independence." Patrick was one for pronouncements. "Once I know where she is, I'll travel there. Right now I'm thinking she's going to turn up in Independence. I've set plans in motion to go there, but there could be last-minute changes. Wherever I go, you're welcome to come along."

Thaddeus had to stifle a groan. He hated to travel on his wounded leg. He'd hoped Wadsworth would go fetch his niece and drag her home. Thaddeus would question her here. But the urgent need to get his hands on Eugenia was alive and well in Thaddeus. "Let me know when we're leaving."

Wadsworth cracked a smile and gave a little nod.

Thaddeus limped from the room, dreading the journey

but too wrapped in vengefulness to even consider for a moment sending a list of questions along with Wadsworth and just staying home.

As he headed back to his office, he decided that wherever they went, he'd take Sykes and give the man one more chance to prove himself.

It flickered through his mind, as it did from time to time, to wonder what in the world had happened to that lunatic, murderous Yvette.

"I found her." Oscar rushed into the cabin.

Beth, gently bouncing a baby, the same as always, asked, "Where is she?"

Mama came up beside her, bouncing Jacob.

"She's in that cave where we stored all that extra food we brought, planning for it to last the rest of our lives. That's how she survived. I followed her tracks, found her out front of that cave, and watched until she wandered off. I slipped inside and found she'd eaten some of the canned goods we stored there. It looks like she lived in the room with the hot spring, and that's how she stayed warm. Her dress is the one she was wearing last summer when she stabbed Rutledge. It's even got a few bloodstains on it."

Oscar said the last with grim satisfaction. Beth suspected Oscar would never dislike anyone who stabbed Father.

"Poor abandoned thing." Oscar seemed to like her overly. "Don't reckon she had a change of clothes or so much as a blanket to make the floor softer."

"The woman who attacked me at Horecroft Asylum

is living in our canyon?" Mama had listened closely to their story about being found by Father. She recognized the name Yvette.

They'd all heard the story of the first time Mama had touched her. The first time and the last.

Yvette had gone mad with a violent assault.

Mama never touched her again. No one in that place ever did except the attendants, who seemed to revel in sending Yvette into a fit of rage.

Mama gave Jacob a soft kiss on the forehead. "What can we do for that poor bedeviled creature? I've said before that some people in Horecroft were truly mad. But it was no place for anyone, no matter the state of their minds." She looked at Beth, then at Oscar. "Do you think we can help her?"

The only response was silence.

Jake came in then. Joseph soon followed.

"I found her," Oscar said as he washed up, then helped set the table.

Jake washed up, too, and afterward took the baby from Beth, kissing both of his girls gently on the forehead. "You eat first. I'll mind our little Marie."

Joseph took Jacob from Mama.

"This is a spring chick?" Beth tasted the soup and wanted to moan with the pleasure of it. "It's so delicious. I can't quite believe those chicks are old enough."

"It's been plenty long," Oscar said, ladling a bowlful for Mama. "You've been busy the last few months."

Beth laughed. "That is the pure truth."

When they were eating, Mama asked again, "What can we do for Yvette? I want to at least talk to her. She has a rational way about her most of the time. Her speech is refined. She always wore beautiful clothes. I wonder how she came to be at Horecroft?"

"She seemed to think she was married to Father. When he referred to you as his wife, she became furious. That's when he hit her. That's when she went berserk and stabbed him."

Stabbed and slashed and hacked away at him. Blayd had shot at her to stop her, which made the Pinkerton agent, coming in after Yvette had been knocked to the ground, shoot Blayd dead. Then the Pinkerton had a badly wounded Father hauled away to town by Blayd's henchmen while the other agents had said they'd find Yvette and see she was taken . . . somewhere.

Clearly McCall had failed.

"She must have somehow followed us right into the canyon." Jake handled the gentle baby-bouncing rhythm perfectly. "I wonder if spending the winter alone suited her or drove her further mad? If it suits her, there's no reason we couldn't just leave her alone, let her live in that cave. Maybe we could leave supplies at the cave entrance. Make sure she's eating right. We could make a mattress for her, sew her a new dress, and see if she's not too addled to change clothes? We just don't know how she's doing, physically or mentally."

"I'm going to talk to her."

"Now, Ginny—" Oscar began.

"I'm doing it." Mama cut him off.

There wasn't much Oscar wouldn't do to protect Mama, and neither was there much he would deny her. He just nodded.

"Let's go then," Oscar said. "Right after we eat. I'll go with you, so will Joseph. But we'll stay well back. So will you. Jake and Beth can stay here with the tykes."

"I want to go. I saw her last fall." Beth, who'd learned to eat fast, was done and pushed back from the table. "Father was talking to me, and for some reason she followed us here. I should go."

Jacob chose that moment to start crying.

The whole table laughed at the baby boy's perfect timing. Joseph said, "I'll stay and help Jake."

Joseph was done eating, too, and took both babies. "I'll see if a nap is coming. Jake, you get your soup."

Mama said, "I've got a spare dress, the blue one. Yvette was of a height with me. I'll take that to her. And I made cookies this morning. I'll take her a plate of those and . . . uh, welcome her to the neighborhood."

It all sounded so friendly and yet Beth was sorely afraid it was going to be anything but.

12

"And you're sure you've never seen this man before?" The sheriff stared down at the body while he scratched his round belly. The lawman looked right prosperous.

"He's a complete stranger," Kat said. She could feel an imaginary noose tightening around her neck. Mr. Etherton hadn't come out to the house, but he'd assured her she wouldn't be arrested and that he'd step in if she was. She was finding it hard to breathe.

"And he had your names written in a notebook he carried with him, as well as an envelope full of hundred-dollar bills?"

Seb nodded, then handed the sheriff the dead man's notebook and money.

"Welp, he's a no-good varmint to put his hands on a woman thataway. Reckon he got what he deserved. He's no one I recognize, but then new folks are coming into town all the time. I'm gonna ask around, see if anyone's talked to him or if he was seen getting off the train. If he was staying at the hotel, he had to sign the register and might've left a satchel. The hotel may even know where he's from so we can notify his kin. You don't have to worry about this none, Mrs. Jones."

The imaginary noose loosened, and she took a deep breath.

"My deputy is coming along with an extra horse. Did you see a horse he left around here?"

"No, and we showed you where he grabbed me. He may have a horse tied up out there somewhere."

Nodding, the sheriff said, "We'll scout around. This fella we'll haul to town and dump him in a hole in the ground. If we can't find any family, the money is yours. I'll look for wanted posters, too. If he's a hired killer, he's prob'ly wanted somewhere for something, I reckon. You might get some reward money, Mrs. Jones."

"We want to leave town, go have a talk with the only person I told where we were." Seb crossed his arms and gave the sheriff a tight look. As if he expected to be told not to leave town.

"Hope you get things settled and get back to your cabin before winter settles in. Good luck to you."

The deputy rode up while Kat and Seb packed and saddled up. Kat got the impression that a woman could do most anything in this state and not end up arrested. Probably not a lesson women should learn, or the state might be flooded with the worst sorts.

When they'd gone for the sheriff, they'd checked and found an eastbound train was due in later that day, so they didn't stay long at the homestead. And anyway, if one man had found them, another might show up at any moment. Maybe there was a bounty on her head or Seb's or both of them? Maybe there was a stampede of hired killers heading for Cheyenne.

Good thing they were on the train and heading east before nightfall, leaving Cheyenne behind them.

"We'll reach Omaha tomorrow night and then we'll take a steamer ship south to Independence." Seb ran a hand through his dark blond hair.

"You need to visit a barber, husband. You look for all the world like a man who hasn't had his hair cut in over a year."

Nodding, Sebastian said, "Let's see what Omaha brings. Maybe we can find time for a haircut before we sail. I should probably try not to look too disreputable when I go punch those gentlemen lawyers Sterne and Morris right in the nose."

"A change of clothes, too, for both of us." Kat looked down at her bedraggled blue calico dress. It wasn't the only one she owned. She'd bought fabric and sewn a dress for herself in Cheyenne. But she'd forgotten about it when they'd shoved a few things in their satchels and caught the next train passing through town. This dress was a tattered thing Beth had provided for her when they'd first met.

They sat side by side on the back bench of the last passenger car. Probably, now that Kat thought about it, a sign they weren't eager to reach their destination. Or maybe a sign they wanted to be near the door in case someone else tried to seize them.

They had a lot of reasons to be all kinds of worried.

No one sat close to them. The train car wasn't particularly full. They'd opted not to pay for a sleeping berth because Kat didn't want to sleep. She was afraid to close her eyes. Afraid to be cornered.

"We have our guns." She patted her Springfield rifle that rested between them on the bench. The Peacemaker was tucked in her pocket. She'd watched Seb pack his as well. "You know how to shoot?"

"Nope," Seb said.

"Maybe we need one of those under-the-arm holsters like my attacker had. And more bullets."

Silence strung out between them. It had been late in the day when they'd embarked on their journey. Kat wondered if she could make it through the night without sleep. Maybe they could sleep in shifts. Yet every time she closed her eyes, she would picture that man she'd shot, bleeding, dying, eyes open and fixed on the sky.

"Tell me about the asylum, Kat."

She thought she'd told him enough, but then remembered her vow to talk more about her past with Seb. "Do you remember the story Ginny told about that woman getting upset when Ginny lightly touched her on the arm just to be friendly?"

"Yep."

"Nothing happened like that to me. Or mostly nothing. The orderlies and nurses were often cruel for no reason, but I never fought back. Never spoke up in defense of myself or anyone else. I was a model prisoner . . . I mean, a model patient."

"Stick with prisoner—it's closer to the truth."

"I wasn't in as long as Ginny. A year only. Ginny was so smart and so honorable. She lived out her faith every day in that place. She encouraged others in small ways, but the attendants took it all as rebellious and disobedient, and I suppose as proof of insanity. Ginny couldn't quit, though. She was well-behaved, wanting to take care of everyone. She was even kind to the attendants. Not me."

"You weren't kind to the attendants?"

"I was silent. Obedient. I listened all the time, but only spoke if I was asked a direct question by someone in charge of me. At first I was grieving and felt like I deserved to be locked away. Then, as my thoughts cleared, I became so afraid that I made myself into a mouse. Outwardly I remained a mouse the whole time I was there. But after a time, inwardly I began to rebel. I realized if I was sneaky about it, I could do some small bits of defiance. I started with learning to pick the lock on my door."

Seb smiled broadly. "Good for you."

"I used a hairpin to pick the lock. I listened for the women who'd patrol the place at night. There was one on duty per night, and all of them were slack and usually just walked up and down the halls once each night. I'd hear the night guard pass by, then pick my lock and sneak around. Whoever was on guard did their one walk-around and then returned to the front desk where they'd fall asleep."

"What if they'd caught you?"

Kat shook her head. "Everyone was locked up, and those guards didn't much think of us, let alone care about us. I often wondered what would happen if the place burned down. Would they make a single effort to get us out? I suspect they'd let us burn to death in our locked rooms."

Seb shuddered.

"I also learned where they hid the room keys and where they kept medicine. I got into the doctor's office and read through my files. I even found a way out. But that's where my rebellion ended. I was too afraid to run away. I didn't know where I'd go. I was tempted. I considered it. I tried to think of a plan, but what would I do once I escaped? I had no money. My parents were dead by this time, and I had no other family—at least none I thought would help me. So I'd go back to my room, and I'd think and think, plot and plan. And then one night while I was doing my sneaking, I ran into Ginny slipping down the hall. I found myself a woman with a plan. I tagged along."

The conductor came through the door at the front of the car. One hour earlier, he'd walked to the back to check the passengers' tickets. Then on through, there were baggage cars, cars for livestock, and finally the caboose on past Kat and Seb. This was the conductor's second time through. Kat fell silent. She didn't have much more to say anyway. The conductor made his way toward them, nodded in a friendly way, then went on through the back door of the car, inspecting the train maybe. He seemed more vigilant than the asylum attendants.

"We took a cattle boat from Chicago to Independence."

Seb turned, startled. "A cattle boat? I've been on one of those. The stench was terrible, and the animals never stopped lowing."

"Beth was sure her father would expect her to travel in comfort. He'd look on the train and on passenger boats, but he wouldn't think of their traveling in such a way. That's why she chose the cattle boat and the wagon train. Beth had arranged jobs for her and her mama on the boat as cooks, while I stowed away. Except Ginny was a failure as a cook. Since no one knew us, Ginny hid in our cabin all day, and I cooked with Beth. When we landed in Independence, we walked to a prearranged spot to pick up the horses and supplies Oscar had left for Beth and Ginny. On our way, we heard you crying for help. Ginny and I stopped to care for you. Beth went on to get the horses. She bought a couple of extras and that cart we carried you in."

"I have only the faintest memory of you finding me," Seb said. "I remember you did some doctoring on me and declared it wasn't serious and that with care I'd live. I'd already resigned myself to death. I'd been shot. I climbed out on the roof of the warehouse where I had my laboratory, three stories high. I could jump or wait for the man hunting me to finish me off. A wagon passed beneath me, and I jumped."

"That explains why you had badly cracked or broken ribs. That hurt worse than the bullet wound."

Seb shrugged. "Maybe. The bullet wound hurt plenty."

"And you had a terrible lump on your forehead."

"I must've landed facedown on that wagon when I jumped out the window."

"The ribs were agony, but the blow to the head was what kept you addled and in and out of consciousness for so long. So we loaded you up, and on the way out of town, afraid because she was bringing two extra people with her, Beth stopped and bought more supplies and whatever else she thought might help." Kat patted her husband on the arm. "Beth wanted to patch you up and leave you at an inn, pay for you to be looked after. She said if it was good enough for the Good Samaritan, it was good enough for her."

Seb rested his hand on top of hers. "She was probably right."

"I insisted we take you. Not hard to do when you were unconscious, and we already had the cart."

"When I came around in the alley, I didn't know how I'd gotten there, what part of town I was in, or how far I'd ridden in that wagon. All I knew was that I was dying and that packet of mine had the notes to my latest invention. The address I scrawled on it was to Marcus Coleman."

"I remember his name on your packet. He's the one you've been corresponding with—another person who knows where we are."

"That's true. We spent all our time together in the lab, comparing notes, challenging each other, brainstorming ideas. We started out working on batteries, then he turned his attention to electricity generated from a steady source like a waterwheel or a steam-powered engine. I focused on a battery that could store electric energy and be transported. We corresponded after I came home to Independence, and he stayed on in St. Louis. Inventing was never about earning a living for him. It was always in pursuit of making the world a better place. Even though he'd quit his battery experiments, I thought he'd understand what I was working on and might be the one person who could finish it. I added pages to it in Hidden Canyon, and I've added more since Cheyenne. I feel like I'm getting close to a breakthrough."

The door behind them opened. The conductor came back in, paused, and smiled down at them. "We've got a long quiet stretch coming. We'll have to stop and take on water every once in a while. But there's no stop for meals or such things overnight. The stops will be short. Your tickets are to Omaha, so you can sleep through the stops and get some rest."

"That's good advice, sir," Seb said. "The whole train seems settled in for the night."

"It's a racket as it rolls along, but there's a steadiness to it that for some folks is almost like being rocked in a cradle." With that, the conductor said good-night and moved on to the other passengers, most of whom were sleeping already. A few moments later, he left the car.

"Kat, scoot closer to me. Rest your head on my lap."

She whispered, "One of us needs to stay awake. Most likely there are no hired killers on the train, but I'd prefer not to find out I was wrong while I'm sleeping."

"We'll take turns then. I'll take the first watch. I brought a new book with me in my satchel."

"Not Plato's *Republic*, I hope. I didn't notice you carting ten volumes along."

He removed the book from his satchel. "No, *David Copperfield*. It was the only book I could find in the general store. I suppose they had more packed away, but we were in a hurry."

Kat lit up. "Charles Dickens? That sounds wonderful."

Seb kissed her. "Wonderful? I doubt it. The main reason I bought it was because it sounds like a book that will put me to sleep."

She gently cuffed him on the arm. "Just read."

"Yes, Mrs. Jones."

Smiling, she slid up against the window to give herself enough room, then leaned sideways to use Seb's thigh as a pillow. He squeezed her shoulder and opened the book to chapter one:

"'Whether I shall turn out to be the hero of my own life, or whether that station will be held by anybody else, these pages must show . . .'"

Seb took first watch and read about someone else who'd fallen on hard times.

13

"Do you remember how long it took us to cross Nebraska on the wagon train?" Kat marveled at the speed of their travel as they stepped down from the train in Omaha. They were near enough to the river that she could see the steamboat docked just a few hundred feet away.

The people of Omaha had yet to build a bridge across the Missouri River for the train to continue eastward. Instead, eastbound travelers were forced to off-load their possessions from the train, take everything with them aboard a ferry across the river to Council Bluffs, Iowa, and catch the train there. It was a cumbersome process, and the river was more mud than water, its banks prone to flooding. Yet despite that, the bridge was proving to be a monumental task. Still, the same hardworking and determined folks who'd laid the tracks for the railroad all the way across the country would also see that this bridge got built.

"No, I don't remember much of that leg of the journey.

I was unconscious for most of it. But what I do recall was the boredom."

Kat turned somber. "The least boring day of that trip was when O'Tooles' wagon broke a wheel and rolled over in the creek."

"I do remember that." Seb nodded thoughtfully. "It was good to see the O'Tooles, especially after they'd had some time to heal from losing Shay."

"They're enduring all right, but then what choice does anyone have in this life but to endure? Having Bruce there to show them how to get by sure helps. But there'll always be an empty place in their hearts. I'll always remember that day, no matter how hard I try to forget it."

Seb turned to study his wife. "Your knowledge of what to do with someone who'd drowned saved most of that family, Kat. Did you learn that from your father back in Chicago?"

"Yes. We came running once when a child fell into a water tank. Pa saved him. I can remember a couple of other times, too, when we lost a few. I learned hard lessons back then." Kat thought of how devastated the O'Tooles had been when Shay couldn't be revived.

Neither of them could manage a smile as they made their way down the platform steps at the train station. Seb walked beside her, both of them exhausted, hungry, and in need of washing up. "Let's go see when the next boat heads south to Independence," he said.

They found the ticket office and learned that the boat was scheduled to set sail tomorrow morning at first light. That gave them time to rest, eat something, and get cleaned up for the journey ahead. As they left the office with their tickets, Kat leaned her shoulder against Seb's. "I suppose we should be grateful the boat isn't sailing right away, only now I've got just enough time to worry. I'm frightened of what could happen."

"Don't be scared. There's no possible way someone sent to Cheyenne to kill or kidnap us could know we're on our way to Independence."

Both of them looked around nervously, as if Seb's confidence might be enough to bring on trouble. No killers seemed to be bearing down on them, though it was hard to tell in the bustling river town.

"Keep talking," Kat said. "Maybe I'll believe you if you say it enough."

Seb gave her a tired smile. "How much sleep did you get last night?"

"I had my eyes closed for two hours on two separate occasions. I'm not sure there was much sleep involved. And I dozed for a bit earlier today before we arrived."

"I'm about a match for that. Although I don't remember a thing about the trip from North Platte to Fort Kearny—except for stopping for water."

"Every fifteen miles all night and all day. I don't believe I slept through a single stop. Why don't you spend your time inventing a train engine that can run for days without stopping."

"I'll put it on my list. But the trains need to stop to pick up and let off passengers, and to load and off-load supplies. They'd still have to stop."

"In some ways, tearing across the country so fast makes it less real than walking the whole way. It makes Cheyenne seem like a place we've left behind forever."

"We'll get back there, Kat."

He hesitated, and that drew her full attention. "What is it?"

Omaha was a hectic boomtown like so many that had gotten the train. Carriages and freight wagons rushed along. Voices shouted, and the clip-clop of horses' hooves created a din. The train chugged behind them, turning around to set out again across the nation. Nearby the river flowed along, making its own steady roar beneath everything else.

In the middle of what amounted to a riot of noise, Seb asked, "What do you think will come of your talk with Mr. Etherton?"

Kat shook her head. "We ran off so fast, the man hasn't had time to look anything up."

"Well, Beth thinks you should be able to fight your uncle. He had no right to lock you away in that asylum."

"Her words were mainly for Ginny. She's the one who's in danger."

"And yet you're afraid of him."

Kat shuddered to think of Uncle Patrick.

"You're right about his being a powerful man, but you're a married woman now, Kat. I'd go with you and face him. I know you're afraid, but in the end we'd win. No jury could look at you and listen to you for a single minute and not recognize that you're sane and capable of being on your own."

"Yes, he had no right. And there's no law that could declare he has any power over me. I'm still afraid, though."

"What if it turns out he's behind that man coming after you? We'll have no choice but to take him to court. Either that or run for Hidden Canyon."

"For now, I'm content to believe all this trouble stems from you."

Seb laughed. "It probably does."

Kat took his hand. "Let's face Independence first. We'll spend tonight cleaning up, resting, sharing a meal, and getting ready to go meet your lawyer."

Seb nodded, then pointed at a dry-goods store down the street. "Look, there's a ready-made dress in that store's front window. Let's see if they have your size."

"Yvette?"

The woman, fifty or so feet away, startled like a wild animal when Mama called out to her. They'd tried to bring her supplies right away after the first time they'd seen her. But when they'd come to the canyon, she hadn't been around until now.

She spun to face the voice, then froze. Her white-blond hair was a bush. She stood just outside a grove of trees, not that far from the mouth of the cave.

Beth remembered her perfectly styled hair last fall. At the time, Beth had assumed she had a lady's maid, but if no one could touch her, then no. Her dress wasn't dirty. She must be washing it in the hot springs and bathing regularly. She was thinner than she'd been last fall, yet she didn't look as if she were starving. And her eyes looked as frightened as a young doe.

"Do you remember me? It's Eugenia, from the asylum."

"I'm not going back there." Yvette's voice had been refined last fall, very proper until she started screaming. Now it creaked like a rusted hinge.

Beth had to wonder if those were the first words she'd spoken in six months.

"I'm not going back either, and I would never try and make you go back," Mama said. "We both got away. We're staying away forever." Yvette's eyes slipped to the left, where Oscar was standing. He'd stayed back, but not all that far.

Beth stood at Mama's side.

"Can I talk to you, Yvette? I brought a gift for you. I'd like to help you." Mama lifted her arms a bit to show her a neatly folded dress. They were of a similar height, though Yvette was slimmer. On top of the dress was a plate that held a comb and a bar of soap, and beneath the dress a blanket.

"And I brought sugar cookies," Beth said. She prayed silently, wondering what God would have them do for such a wounded creature. Based on Mama's stories and what Beth had witnessed last fall, Yvette seemed thoroughly mad and very dangerous, but could she be helped? Could she accept friendship and kindness? Could a person's sanity, once lost, be regained? Beth had no idea. If it could be done, God would have to guide them.

Mama took a few steps forward, slowly.

Yvette tensed, watching, as if ready to take flight at any moment.

"If you want me to stay away, I will. I'll leave the gifts here, and we'll leave you alone. The cave you're living in is a decent enough home, with hot water and a warm room during the winter. But we invite you to join us for meals, Yvette. And for company if you're lonely. You could live in the cave and come eat with us. We have plenty of food, vegetables, and fresh milk. We'd be glad to share."

Mama kept inching forward as she talked, closing the distance between herself and Yvette. Beth stayed back, watching for the knife Yvette had wielded last fall. She tried to remain calm and let Mama reach out to someone so fragile.

Mama must've been wary, too, because she stopped, crouched, and lowered her armload of supplies to the ground ten feet away from Yvette, the wrapped cookies on top. Mama then backed up and sat on the grass. "Come and eat, Yvette. I'll bring you food for every meal if you want. I'd like to talk with you, offer you friendship."

Yvette looked between the cookies and Mama, her eyes finally locking on the cookies as if they were too much to resist. She moved cautiously to the plate, then sat and curled her legs beneath her, keeping her distance from Mama. She unwrapped the cookies, grabbed one, and took a bite. Her eyes closed, a blissful expression on her face.

Beth knew about the food in the cave: cases of canned vegetables, lots of beans, things they hadn't needed yet but had brought along to store for later.

Yvette's eyes opened, and she focused on Mama. After that first bite, she ate tiny nibbles of the cookie and chewed slowly as if to make it last as long as possible.

"I know you've been hurt, Yvette. I was hurt, too. Dr. Horecroft was cruel to us both. My daughter helped me escape." Mama gestured toward Beth. "You managed to get away, too. I know Thaddeus Rutledge brought you out here."

They'd talked about just what to say. Yvette had been upset when Father had talked of his wife. Yvette seemed to believe *she* was his wife. But she hadn't truly gone wild until he'd struck her. After that, she'd had what Mama said was her "usual outburst" whenever anyone touched her. If a raging knife attack could be called *usual*.

Yvette blinked and said quietly, "I-I like the cookies."

Beth realized then that, beneath the unkempt hair and limp dress, Yvette was an unusually pretty woman. If Yvette had been terribly hurt, physically or emotionally or both, Beth wondered if that was what had driven her mad. And if so, could she be brought back to her senses by their showing her kindness? And if she did join them, could Yvette ever be trusted? Could she be touched without a blinding rage consuming her?

How dangerous was she?

"And I like the cave."

"I'm glad you found the supplies in the cave and used them," Mama said. "I'll come back and bring more blankets and a mattress filled with dry prairie grass so you can have a comfortable bed. What else do you need?"

Yvette started humming. She finished her cookie and picked up another one. As she sat eating, humming, she reached into her dress pocket and pulled out Father's knife. She stared at the blade.

Beth braced herself to rush to the woman if she cut herself. Or to defend Mama if Yvette attacked her. For now, Beth stayed back and listened to a haunting melody coming from Yvette, barely audible. It was the same one Yvette had been humming when she and Jake had first seen her.

The melody niggled at the edge of Beth's memory. Yvette hummed just a few notes of it, over and over again. But no matter how hard she tried, Beth couldn't place it.

A few minutes later, when the cookies were gone, Yvette stood and said to Mama, "Thank you. I'd like a mattress."

Mama smiled. "I'll bring it right away. Won't it be nice to sleep in a soft bed again? One more thing—we have a worship service every Sunday morning at our cabin. Have you seen our cabin?"

"I know where you live. I've been watching you. You have babies in the cabin."

A chill rushed up Beth's spine.

"Tomorrow is Sunday." Mama's voice remained kind, but Beth knew her mama well. There was a thread of tension in the invitation. Could Yvette be trusted near the babies? Could she be trusted near any of them?

"Come and join us early enough for breakfast, then stay for church. We'll hold our meeting outside, and you can stay well back if you wish. But you can worship the Lord with us and listen to our Bible reading. We're all so thankful to have gotten away from the asylum. To have found this place we call Hidden Canyon, where the men who hurt us can't find us."

Yvette jumped just a bit when Mama mentioned those men. Then she began humming again, picked up the dress and blanket and other things, never taking her eyes off Mama. She whirled and dashed into the grove, probably heading for the cave.

Mama turned and walked back to join Beth and Oscar. It was only when Mama got close that Beth could see she was crying.

14

Sebastian and Kat sailed for Independence at dawn, clean and rested, decently dressed and with full bellies. The steamboat made good time on high water. Seb had to admit he wasn't in a hurry, but the boat steamed along at a surprisingly fast clip.

When they disembarked, Kat said, "I can't tell if I'm unsteady because I've been on a boat or because my knees are shaking with fear."

Kat had on a green calico dress, smattered with pink-and-white flowers. It was high-necked and long-sleeved and very pretty. She wore a straw hat with a green ribbon tied tightly under her chin or the wind on the boat journey would've blown the hat from her head.

Seb didn't spend much time noticing clothing, but his wife, in this dress, with her blond hair pulled back in a tidy bun, along with those bright blue eyes of hers, all made Kat an eye-catching woman. A wealthy, well-connected woman through her husband's family, smart and hardworking, kind and a person of faith. He felt a sudden surge of thankfulness that he'd ended up married to her.

He rubbed her back to buck up her nerves. "You look beautiful this morning."

Her blue eyes darted to him, surprised. "Thank you."

Had he never complimented her before? He really was a lunkhead of a husband. He put that aside for now. "It's not far to my lawyer's office." Seb looked around the city he'd spent his life in. "It's odd to be back and carry along the memory of being shot. To be suspicious of the men I've trusted. It'll die, won't it?"

Kat looked at Seb. "What will die?"

"Independence."

"Why would it?"

He stared at the Old Main Courthouse, part of the image of his youth. "Without the wagon trains, without this being the jumping-off point, what is there left?"

"It'll survive. It won't be the bustling place it once was, but that might be for the best. Being from Chicago, I must say bustling can get very old."

Seb drew himself out of his own dark thoughts to smile at her. "Somewhere between being trapped in Hidden Canyon and the raucous noise and motion of Chicago . . . is that our goal for a home?"

"I think we can find a middle ground. I like the homestead we were living on, except . . ." She fell into silence and looked away from him. "Let's go see your lawyers."

She took a step, but Seb reeled her back in. "Wait a minute. What do you mean by 'except'?"

She stared at the courthouse as if it were riveting. It was a pretty building, but not quite that interesting. He rested both hands on her shoulders and stepped directly in front of her. "I can tell by all you're *not* saying that the 'except' part is important."

She drew in a deep, slow breath, then turned to face him. He thought she looked false somehow. "I'm excited for you, excited to see what you'll invent. But it gets a bit . . . quiet in the house. I may get used to it. But I need something else—a friend, a group of friends, I don't know."

"I'm glad we're going to church now. It's good to spend time with people of faith. I'm sorry I let my work consume so much of my time." Seb knew he got lost in his experiments, so much so that he often forgot what day it was.

"Parson Roscoe's wife mentioned a lady's sewing circle. I'm going to join that. And since Cheyenne is the territorial capital, I'll see about learning whatever it is that swirls around a capital. Maybe Mr. Etherton would know how I might get involved. I can see if they need . . ." Her voice dropped in a way that drew his avid attention.

"Need what?"

She lifted her eyes, and they seemed overly bright, like maybe without much trouble she could start crying. "Maybe they'd need *me*."

He was stumped. Did she mean . . . ? "I need you, Kat."

She pulled free of his grip and turned away again. "No you don't. Not really. You need meals and clean clothes, so there's that. But the days get very long for me. If I want more, if I want friends and companionship, it's my job to find those things, just as you've found your job."

She swiped the wrist of her pretty green dress across her eyes briskly.

She went on, "I'm not going to wonder about livening things up when I've possibly got a killer after me. When we get that ironed out and get back home, I'll need to see about finding my own life."

Which meant she needed more than him, locked away and inventing twelve hours a day. Maybe she needed to know she had a husband who put her first, who cared dearly for her. He vowed to do better.

"Kat, do you—?"

"Sebastian!" His name, shouted from down the street, cut through the chaos of Independence and the tumultuous thoughts in his head.

"Sebastian Jones, as I live and breathe."

Seb turned to see his lawyer Lloyd Sterne striding toward them on the busy sidewalk. His big smile, his wavy brown hair. Dark eyes that didn't seem to be smiling even though his mouth was, but then maybe Seb was just seeing what his suspicions told him to look for.

The time for talking things out with Kat, promising to do better, would have to come later.

"Lloyd." Possibly a man who'd hired a murderer. Kat stepped ahead of Seb, almost like she was moving in to protect him. He caught her hand and drew her back to his side as they walked toward his old friend.

Lloyd reached them, his hand extended. Seb shook the man's hand, but his expression was blank, no smile. Lloyd kept on shaking his hand, then started shaking his head. "You vanished, Sebastian. Deacon called the police and had them break a window to get into your house. Then we found a trail of blood in your laboratory."

"You missed me then?" And his laboratory had been secret. How had they found it?

"Yes, by the great horn spoon, of course we missed you. You were coming in almost weekly with questions about your patents, and you'd end up having dinner with us. Then you just vanished." Lloyd made a dramatic sweeping gesture with both hands, fingers spread wide. The kind of thing a magician might do. "We went by your house, and it was locked up tight. A neighbor told us she hadn't seen you in weeks, so we called the police."

It had taken them *weeks* to miss him? Well, he spent most of his time alone, doing experiments. Much like he was behaving in Cheyenne. He thought of Kat's desire to find her own life.

"Your house was empty. Nothing." Lloyd's face was very expressive, his eyes wide, all of him in constant motion. This was the same Lloyd. "Including no sign you'd traveled anywhere, though we were sure you would have told us if you were leaving town." Lloyd hesitated. "Let's go to the office. Deacon will want to see you." Deacon Morris, Lloyd's partner in the law firm. "We can talk as we walk. I'm eager for him to see you're back. So, where in the world have you been?"

Seb exchanged looks with Kat. He almost felt like it would be best to have this talk out in public where no one could slit his and Kat's throats behind closed doors and then hide their bodies. No one knew he was back. No one would even consider that something had happened to him now because they'd already accepted the fact that he was gone.

Seb decided to go along, though he wasn't sure if he'd

go inside. He had a few blocks to weigh what to do then. He drew Kat close and kept pace with Lloyd. The man was walking fast. Was it to minimize the chances of anyone else Seb knew seeing him?

But then Lloyd was a fast-walking, fast-talking man. If he stood still and was quiet, he tended to bounce.

"We found the address of the laboratory in your house. We didn't know it was your laboratory when we found the bill of sale, only that you'd bought a warehouse."

"You own a warehouse?" Kat asked.

"A small one."

"And a house?"

"My parents' house. The house I grew up in." Just more details he realized he'd never told Kat. Once he'd gotten back into his laboratory, he'd talked mainly about science rather than his past.

"Anyway, we visited your warehouse," Lloyd continued, talking over their exchange, "and there we found a door standing open." He hurried ahead of Seb, stopped, and grabbed Seb by his upper arms. "We were scared to death. We found blood, and the place was a wreck."

"Someone shot me."

Lloyd froze, but he couldn't stay still for long. Shaking Seb, he cried out, "You were shot? Why? By who? How'd you survive?"

Seb was in no mood to trust anyone. "You remember that diner about a block from your office, the one we always went to with the chicken-noodle gravy?"

"Sure, sure. Conway's Diner."

"Well, we're going inside, Kat and I. We'll get a table and wait for you there. Go get Deacon."

"Okay, sure, if you're really hungry."

"We're not *really hungry*, Lloyd." Seb tore himself free of Lloyd's grip. "Someone tried to *kill me*."

Lloyd, already overwhelmed it seemed, didn't respond.

"Last spring. That's why I ran. Now this summer, less than a week ago, someone attacked Kat out in Wyoming, and they had her name and mine written in a notebook, along with five hundred dollars. You were one of the only ones I told where exactly we were. So I'm not inclined to trust you. I'm not inclined to let you lead us anywhere. I'm not inclined to shut myself and my wife in a room with either you or Deacon."

Lloyd's mouth went slack as if shocked beyond speech. That didn't last long either. "Well, for heaven's sake, Sebastian. How could you—?"

"In there." Seb cut him off, jabbing a finger at a doorway with the words *Conway's Diner* painted on one of the place's front windows. The building was red brick with a white-painted door in the center. "We'll wait for you there. Then we'll talk all this out."

"Seb, you can't think . . ."

"I don't know what to think, but I don't trust you or Deacon Morris. You both had more knowledge of me than anyone else. I'll be interested to find out what you did with my house and my warehouse. I owned them both. Did you sell them and keep the money for yourself?"

Lloyd quit talking but, as expected, kept bouncing. He jiggled his knees, crossed his arms, then uncrossed them. A fidgety man. "I'll get Deke and be right back." He turned and walked at a pace next to running. But it was his usual pace. Nothing suspicious in his behavior so far.

Seb gestured toward the door. Kat came along.

"That was remarkably blunt," she said.

"I apologize. I've got manners, I think. I just didn't bother with them."

Kat went through the door when Seb opened it. "Getting the door for me is good manners. You're doing all right."

The diner was spacious but plain, nothing much fancy about the place. But the food was good, served fast and hot, and there was plenty of it. It was midmorning and not overly busy. Seb and Kat found a table that would seat four, well away from the front windows.

A waiter came up, and Seb said, "We've got two more joining us, but they might be a few minutes getting here." Time enough, he thought, to alert anyone they'd hired that Seb was in town along with his wife, Kat.

"Would you like coffee while you wait?"

"Yes, please." He looked at Kat, who nodded.

"Do you have chicken-noodle gravy?" she asked the waiter.

"We do, served over mashed potatoes with biscuits. It's our specialty."

"Can I order that while we wait?"

"Right away." The waiter turned to Seb.

"The same for me, thanks," he replied, then looked toward the windows and the street beyond, wondering what danger they might have brought on themselves.

Patrick Wadsworth as good as crashed into Thaddeus's office. "I found them."

"Where?"

"Independence, Missouri. I'm told she arrived there

from Wyoming just this morning. I'm leaving at sunset. I'll need all day to make plans for while I'm away."

Thaddeus needed that much time, too. "I've got an engine arranged to pull my private train cars. I'll be able to ride on my own schedule. You're welcome to come along."

"Let my people know which station. I'll get my own cars hooked up to your engine and meet you there at sunset." Patrick jerked his chin in agreement and stormed out.

Patrick wanted his mad niece. Thaddeus wanted information from the fool woman. He hoped she wasn't as far gone as Yvette.

Once Thaddeus had recovered enough from his wounds, he'd hired men to scout the countryside. But winter had made the search difficult, and spring was late in coming. They'd been back at it only a few weeks. He had others track down the folks on the wagon train to dig up more clues but heard back nothing but bad news. Apparently, his daughter had vanished into the Idaho wilderness.

Now Katherine Wadsworth had popped up in Independence, Missouri, the place where wagon trains left for the wilderness. That was where Eugenia and Elizabeth had gone, he was sure. Then onward to Idaho, of all ridiculous places. Independence would be the worst kind of backwater town. Thaddeus had been to St. Louis, a thriving big city although miserably hot in the summer. But Independence would be both miserable and small besides.

Rubbing his leg in grim acceptance of what lay ahead, Thaddeus rang for his secretary and began barking orders. Including orders for his valet to pack and for Sykes to get ready to travel.

Time to see just what his man Sykes was made of.

15

Lloyd burst into the diner with Deacon Morris on his heels.

Lloyd was a skinny man, probably from the constant motion, and dark-haired, forty-one years old. Deacon was fifty at least, the senior partner in the men's law firm. He was stout, his hair thinning and turning gray at the temples, with wire-rimmed glasses and muttonchops. Deacon was more deliberate in his speech and movements, wore fine suits and kept his hair trimmed short. Both lawyers were ambitious, hardworking, and prosperous. Deacon was married, a father to six children, all of them grown now. Lloyd had never slowed down long enough to find a wife.

Seb knew these bare-boned facts, but beyond that, he knew little about the two men. They seemed to be honest, though, so why would they try to kill Seb for his inventions? He wanted to trust them. It twisted his gut to look at them and remember that gunshot last spring, the attack that had sent him running for cover.

How could he be sure? Well, he was very sure of one thing . . .

Kat raised a hand and drew the men's attention. Sebastian had deliberately claimed a table away from the front windows, with his and Kat's backs to the wall.

Lloyd hurried over to them, his face red. With anger? Seb hadn't spoken carefully to the man. He didn't intend to start now. Lloyd pulled out a chair and sat. He was still fidgeting and getting settled when Deacon took a chair.

Seb and Kat were halfway through their chicken noodles poured over the best potatoes in Missouri.

Deacon started right in. "What's this I hear about you thinking we're involved in what happened to you last spring, Sebastian? And what did happen to you? All we knew was that you disappeared and left a ransacked warehouse behind that smacked of being a crime scene."

The waiter came over. The two lawyers ordered the same as Seb, and the waiter, clearly sensing the tension, scurried away.

"I sent a telegram asking for my money to be transferred and mentioned I'd gotten married. And you, Lloyd"—Seb jabbed a finger at the lawyer—"responded with odd questions and asked for Kat's full name. That name was written in a man's notebook, the man who attacked her. Just one person knew the full name of the woman I was married to. Which means you were careless with her name. Somehow, someone found out who she is and then hired this stranger to come hurt or kill the both of us. I'm sure you'll want to pretend you're innocent, but you must've repeated her name to someone who is *not* innocent. It has to have come from one of you."

Deacon opened his mouth to speak just as the waiter approached, carrying two plates. He set them down, turned and walked away, but was right back with a pot of hot coffee and two cups. The poor man didn't want to interrupt them, but he seemed to fret about not serving them properly.

Seb went back to eating, while Kat was mostly done with her chicken.

"Tell us what happened when you disappeared, Sebastian." Deacon sounded as if he sincerely wanted to know.

But Seb couldn't read honesty in his expression, nor dishonesty. Lawyers could be tricky that way.

"A man broke into my lab—the warehouse. He wore a mask and came in shooting. I do my work on the ground floor, but the gunman had that exit blocked. I got out of the room with only one gunshot wound. In my belly."

Kat shook her head. "It was in your side. It was awful, but not a mortal wound."

"So I climbed upstairs," Seb went on, patting her hand, "the intruder coming hard after me, and got to the office rooms on the third floor. Then I threw myself out a window."

"You jumped from a third-floor window of your warehouse?" Lloyd's eyes went sharp with concern. "Those ceilings are high. That's a terrible height to fall from."

"I was lucky enough to land on a freight wagon carrying hay. Soft enough that the fall didn't kill me."

His wife shook her head again and said, "You had broken ribs. You took a blow to the head that made you very sick for a long time. Add the ribs to the head wound to the gunshot wound, and you were badly hurt."

"Kat and her friends were passing by and found me. They loaded me into a cart and headed west. I ended up part of a wagon train before my wounds healed enough to consider whether that was what I wanted. Then, scared to come back here, I stuck with them through the winter. And this spring, Kat and I got married." He smiled at her. "The best part of this story. We've settled on a homestead in Wyoming."

He decided to skip over everything about Beth and Ginny and Hidden Canyon. He didn't mention Thaddeus Rutledge either.

"I set things up to work on my experiments. We weren't sure what to do about the man who'd tried to kill me here in Independence. Then Kat was attacked by a man who snuck up behind her. She won that fight, and later we found a notebook on the man with our names in it—including Kat Wadsworth Jones. I'd said that name to no one except the parson who married us. And I'd wired it to you, Lloyd, at your request. Within weeks there was someone searching for us in Wyoming with Kat's full name, the name she had before she married me. So one of you sent the attacker with no good intentions, or you told someone."

Seb studied each man's face, wondering if they'd try to lie.

Lloyd cleared his throat. "I told a few people you'd come back from the dead. It never occurred to me to keep that secret."

"A few people?" Kat asked sharply.

Seb jumped in. "I want a list of names. Every single person you told. And think back to last spring—not a few months ago, but a year and a few months ago. That I had a laboratory in that warehouse wasn't a generally known fact. I'm aware of the spying that goes on among a certain type of inventor, so I was discreet about where I worked. How did someone find me there? Who did you tell about that?"

"We didn't know about the warehouse before you went missing," Lloyd protested.

"So you say," Seb grumbled, then reached for his napkin. Conway's might be just a diner, but it was a nice one. No need to wipe his mouth on his sleeve in here. "Tell me, do I still own my home and warehouse? What happened to them? And what happened to the money from my patents?"

Deacon lifted both hands as if to slow him down. "Everything is in order, Seb. We even repaired the damage we did when we broke into your house; we fitted new locks on both doors." He produced two keys and handed them to Seb. "The taxes were paid out of your income and that money, and what we didn't wire to your Wyoming bank is sitting in your account here. In fact, you can go sleep in your house tonight. It might need dusting. The food in the cupboards is all a year old. We went in once, but never again. We hoped and prayed you would turn up alive."

Or maybe, Seb thought, they'd been cautious and bided their time before starting their thieving. Seb eyed the two men for a long moment, then stood. "I came here to find out who wants Kat or me or both of us captured or killed. I'm not sure staying in a place I'm known to own is wise. We'll send a note to you later to meet us again. I'll expect a list of names. Or a confession."

He reached down for Kat's hand without taking his eyes off his lawyers. She took his hand firmly. He tossed money onto the table, and the two of them strode out of the diner.

As they headed down the street, Seb said, "I know we came here to face our troubles, but now that I'm here, I'm not sure exactly what to do. Should we go to the sheriff, or should we arrange to sell everything and leave town? Go somewhere else. We could have the money sent to Cheyenne but live away from there. Along the train route would make the most sense, so we could get to Cheyenne easily whenever we need more money."

Kat said quietly, "For now, let's get away from here and keep an eye out behind us. It takes barely any time to send a telegram to someone to have us followed. And Lloyd was certainly gone long enough."

Seb's gut twisted as he glanced around them. A carriage drew up close, but Seb said, "Let's not get on the first cab that rolls past us. Even that could be arranged."

Instead, they dodged down an alley and onto another busy street, then walked up that street in the direction they'd come. "Over there," Kat said, pointing. They darted into the deeply inset doorway of a bank. Looking up at the sign over the door, she asked, "This isn't your bank, is it?"

"No. I know Independence well, but I've never done business in this bank in my life. You watch to the right in case someone's ahead of us somehow. I'll watch left. We should be able to see if someone was set up outside the diner and now comes hurrying toward our last known location."

And there they stood as people came and went from

the bank. He focused on their faces but saw no reaction from any of them. They just walked right on past and disappeared into the bank building. Folks also walked past the bank on both sides of the street. Wagons and carriages rolled along, heading in both directions. No one appeared to notice the couple huddled in the doorway of the bank.

No one was looking out the second-floor windows across from them. Nothing happened to make Seb suspicious. And yet he was. He most certainly was.

"Instead of a cab," Kat said, "we should buy horses and ride. That way we'd be more in control of our own fate. And I know just the place to buy them."

Seb nodded. "A wise choice, buying horses." He released a long sigh. "Well, no one's come along who seemed to be watching us. I think it's time we moved on, and since you know where you want to move to, lead the way."

"She's here. Don't look," Beth hissed. Everyone halted their eating, frozen in place. They'd dragged the table out of the cabin so as to have their breakfast in the open air.

Beth almost smiled when she realized how unnaturally they were all acting. Because she was facing west, and Yvette came from that direction, it was fitting she'd greet their guest first. "Yvette, hello. Come join us. We're having eggs and bacon with biscuits. We've got butter, jelly, and milk or coffee to drink."

Mama and the others looked up and smiled. Beth saw the suspicion in Yvette's whole body. She stood behind the tree nearest the cabin, leaning out, watching, wanting.

Whether biscuits with jelly or just companionship, it was hard to tell.

She wore the new dress, a simple blue calico one that Kat had helped Ginny sew last winter. Kat could work circles around both of them with her cooking and sewing, and they'd learned so that now Yvette had a dress. Beth had included a lot of fabric in her supplies.

The dress Yvette had worn before was elaborate and very beautiful. But she'd worn it all winter. She looked better dressed in the calico. It buttoned down the front, making it much easier to wear than the dress she'd had before.

Yvette's hair was much improved, too. It was rolled into a bun at the base of her neck. Beth thought of the rat's nest her hair had been, looking as if it hadn't been combed for an entire winter. How long, how many painful hours, would that have taken? Such a frustrating task might be the wrong thing for a mind so fragile. Or maybe bringing order to her hair somehow helped to bring order to her mind.

If Yvette wouldn't let anyone touch her, it stood to reason she could manage her own hair. Though it had been in such a state, it might have taken a while.

"I'll bring you a plate if you don't want to sit with us." Mama didn't wait for her offer to be accepted. They were no doubt all afraid Yvette wasn't going to talk or join them, and a decision about coming near was beyond her.

Mama stood from the table, filled a plate, and headed for Yvette.

Under her breath, Beth said, "The dress isn't a good fit. I'll make her a better one, not on the Lord's Day but starting right away tomorrow."

Beth saw the poor, frightened woman tense, her gaze riveted on Mama.

When Mama was about the same distance from Yvette as yesterday, she walked to a boulder that was about waist-high and reasonably level on top. Mama set the plate there, along with a fork, which now seemed a bit too much like a weapon to Beth.

Mama backed away, talking. "We're going to have church services now. You come and sit on this boulder and eat. We'll start off with singing. You can join in or just listen. Your choice."

Mama backed away, mostly, Beth thought, to not make any sudden moves, like turning around might've been.

Then Mama slowly turned her back on Yvette and came to the table. Most of them were done eating. Jake had Jacob in his lap. Oscar had Marie tucked in his elbow.

Joseph got out his harmonica. Quietly he said, "My heart breaks for that woman. I wonder who hurt her so badly, it turned her into this frail, frightened waif? I was married years ago, though not for long. My wife died birthing a baby. My baby girl would be about Yvette's age."

Joseph played a single verse of "O Come, All Ye Faithful." It was a personal favorite of his and one he played especially well. Though it was considered a Christmas carol, it was a wonderful way to be summoned to a worship service. He could manage most simple hymns, and the instrument always lifted Beth's spirits. Once Joseph finished playing that song, he began the Doxology: "'Praise God from whom all blessings flow . . .'"

Beth remembered Bedelia McDaniels, the wife of Parson McDaniels, both of them riding west with their wagon train. She'd used the Doxology to the tune of "Old Hundredth" as a call to worship, and often just a call to the beginning of a new day of travel. Joseph had taken to accompanying her if he wasn't too busy, and he played it very well.

"'Praise him, all creatures here below.'"

The McDaniels were heading for a mission field in Oregon.

"'Praise him above, ye heavenly host.'"

The singing woke Jacob, and he began to fret.

"'Praise Father, Son, and Holy Ghost.'"

Afraid a man moving around might alarm Yvette, and knowing some pacing and bouncing would be required to keep the baby from crying, Beth stood. "I'll take him," she offered.

Jake's eyes met hers. She'd told him about Yvette's interest in the babies, and they both knew to be very careful and at the same time hope that the infants might touch Yvette's heart in a good way. They were adorable children, now nearing three months old. They were smiling and cooing when they got attention, and it would take a very hardened heart indeed not to find them appealing.

By the time Beth had her son and was doing her usual bouncing, Yvette had approached the boulder, taken the plate, and sat down to eat.

It crossed Beth's mind again that Yvette hummed a strange tune. Beth wanted to know what it was. It must be special to the woman, and if Beth could figure it out and sing it, Yvette might join with her. She always hummed the same few lines over and over, as if she were trapped in that small circle of music. Maybe a different song would pull her away from this one. Or if Beth could figure out what song it was, maybe she could break this strange cycle of repetition.

It struck Beth hard that what Yvette needed above all else was to feel safe. Right now she'd decided that the way to feel safe was to be alone. How might they help her? And if she felt safe for long enough, could her broken mind be mended?

16

Being unpredictable is the right idea. Good work."

The two of them rode horseback out of the same livery stable where Beth had bought horses and a cart to haul an unconscious Seb a year and a half earlier.

"And now we go to the boardinghouse the livery stable owner recommended. If someone is following us, they're very good. I haven't seen anyone. If they are that good, we've got bigger problems than where to find food and a roof."

The livery man said the innkeeper had a barn out back and would supply food and a stall if her renters cleaned the stall and cared for the horses.

Kat led Seb to the alley where he'd been lying shot that spring day long ago.

"I was in there?" Seb stepped into the narrow alley, which was little more than a pace between two buildings.

"Yes, you called out 'Help me.' Ginny went rushing right in. Beth looked horrified. I went along more cautiously, but I did go. I saw you clutching your belly. You tried to thrust that packet into my hands and said something about dying. I soon cleared that nonsense out of your head."

"This is miles from my laboratory. I have no memory of getting here or getting off that freight wagon, assuming I'd been carried here in one." Seb, a few steps in front of her, turned and smiled. "You decided you could save me, huh?"

"Yes, I knew I could," Kat said. "The bullet wound in your side, it was bleeding terribly, yet the bullet hadn't hit any internal organs. It was more of a flesh wound. I told Beth to give me something to use as a bandage. She handed over what I now know was her only spare dress. Then I ordered her to go get the horses and told her to find a cart and a spare horse." She paused and shook her head. "It was odd. I was so quiet and willing to work at anything to stay out of that asylum. But then I saw you wounded, and I started snapping out orders—to you, to Ginny, to poor Beth. I had more nerve than I should have."

"And there I was, taken into the care of a Good Samaritan." Seb took her arm and led her out of the dark alley. "Thank you, Kat. I would probably have survived my wounds and staggered out into the open and gotten shot again. You three generous ladies saved my life."

"Well worth it, husband." She grinned, and the sass made him chuckle. "Let's go find that boardinghouse."

They followed the stableman's directions away from the docks until they reached a decent-looking neighborhood and a house with a sign out front that said, *Aunt Vivian's Inn*. A good-sized white house with a second story and a front porch. An elderly woman sat on the porch, rocking away. Aunt Vivian perhaps?

"This is a good distance from both my house and my laboratory. No reason anyone watching those places would spot me here."

They dismounted, tied their horses to a hitching post out front, and went through a gate in a white picket fence to approach a gray-haired woman, who kept on rocking as she watched them. She was small, thin, and had a genial smile.

"Are you looking for a room?" She rose from her chair and came to the top of her porch steps. She had a fine way about her. A bit prim, her words very clear, like maybe a woman who'd been a teacher in her earlier years.

"We are, ma'am." Seb drew his hat off his head. "And a place for our horses. We're not sure how long we'll stay. If you have room, we'd be obliged."

"I do indeed have a room. I'm Vivian Wayne. Come in, come in. You can get settled in your room and then come back out to put up your horses." She waved them up the four steps to the broad front porch. She had the door open, but Seb took it from her. "Go on ahead. I'll hold the door, Mrs. Wayne."

See, he did have manners.

"Call me Aunt Vivian. Anyone who stays here is required to do so." She had a friendly twinkle in her eyes.

They were soon checked into a room under the names of Joe and Ann Williams. Dinner was four hours away.

Seb couldn't settle down. "Do you think I dare go to my house? I'd like to see how things are."

"I thought you wanted to be unpredictable." Kat removed

the neat little bonnet she'd bought along with the dress. It was straw and had a green ribbon around it to match her dress. She laid it on a round table by the window. She sat in one of two chairs at that table and studied him like maybe he was a failed experiment.

"If we're careful, and no one sees us, then we get back here without being followed—we'd be back to unpredictable. But there are things in my house I'd like to see to."

"And your laboratory? Do you want to see that?"

Seb shrugged a bit sheepishly because he would like to see how it had held up after being abandoned for a year. "I've some notes hidden away at home. If Lloyd and Deacon were telling the truth and there was no sign of the house being searched, even if someone went through it, they might not have found my notes. I'd like to get a few things to take back to Cheyenne with me. I had one patent in those notes ready for me to apply. I'd like to get the process started."

Seb lifted his eyes to meet hers. "And I guess, well, I guess I'd like you to see it. Is that foolish? It's my boyhood home. Maybe you'd feel like you knew me a little better once you see where I grew up. It's a nice house. My father was a successful man. Not wealthy by any means, but a man who'd taken good care of us."

Seb rose and moved to the chair across from Kat and reached for her hand. "I feel like we have shared little of ourselves from before we met."

"Seb, you know more about me than anyone in the world. Well, not counting Uncle Patrick, and he doesn't know me lately."

Seb gave her a sad smile. "Same for you. I've told you

a lot about myself. But as I sit here talking, I realize even with you knowing the most, you still don't know much. It's time we got to know each other better, Kat. We can check out the house from a park nearby. If we think it's safe, we'll go inside."

"Is four hours enough time? I'd hate to miss Aunt Vivian's supper."

"More than enough."

"Let's leave the horses. It's easier to sneak around without them."

"But slower if we have to run for our lives."

Beth's eyes dropped to the gun Seb now wore in a holster strapped around his waist. Bullets filled every loop on his belt. "I should probably buy a smaller gun, besides the one in my pocket. I could carry it in my reticule."

"Let's do that first. We're not nearly dangerous enough, and I say that even knowing you shot a man a few days ago."

Kat gave him a bleak smile. "Yes, I did."

"An accident, Kat."

"I hope God considers all the gray areas." Her shoulders squared. She was sure He did. Yes, God would forgive even a broken commandment if a sinner came to Him asking forgiveness.

"And now I'm thinking we need to arm ourselves even more." Kat frowned at Seb. "I feel incredibly guilty about that. 'Thou shall not kill,' and yet I want to be prepared for just that."

He took her hand. "We're not going out looking for someone to kill. We're going out ready for trouble if someone brings it to us."

"And that's enough? I still feel guilty."

Seb shook his hand. "Hard questions, Kat. But I think, under the circumstances, I'd rather fight someone who attacked us than just stand there helpless. Let's pray about it while we walk over to my house."

~

"That is a very nice house. I have to reassess just how much money I married. You don't have any scheming uncles, do you?"

"I don't have anyone." His heart pounded to think of how alone he was in the world. Then he turned to Kat. Their eyes met.

"I don't have anyone either." She drew a trembling breath.

He saw so much there. So much loneliness. The death of her husband. The death of her parents. The misery of her year in the asylum. The wild escape with Ginny, and the run across the country with strangers. It was all there.

But it wasn't true anymore. "We have each other, Kat."

Her eyes held. They looked deep. Maybe seeing in him the same things she held inside herself. "Do we have each other, Seb?"

He nodded, just a bit at first, then with more assurance. "Yes, Katherine Jones. We have each other. We have and hold and will as long as our lives last. And I'm glad of it."

She kissed him on the cheek. "It's good to have someone. I'm glad of it, too."

The moment stretched, full of sweetness. But with their constant danger and worries, it couldn't last for long. They both turned to look at Seb's house.

It was a part of town with big yards and old trees. The house had two full stories. Gabled roofs faced the front of the house, and Seb knew there were two matching gables on the back. A porch wrapped around the whole house, and it shone white because Ma had seen to it that it was always freshly painted. They stood looking at the south side with the big front door up a flight of ten steps. There were picture windows on both sides of the door, but the one to the left was boarded over. Seb wished Lloyd had chosen a smaller window to break.

"I can't take credit for the house. It belonged to my parents. Pa was a successful schoolmaster. He earned good money as the lead teacher for the older students in the Independence school. And he'd spent it wisely, as did Ma. She made it a comfortable home for us. She loved her pretty doilies and overstuffed chairs. Lots of flowery fabric and comfort. That was Ma. I didn't care to have flowers all around, so after she died I banished them from my room. She had screens put on the doors to let in the breeze on a sticky summer night and keep out the mosquitoes."

Seb stared at the house. In some ways, it had an abandoned and neglected look about it. "I know Ma missed my older brothers and sisters. She said losing them to the West and to war was the way of the world and a hard way. But she believed life was about more than keeping a family close. She was a woman of strong faith, and she had great hopes that her children, wherever they were, in this life or the next, were people of faith and that was what was important. But I realize now I stayed close in part because of how much she missed them."

"Would you like to try to find your family? I'm not sure how, but we could search for them. You said your sisters got married and went west. You probably have nieces and nephews you don't know about. A letter can race across the country now with the train. Once we find them, you could stay in touch. We could even visit."

Seb looked away from the house. "It's been so long, Kat, and I was so young when they left. I don't feel like I'd even know them."

"We could look for pictures. Maybe we could find your sisters' married names. Maybe your Ma wrote down where they were headed, or even got a letter from them telling her where they'd settled."

Seb nodded silently, thinking about it. "It would be worth a look. But maybe I'll put that off for now. Today I'd like to just get in there, find my papers, and leave. I'd like to see if there are any pictures or letters, though. I've never thought of that before. Inventing took all my attention. When I got home from college, Ma had passed. Pa was struggling to keep the house as nice as it had always been. Moving in with him was the most natural thing in the world. I helped care for it inside and out. I always mowed the grass." He smiled. "I'd seen a lawn mower at college and came home and built one of my own. Even invented a basket to catch the clippings."

"You built a lawnmower? I don't know if I've ever even seen one. I can't remember for sure ever hearing of one. I think in Chicago, the grass was scythed or sheep were let out to do the mowing."

"It's a fairly simple machine, but it was already patented. I just built it for my own use because they were expensive and hard to find. But mine worked. I kept the walkways graveled and tidy. The bushes clipped. Now there are weeds coming up everywhere. The grass has gone to seed."

The bushes he once trimmed were now overgrown. There was a vine growing over his porch. The house had faded patches in the paint.

"There are trees in the park and trees in my yard." He swallowed hard. "Plenty of places to hide. How do we know if it's being watched?"

"Someone was watching you last spring, and then they found us in Cheyenne. If word has reached them that you're back, someone with ill intentions almost certainly will have found out. Even if they'd given up before, they certainly would think to watch it now."

"But Lloyd and Deacon said they had to break in." He saw the window beside the front door was boarded over. They'd fixed it, but not well. "So, since it was weeks after I'd been shot before they broke in, no one else had done that. At least they'd left no sign of breaking in and searching the house. Maybe my would-be killer believed I was dead." Then he remembered something and snapped his fingers. "Lloyd said they'd talked to a neighbor who hadn't seen me in weeks."

Seb rested a hand on Kat's shoulder and turned her toward the west. A house was visible behind the trees. "Mrs. Gundersen is a sweet old lady who gave me cake or cookies now and then when Pa was failing, and she kept at it after he died. I'd stop in for coffee and fix anything she had that needed repairs. Little things like a wobbly chair leg or a creaking front step. I used the lawnmower to cut her grass when I did mine. She was a kind woman. I really liked her. In fact, because all I did was work in my lab, then come home to sleep, visiting her made her about the only friend I had."

Kat sounded sharp when she said, "Except for your lawyers who now may be trying to kill you."

"Yep, except for them. She'd lived in the house next door for years. They both back up to a wild land and the river. Far enough away to avoid the spring flooding, but they're the closest houses to the water. She was good friends with my ma their whole lives, but she was also lonely and spent a good amount of time looking out for the neighborhood. She'll know if anyone's been around."

Seb drew Kat back behind a grove of trees in the park across the street just south of his house. He walked behind the trees with her and stayed hidden as they made their way to Mrs. Gundersen's back door and knocked.

She was a slow-moving woman, but Seb heard her coming. When she opened the door, she beamed. "Sebastian Jones! My boy!" She threw her arms wide.

Kat was a step behind him, and a good thing or she'd've had to move fast to get out of Mrs. Gundersen's way. Seb was engulfed. He glanced back and saw a genuine smile on Kat's face as she watched the elderly lady.

"I've worried so about you. I've not heard a word." Mrs. Gundersen's voice broke. Then she inhaled slowly to steady herself. She was a plump woman, fond of her own good cooking it seemed. But spry and probably not as old as Seb had always figured. His folks were close to seventy when they died. She was most likely the same, though he'd always considered her grandmotherly.

"I was sure you wouldn't just leave without a word, which meant it must have been something bad." Her gray hair, always in a tidy bun at the base of her neck, seemed to quiver with her excitement at seeing him.

She wore gold-framed glasses and a pink calico house-dress that seemed like the same one she'd always worn. But it wasn't faded, so it might be a new one.

Seb hugged her tightly and reconsidered his whole life. Yes, he'd been alone in the world after his parents died, but not completely. Not as long as this neighbor loved him. Hugging her, he said, "I had trouble and had to run, Mrs. Gundersen. I finally was able to get back."

She straightened away, her eyes damp with tears, her smile as bright as the break of dawn. "Trouble, was it? I suspected something happened."

"I should have written, but I ended up on a wagon train heading west and thought it best if I vanished for a time."

"A wagon train west? But now you're back?"

Seb slipped gently from her grasp and turned to extend a hand to Kat, whose eyes looked a bit too bright. "Meet my wife, Mrs. Gundersen. This is Kat Jones. I met her on the wagon train. I was hurt, someone . . . attacked me, I think to steal my inventions. Kat nursed me back to health, and when we both decided to come back east, I convinced her to marry me."

Kat blushed and shook her head. "I wasn't that hard to convince."

"Married. Well, and about time." Mrs. Gundersen let him go and gave Kat almost as big a hug as she'd given him.

Seb looked on and smiled. Neither he nor Kat had had

a mother for a long time. Mrs. Gundersen's hugs felt wonderful.

"Come in! I'll put coffee on, and we'll catch up."

"I would like nothing better, but the trouble that drove me away from Independence might still be near."

The smile vanished instantly. "How can I help?"

Seb hugged her again. "I love you, Mrs. Gundersen. Thank you. When I tried to think of whether it was safe to get into my house, in the event it was being watched by the men who attacked me before, I thought of you."

Kat asked, "Have there been people around his house? Have you noticed anything either back when he was attacked or more recently?"

Nodding, her eyes sharply intelligent, she said, "I watched those friends of yours break in. They'd been here to ask if I'd seen you before they broke your window. I was worried sick. They had the police with them, so I decided not to object. At first, another man came around. He asked if I'd seen you, but I hadn't, so he left me alone. I didn't like the look in his eyes. Later, I saw him hiding in the shrubs behind your house. Before your friends came. I kept an eye on him. All I could think was that he was watching for you. I hoped that meant you were alive. If he'd killed you, why would he wait and watch in secret? And then a few days ago, I saw someone again."

"Not those friends?"

"Nope, the lawyers, right? They said their names, but I've forgotten them. I've never seen them again. I wasn't sure if they were trustworthy or not, but just like the first man, I didn't have to lie because I didn't know anything, except I hadn't seen you. They certainly seemed concerned and acted like they wanted to find you for your own safety. But how can a woman be sure? I never saw them again, and even when I was near expired from curiosity, I didn't go to them and ask if they knew what had become of you."

"Show me the shrubs where that man hid." Seb held Kat's hand and slid the other arm around Mrs. Gundersen's waist. She guided him to her front window. Seb peered out and noticed she had a clear view of his house. Since she liked to sit in this front room and do needlework and look out the window, she wouldn't miss much.

"I haven't seen him for days. He always hid in the same place." She pointed to where he'd been.

Seb looked at Kat. "You stay here with Mrs. G. I'll go look around the house for—"

"No. I'm going with you. If you have to run, then I'll run with you. If you have to fight, then I'll fight with you."

Mrs. Gundersen gave Kat an approving look. "You've picked a fine wife for yourself, Sebastian. I think it would be best if neither of you went over. But whatever you do, you need to stick together."

Seb looked at those bushes again, studied them for a long time, then said, "Let's go." He took out his door key and made sure Mrs. Gundersen was looking right at him. "Be careful. The men looking for me are dangerous."

She nodded and yet looked upset. "You'll come back and see me, won't you, Sebastian? When all your troubles are settled?"

"I will." He glanced at Kat. "If we can figure things out, I'd like to go back to living in that house."

Kat nodded but didn't reply. And now wasn't the time for such a talk.

Seb gave Mrs. Gundersen a hug, then took Kat's hand. They walked quickly across the lawn and down the gravel street that separated his house from Mrs. Gundersen's.

17

Kat tried to get a full sense of the house as she stepped inside. The more she got to know Seb, the more she realized she didn't really know him.

All of their first months together, from his injury to his decision to stay with them as they headed west to their time in the valley, the Seb she got to know first, she knew now had been completely out of character. His true character was the man who spent all his days in his laboratory.

The house, pretty as it was, had held little of his attention. By the look of the dusty but otherwise tidy house, he was a man of order, a man with deep roots. She guessed the pretty flowery paintings and pillows and the old but finely made furniture were all left from when his parents were alive. This wasn't the home of a rootless, obsessed inventor.

Except for the obsessed part.

The mantel above the brick fireplace was lined with framed tintype pictures. Those would be Seb's brothers and sisters. There was one of him as a young man, possibly from when he graduated from high school. There was one of the whole family with a very young Seb sitting on his father's lap.

Had Seb even noticed them there? She'd asked about pictures, and he'd acted like they'd need to look around. This house must hold a lot of things from his past. Kat wanted time to explore but, as Seb had already said, not today.

"Let's go upstairs," he said. "My notes are . . . well, they *were* hidden in my room."

Kat followed him up the stairs. "You hid your notes even though this was your own home? Where you lived alone?"

Seb glanced over his shoulder with a sheepish look. "At the time I felt like I was being overprotective of my work. Now it seems I was being careless with it instead. There are ruthless thieves in the world of inventors. I'd met men who pretended to want to share my enthusiasm. They came to visit and wanted to talk to someone of like mind. Several times, though, I caught them snooping around my house when I went to get them a drink of water or a cup of coffee. More than once I interrupted a break-in. Which is what made me invest in high-quality locks for the house—locks I invented myself and got patented. I've had to sue on two different occasions to stop someone from using one or another of my patents without paying for it. Along with those measures to protect my patents, I hid my notes."

"How many patents did you say you have?"

"I've got quite a few now. Some have expired. A few have been widely used and are very profitable. I have a battery that is enough different from Leclanché's wet cell battery to be granted a patent—that is, if I can just finish it. That's the first step of what I'm working on in Cheyenne."

Kat had heard him talk about Leclanché before. Her mind tended to wander when he went into detail. She vowed there and then to listen more closely, no matter how boring he was.

"And I had one earlier than Leclanché about a specific small change to batteries that he improved enough to earn a patent. Beyond that, I invented the locks. They're quite secure and have sold well. I've worked on pottery containers that won't absorb acid, kerosene lamps and coal oil improvements, and I've used electricity for a few things but with limited success because I can't find a steady supply of power. A good battery would provide that. There's so much out there that's possible with oil and electricity."

He was getting excited about inventions again. She forced herself to pay attention.

"Any new invention you see is usually the product of dozens of small changes that make it better each time."

He led the way into his bedroom, still talking, but she'd lost the thread of his explanation once she was in his room.

She saw a spartan life. A dark blue bedspread, an iron bed frame, no rugs, no pictures on the walls or bric-a-brac anywhere, no curtains on the single window. He'd said he'd banished his mother's more decorative flourishes from the room. Smiling inside, she wondered if maybe he'd locked the door against her with one of his patents.

He had a chest of drawers, a small desk, and a wood chair. There was a closet with its door closed. Seb went straight to the closet, opened it, and dropped to his knees.

He worked over something she couldn't quite see. She leaned sideways to see what he was doing at the same time he shifted aside just enough. She saw a plain floor that swung open on a hinge with no latch she could see. It was a sneaky hiding place.

Packed between the floor joists were packets like the one he'd had tucked inside his shirt when she'd found him bleeding in the alley. His hidden papers had survived his year away.

Lifting the packets from between the floorboards, he set them aside until he'd gathered a stack of them. He closed the little door with a firm snap. He gathered up the papers in his arms. Kat opened her mouth to ask him about them when they heard a window shatter in the back of the house.

Kat's mouth slammed shut. Seb, wild-eyed, closed the closet door, stuffed his papers inside his tucked-in shirt, and moved to close the bedroom door, quickly but silently. He manipulated the doorknob, and she heard what must've been the snick of the lock. He grabbed the single chair in the room and jammed it beneath the knob. He jerked his head toward the window, and she was on his heels as they tiptoed across the room. They moved quietly, but apparently not quietly enough. The intruder must have heard them because they heard footsteps pounding up the stairs.

Seb fiddled with the lock on the window and raised the sash. Kat saw a roof that topped the front porch. She remembered the gables—they were going out of one now.

He climbed out, then reached in for her. She had no idea how they were getting down, but he clearly had it all planned. She followed along, heart pounding but trusting Seb. He guided her to a corner, then turned and scrambled down a few feet.

The bedroom door shook under an assault.

"You're cornered, Jones," a voice shouted. "I've finally got you."

Kat, trembling, crawled outside just as Seb had. He guided her feet, then went down another step as the door to the bedroom rattled and a man roared with gleeful anger. He truly believed they were trapped.

The rest of the way down would have been simple if she hadn't been shaking. But she tried not to let the terror she felt slow her down.

At last her feet hit the ground, Seb grabbed her hand, and they ran. Seb saw Mrs. Gundersen peering out her front window and made a motion to shoo her out of sight. She ducked away as Seb and Kat ran straight for the trees in the park. They could still barely hear the furious battering of the bedroom door, followed by a crash, just as they dodged behind the trees. Seb didn't stop, but scrambled deeper into the safety of the woods, Kat following as best she could.

"Jones, this isn't over!" a man screamed from the bedroom window.

Seb never let up his running, and neither did Kat.

Finally he slowed but continued to stride all the way across town in a maze of turns, and she worried they might be lost until suddenly she knew where they were as he led her up the steps of the boardinghouse and straight on up to their room.

Aunt Vivian called from the kitchen, "Dinner will be ready in thirty minutes."

"We'll be down." Kat did her best not to let Aunt Vivian know she was gasping for air and riddled with fear.

They stepped into the room. Kat was glad to see the door had a lock. Seb went to the curtains and pulled them closed.

Then he turned, dragged a chair away from the window, and sank onto it. There were two chairs. Kat made sure hers was out of sight from someone below searching, then sat to face him.

"We should go to the sheriff," she said.

"Will whoever is after me be watching to see if that's what we do next?"

Kat stood and began pacing. "He predicted we'd go to your house."

"I don't know about the sheriff, but at least we know one thing." Seb ran a hand over his face, then rested that same hand on the papers he'd brought along.

"What's that?" Kat hesitated to suggest they run all the way back to Hidden Canyon.

"The man hunting us in Wyoming was after me."

Thaddeus settled into his private car, ready to write notes he'd need to send back to Chicago to keep his company running. Sykes and two others had their own car, complete with sleeping quarters. This was an overnight trip. But they'd reach Independence early in the morning.

Because of that, Thaddeus hadn't brought his diner car or a cook and maid along. They'd be in Independence for breakfast.

His usual string of seven cars, including baggage and

livestock cars, wasn't necessary. Only the sleeper cars, one for him and one for Sykes, and Thaddeus's private passenger car. Wadsworth had arranged for the private engine and his own set of cars, and the only passengers were those Thaddeus and Wadsworth had brought along.

Thaddeus sat reading business reports and drinking a glass of brandy laced with laudanum, his usual cocktail and the only hope of a halfway decent night's sleep.

A knock at his door surprised him.

"Come in?" It was easier to call out than get to his feet.

Wadsworth entered.

Since it was the rear door of Thaddeus's private sitting car, he wasn't surprised when Wadsworth came in. Thaddeus's three cars had been hooked on before the three Wadsworth had brought.

It was late, and in the rush to make arrangements for his business to operate without him, he'd yet to see Wadsworth. It stood to reason there were details that should be discussed. Then Dr. Maynard Horecroft came in behind Wadsworth.

What was he doing here? In company with Wadsworth? How could Wadsworth trust the man? Katherine had escaped over a year ago, and Horecroft hadn't informed Wadsworth, even while Wadsworth paid a hefty monthly fee to contain the madwoman.

Horecroft must've spun some sort of tale. When Thaddeus had found out about Eugenia's escape, Horecroft had claimed he was searching for them, and searching cost money. So the monthly fees had continued. Thaddeus knew a cheat when he met one. And for all his costly searching for his wife and daughter, Thaddeus's men had yet to report back that they'd found a second search being conducted, one that could be tracked back to Horecroft. Thaddeus distrusted the man and considered him a liar and a thief, but somehow Wadsworth had been convinced the man could help when they found his niece.

"Sit down, gentlemen." Thaddeus gestured toward his blue velvet chairs, which faced his own specially made chair, which had a footrest so he could lift his leg. It tended to swell, and his doctor had suggested he elevate it.

The walls in the car were paneled with burnished black walnut. The furniture was walnut and teak. He had kerosene lanterns, patterned with floral-painted blue chimneys, in sconces on the walls, carefully set so they wouldn't fall if the train ride became rough. That included one behind his left shoulder to provide light for his reading.

There was carpeting underfoot and a table on the far side of the room for when he took meals in the car.

Horecroft went straight for the nearest chair. Wadsworth, unsurprisingly, began to pace.

Wadsworth began, "Dr. Horecroft has had agents searching for my niece ever since she went missing from the asylum. He has been instrumental in finding her."

Thaddeus sincerely doubted it, but didn't say so.

Wadsworth went on. "I want her returned to the asylum with the minimum amount of fuss, and of course I don't want her injured. He's agreed to assist me in retrieving her."

"You understand my position in this, Wadsworth." Thaddeus had yet to consume enough of the laudanum to ease his pain. He took a deep draught of it, then set it and his reports on the table beside his chair. The table was also made of walnut, inlaid with teak in an intricate pattern. There was a holder for his drink, fashioned with ledges all around to prevent papers and other objects from sliding due to the motion of the train.

Thaddeus was surprised that Wadsworth seemed to genuinely feel concerned for Katherine. The man seemed intent on getting her back into supervised care. He seemed to hope she could be cured.

Well, she was a woman, wasn't she? In Thaddeus's experience most women needed to be supervised and probably locked away. Thaddeus regretted he hadn't just locked Beth up right from the moment she'd demanded her mother be returned to the home. Insolent, rude, ill-mannered girl. Just like her mother, she'd betrayed him after he'd given both of them luxury all their lives.

"I am searching for my wife. Your niece will have information that will assist me in my search. I have every reason to believe she spent the winter with Eugenia and knows precisely where to find her. I know your motive is to get her back to the asylum, but I need to talk to her before she's locked away."

"I will make sure she talks to you, Thaddeus." Horecroft spoke when Thaddeus wanted Wadsworth to answer. It was imperative to gain the man's cooperation.

"I did, after all, grant you access to Yvette Hannon last year. She took you to your daughter." Horecroft took a quick glance at Thaddeus's leg, then averted his eyes instantly.

Thaddeus didn't want to talk about Yvette, not in front of Wadsworth. Horecroft's methods to get the madwoman's cooperation had been cruel in the extreme. Long stretches without food. Locked away in a solitary building on the asylum property. Horecroft had never admitted to acts beyond that, but Thaddeus couldn't be sure. The woman responded to being touched with explosive, violent rage. Thaddeus's leg was proof of that.

Everything had taken too long. They had been weeks getting information out of Yvette and then the weeks for the trip and recovering from his injuries. Thaddeus didn't have weeks anymore. The stock market and the Chicago financial climate were volatile, and Thaddeus knew his investments were overstretched. The time was coming when his wife's money was going to be crucial. Any delay, considering the harsh Idaho winters, might put off Thaddeus finding his wife and bringing her home for yet another year.

"Wadsworth, I want your word you'll let me talk to your niece. I want to know where she spent last winter. I've had men exploring the area where I found my daughter last fall, yet none of them have been able to locate her. And where my daughter is, my wife will be. My daughter is a married woman now, and as such she is beyond my reach. But my wife is still mine to guide and control. And I *want* her location."

Wadsworth nodded. "We'll be riding back to Chicago together. I will insist Katherine allow you to question her. Running off as she did is, to me, sufficient evidence she can't be allowed to wander free. Dr. Horecroft assures me he's been searching, too, including in many of the same areas you have. His efforts finally ran her to ground. Yes, I agree you can interview her, and I'll insist she give you answers."

Thaddeus had to wonder if Wadsworth's idea of insisting would be the same as Horecroft's or as effective. Would they glean the desired information or just break the woman, as Yvette appeared to have been broken?

Perhaps Katherine Wadsworth was a bit more fully in control of herself and would therefore be more easily dealt with.

Thaddeus felt his heart speed up to match the chugging of the train's turning wheels. Tomorrow might see the end of his year and a half of searching.

18

"All they do every day is sit like that." Beth looked at Jake, worried.

Shaking his head, Jake said, "I can't believe she let Joseph get so close to her."

Joseph sat on the grass on the bank of the creek, ten feet away from Yvette. Mama sat a few more feet away. They'd been gathering this way every evening after supper, but tonight Yvette had put Joseph between her and Mama and seemed to prefer that.

"And she appears to be talking to him."

"Until Yvette showed up here, Joseph never talked about being married, that he'd lost his wife and his only child, a daughter. Maybe she senses that he knows such pain, too."

They bounced their babies as they paced inside the cabin, taking turns looking out the open cabin door when they passed.

"Can she be helped, Jake?" Beth lifted her little Marie against her chest and patted her back. It was nearing bedtime. Both babies had full tummies. If they could just get a good burp out of the twins, Beth had a chance of getting a full night's sleep.

Maybe.

They'd moved the cribs apart so one was in Mama's room, and one was in Beth's. It helped to keep the little ones from waking each other.

Helped a little.

"I want to believe a mind can mend. At the same time, I'm afraid of her. Afraid especially for our babies." Beth patted and paced.

Jake looked down at his son. "Hey, Jacob is asleep. I'll get him tucked in." Jake paused from looking down at his son to meet Beth's eyes. "The whole world is full of danger, Beth. Rattlesnakes and blizzards and rambunctious cattle and horses. No doctor within any reasonable distance. We do our best to protect the babies and ourselves, but beyond that we put ourselves in God's hands." He paused by the open door and studied Yvette and Joseph.

The woman had walked over to the stream after supper. She'd been joining them for three meals a day, every day for a week, but she'd always eat while sitting on her boulder. As had become his habit, Joseph and Mama followed her to the stream, keeping a respectable distance. Joseph talked quietly with her. After many nervous looks at Joseph, though less every day, she'd started sitting on the bank of the stream. Joseph, with a good ten feet between them, joined her, Mama just beyond them. The two of them talked or sometimes just sat in silence, looking at the western sky and watching as the sun sank slowly toward the horizon.

Jake put their son down, then a few minutes later Marie dozed off, and Beth got her to bed. They both came back to watch Joseph and Yvette.

"Do you think Mama should go out and face Father? Do you think she can be found sane, and he can be forced to leave her alone?"

"She's terrified of facing him. I can't say as I blame her."

"And where we live is a fine place, and I'm glad to stay here. But it's a weight she has to carry on her shoulders every day, one she shouldn't have to."

"Would she have to return to Chicago to face him in front of a judge and jury? Or as a resident of Idaho now, could she see a judge out here? Without your father there or that fool who runs her asylum, I can't imagine your pa would even know there'd been a ruling, unless he was informed by mail long after the fact. And then, as long as she was found sane in Idaho, would she have to stay here? Would she have to prove her sanity in every state she traveled to? Because if Idaho was enough, at least she could go to town or go visit the O'Tooles without her being in danger."

"I've talked to her several times. I can't get past her fear."

"Then for now, we stay here and live in this lovely Hidden Canyon, and we wait until it's what she wants to do."

Yvette surged to her feet. She had her knife, or rather Father's knife, in her hand. Joseph stayed seated, looking up at her.

Mama stood slowly, trying not to draw Yvette's attention.

Yvette's voice was loud enough that Beth knew she was shouting, although she couldn't make out the words. Beth glanced at Jake, and their eyes met, both worried. Then they watched.

Movement beyond the drama caught Beth's eye, and she saw Oscar standing by the cave-house entrance, watching, his arms crossed tight, as if he were holding himself back from running to save his brother.

Just as suddenly, Yvette dropped the knife, broke into bitter sobs, then fell to her knees, her hands over her face.

Joseph stayed where he was, a solid presence. Mama took two steps toward Yvette, but Joseph put an arm out and shook his head.

Beth could see the war in Mama. The need to go to Yvette, hold her, let her cry on someone's shoulder. Yet they couldn't touch her, they didn't dare. What a bitterly lonely way to live.

Neither Mama nor Joseph went to her. They never touched her. Never got closer. But they didn't leave her either.

Jake rubbed his forehead, then moved closer to Beth, slid his arm around her waist and pulled her close while they watched and wondered.

"I'm afraid we're putting Aunt Vivian and Mrs. Gundersen in danger. We have no business being comfortable here or visiting my old neighbor when someone is out there searching for me." Seb paced back and forth in their room. "I waved Mrs. Gundersen back, but what if that man saw her? Or what if he went to her house to question her?"

"She got back from the window. I saw her. She was gone before we ran past the trees. And we were gone before the man got into the room."

The dinner was delicious. Aunt Vivian was friendly and welcoming. Their bedroom was comfortable. The summer night had turned cool enough to make sleeping pleasant. But Seb couldn't settle in for the night.

Neither of them had changed to get ready for bed.

"I've got an idea." Kat sat in one of the chairs by the small table, still fully dressed. "We're leery of contacting the law here in Independence." Kat clapped her mouth shut for a long moment, then said, "Let's go out for a ride."

The sun was still up. The summer nights were long.

"Let's tell Aunt Vivian we want to explore the countryside and sleep by a campfire, so she shouldn't bother waiting up. We'll tell her we will pay for the room because we want to leave our satchels here and retrieve them tomorrow."

"Where are we going?"

"I'll tell you once we're riding."

Seb decided it was as good an answer as any. He and Kat had their horses saddled and were west of Independence in minutes.

"Why are we out here, Kat?"

"Because we're going to Kansas City."

"Um, why Kansas City?"

"We need to talk to the law, and we don't want to talk to the sheriff in Independence. So we'll do something unexpected. We'll make sure we're not being followed. We'll find a place where you can look through your notes."

Seb rested a hand on the packets of papers he'd left in the room while he ate but had taken along for the ride. "I would like to study them. But I'm reasonably sure they're all here."

"Then we'll mail them to Alton, addressed to the O'Tooles in care of Jake Holt. The O'Tooles will hold them for Jake. That way no one can steal them from us or get their hands on them if we run into trouble. If something terrible happens, Jake will get them, or maybe Bruce will deliver them someday."

"They've sworn to never leave Hidden Canyon while Thaddeus Rutledge is alive."

"I know, but even so, I figure they won't last out the summer. They're bound to need something or just go visiting, and whoever goes can fetch the mail. I told Beth we might write to her."

"And she told you she'd never see the letter because they've sworn to never leave Hidden Canyon."

Kat shrugged. "If they don't get it, the letter will sit at the O'Tooles. And when our business is settled here, we'll ride on past Cheyenne for a couple of days, retrieve your packets, visit Hidden Canyon—assuming we can find it—see how big the twins have grown, and then go back to Cheyenne."

"Then we'll go to the sheriff in the nearest town. Kansas City."

Seb clamped his mouth shut because he had no ideas that were better. And he was glad to be out of Independence.

"We've got a few miles to ride. Do you mind if I think about all this for a while?"

"I don't mind. And once we hit a nice level spot"—the hills tended to roll, and the trees were thick—"we can stop, and you can study your notes and think about if you're willing to part with them."

Kat and Seb settled in to find a clear stretch, and they were a while finding one. The sun was getting low in the sky before Kat felt safe enough to stop.

Seb must have agreed with at least part of her plan. "Let me go through these papers."

Kat reined in her horse and swung down from the saddle just as Seb did.

"You sit down and read. I'm going to water the horses in that creek over there, then let them graze. Take your time."

She didn't want to be far from him, but she wanted a good field to watch for pursuit.

By the time the sun was setting, Seb was packing away his notes.

They were on the way again.

"Everything is here, and it was good to study the notes and refresh my memory. I can mail them off. Let's send them to the O'Tooles, but include Jake's name and mine."

"A letter can have a few names on it, I think."

"When we get to Kansas City, I'm going to wire Lloyd and tell him I'll be ready to read that list tomorrow.

"I'll tell him I want to meet at noon, and at the last minute, once we're back in Independence, I'll send someone with a note to his law office to tell him where we'll meet him. Then we'll talk to the sheriff."

Kat jerked her chin in satisfaction. "Sounds like a good plan."

"Let's ride. We can think about it on the way."

They galloped on, away from the trouble Kat knew was waiting for them. But they had to face it soon. Or maybe not. Maybe they should just run.

She hated that the trouble was coming for Seb. It would have been better to have found out the source of all this was that awful Patrick Wadsworth or even that despicable Thaddeus Rutledge.

~

The train drew to a stop in Independence. Thaddeus wasn't sure where exactly they needed to go in town, and he wished now he'd taken his carriage and team. He always took it. He'd had a new carriage specially built to be comfortable for his bad leg. It was much more luxurious than the one he'd owned before he was attacked and injured.

He descended from his private car and sent Sykes to find proper transportation while Thaddeus went to discuss what was next with Wadsworth and Horecroft.

"I've sent my men to the livery to rent horses. We'll be on Katherine's trail in a few minutes."

Thaddeus eyed the talkative man with near lethal irritation, and there stood Horecroft beside him, the smug, thieving liar.

He was somehow still in Wadsworth's confidence, which made Wadsworth a foolish man. But a wealthy, influential foolish man and Thaddeus curbed his temper, something he rarely bothered to do.

"Sykes will have to rent a carriage. I'm no longer a rider." It made Thaddeus feel weak to admit that, which put him in an inferior position for needing the help. The whole situation made him almost killing mad.

He looked at Horecroft then and decided the word *mad* wasn't one to be bandied about.

19

A man tried to kill my wife and me back in Cheyenne." Seb leaned on Sheriff Gillem's desk, both hands fisted. "A man who knew my wife's name, which was not widely known and is a distinctive name. We bested the man who attacked us, and now he's in Boot Hill in Wyoming. The sheriff there was going to try to find out who he was. We are hopeful he's a wanted criminal, and lawmen can mark him off their list. But with his dying words, our attacker told us someone else would be sent. We will have no peace until we get to the bottom of who's after us. Yesterday, someone attacked us in Independence, another unknown man."

"Did you report that attack to the sheriff of Independence?"

"No."

Gillem ran a hand through his thinning hair with a disgusted look. "We can't arrest someone if we don't know he's been accused of a crime."

"That man came after us, and we ran, Sheriff. We got

out of town." Seb took Kat's hand. "So that's your advice? That we go back to Independence with a man after us, who might get to us before we can get to the sheriff there? It's not that big a town. The man, who was almost certainly hired to catch or kill us, might easily run across us if we go back."

"I admit that's a danger." The sheriff tucked his thumbs through a pair of black suspenders over his brown broadcloth shirt.

"What do we do, Sheriff Gillem?" Seb flung one arm wide. "We've come to the law here in Kansas City because we wanted to get away from Independence."

Kat told her side of the story, at one point slapping a wanted poster on the table in front of the sheriff. Kansas City was spreading out, and they'd ridden to the first sheriff's office they could find.

Gillem eyed the poster from where he sat, tipped back in a wooden chair, relaxed beyond any respectable measure.

It's possible they should have ridden farther.

The sheriff looked like he wished they'd just move on. Then he saw the reward and sat up straight. "Ten thousand dollars? And you know where she is?"

Kat saw the dollar signs in the man's eyes.

"She's out west—far beyond your reach, Sheriff Gillem. And this wanted poster is a fraud."

The sheriff subsided in his chair. It appeared he was no longer interested. "You're saying the man falsified this wanted poster?"

"He did." Kat and Seb had debated what approach to take while they'd waited for the sunrise, then mailed Seb's papers off. "I know Elizabeth Rutledge well. She isn't a criminal and most certainly isn't wanted for any crime. We consulted with the Pinkertons regarding this. The man who printed these posters is her pa and wanted to get his hands on her because she's wealthy, and he wants her money. He believed if he moved well away from Chicago before he put up these posters, where no one knew her, he could lie about her being wanted, and the reward would help find and capture her."

"That's a crime." The sheriff tapped his finger on Beth's face on the poster. It was a fine quality wanted poster. Not the usual hand-drawn picture, if the poster even had a picture on it. This was a photograph that had been made into an etching with great skill. Anyone who saw this poster, then saw Beth, would recognize her. "You can't just lie about someone being wanted for a crime as a way to stir up a manhunt. Although if she's his daughter—"

"This woman, Elizabeth," Kat cut him off, "is now married and beyond her father's reach, especially since he admitted to the Pinkerton agent that the wanted poster was false."

"False? You're sure?" The sheriff raised both eyebrows.

"He said exactly that. Now we're afraid Rutledge is after me because he's heard I've returned from traveling west with Beth and I know where she is. Two attempts have been made on our lives already. We want the law involved to protect us from Thaddeus Rutledge."

While Kat's main fear was her uncle, Rutledge was also a danger. He was the one who'd created the wanted poster. And the wanted poster was an actual crime. Rutledge had lied to the law and to the Pinkertons when he falsified the poster to catch Beth and Ginny. Chasing after Thaddeus

Rutledge was something they might convince a lawman to do, or at least the law might step in to protect Kat from him.

But what about the man who'd broken into Seb's house? They had no proof that man was after Kat, and Seb didn't have a known scofflaw pursuing him. But he'd been shot a year ago, long before either of them knew Rutledge existed.

"Can we find someone here to help us or to work with the sheriff in Independence? If you don't have a man to spare for that, can you think of someone who'd be willing to earn money riding along with us for extra protection?"

The sheriff nodded while he studied the poster again. "I know a man, more a hired gun than any kind of Pinkerton agent. But he rides for the brand. If you hire him, he'd be loyal. And he's tough. He'd be a good one to have in a fight."

"One man?" Kat rested her hand on her throat. Honestly, she clutched her throat more like. "I had a vision of a larger group. A cavalry division maybe."

"When the one man is Huey Jessup, that's quite a few." The sheriff ran his thumbs up and down his suspenders. "And I honestly don't know if you can trust the Pinkertons."

"Why not?" Seb exchanged an alarmed look with Kat.

"We've got a small agency in Kansas City, but if Rutledge hired as many Pinkertons as you say, they might be among them. They might refuse to take your word for his wrongdoing just because they've taken his money. At the very least they might hesitate to throw in on a fight against him."

"Where do we find this Huey Jessup?" Seb asked, sounding grim.

A groan from the room behind the sheriff broke in.

The sheriff looked over his shoulder at a closed door with the word *Jail* painted on it.

Kat followed his gaze to the door and had a dreadful premonition.

"That's him."

"He's one of your prisoners?" Kat's grip on her throat tightened.

"Not a prisoner exactly. He got in a fight last night, and I usually let him recover here in the jail. He doesn't like getting blood on his own furniture."

A deep voice as rough as coarse sandpaper joined their conversation. "You hirin' me out again, Sheriff?"

"I am for a fact, Huey." The sheriff talked to the door. "You had oughta get out of town for a while anyway. You've made the wrong people mad this time."

"That Sawyer bunch had it coming. Every time those cowhands get into town, they drink too much and run their mouths until someone's gotta shut 'em up with a fist. They think they're big men, and I like cutting 'em down to size."

"And you did a fine job of it. Neville Sawyer is still at the doctor's office, probably with broken ribs, and he's yet to wake up. And word is three of their cowhands are still in their rooms above the Eagle Talon Saloon, nursing their aching bellies and black eyes. Piketon Sawyer will come into town looking for his brother, and when he sees him, he'll be loaded for bear. But they can't stay here forever. You've shown 'em they can be beaten, and if you up and vanish, they'll have to head out with no chance to pay you back. Sounds like a fight you'll go down as winning, and they might think twice before coming into town to tear things up."

"Probably not, but I'll take the job regardless," Jessup said.

Kat wondered if that meant the decision to hire him was made without Kat or Seb's involvement, beyond paying him of course. This Huey Jessup might be a hard man to fire.

On the other hand, he didn't sound like he was a man to get pushed around easily. He might be a fine addition because it sounded like she and Seb needed to finish a war they hadn't started.

Sheriff Gillem plucked the keys off a nail in the wall, went back through the jail door, and with a creak of metal unlocked the door. He led his prisoner—or maybe his guest, hard to say—out of the jail cell.

And he brought Mr. Jessup into the front office.

Seb had a hired gun. Not a situation he'd ever expected to face.

"Sounds like you got your share of enemies." Huey Jessup was a man who looked as rough as his voice sounded. He had a week's worth of bristle on his face. He wore a faded red shirt and well-worn blue denim pants. He'd come out of the jail wearing two six-guns, which lent credence to the sheriff letting him sleep off a fistfight in the jail, though the jail door had been locked.

He wore a gray Stetson that had seen better days. Boots that had thongs tied around the toes, probably to keep the soles from flapping. He was long and lean and dark and had eyes as sharp and bright as the edge of a razor.

He didn't talk much, but every word was worth hearing. And now, after listening to the whole story, including Kat's uncle's name, which they hadn't told to Sheriff Gillem, Jessup reacted to the Wadsworth name.

"And you say you escaped from an insane asylum?" He studied Kat with those sharp eyes. They'd been riding toward Independence for an hour and were still going over Seb and Kat's story and trying to plan.

"I did in fact do just that, Mr. Jessup. A year and a half ago. My low-down uncle locked me away and has spent the last year in complete control of my half of his company. No, make that *our* company. My husband had owned half, and after he died, I inherited it. But Uncle Patrick didn't want to share or have the cost of buying my half."

"And you," Jessup said, looking hard at Seb, "let me see the bullet wound in your gut."

"It was in his side," Kat said, "not his gut. I worked alongside my father, who was a doctor. I've tended a lot of wounds. I checked Seb over and didn't believe his wound was mortal."

Seb let Kat talk. He untucked the front of his shirt and showed Jessup the scar.

"Bullet wound, all right. Got a couple of them myself. You're lucky to be alive, no matter what she says. Getting shot is serious business, even if the bullet didn't pierce your liver or lungs."

"I am lucky," Seb agreed as he tucked his shirt back in.

"Now"—Huey Jessup gave the trail ahead a sharp look as if he were reading every inch of it—"here's what we're gonna do . . ."

20

Beth decided it might be best for Yvette to get closer to someone in addition to Joseph. She seemed to reject any attempt Mama made to be friends.

After the weeping, she thought Yvette might be making a breakthrough. Either that or becoming more dangerous. When Joseph traipsed after Yvette to sit beside the stream, Beth told Mama to let her follow this time.

Glancing back, she saw Jake and Mama holding both babies. Jake had agreed to let Beth go to Yvette on the condition that he was close to hand. And someone had to be ready to take the baby. As Jake's eyes met hers, he handed the baby behind him to Mama so she held both, then stepped outside the cabin. He leaned back against the wall between the door and the window and watched. But he didn't try to approach Yvette.

Beth smiled.

He crossed his arms and gave her a firm nod.

Then she went on down to the stream. Yvette sat farthest to the right, then Joseph, then Beth.

Yvette saw her and gave a startled wide-eyed look. A blue-eyed elk spotting danger.

Beth sat down beyond Joseph, and Yvette started to talk.

"When he hit me the last time, I fell down a flight of steps and my baby died inside me."

Joseph had told them what she said. She spoke of a cruel husband who abused her in every possible way. She also spoke of a father who was of the same temperament. She'd lived all her life under the brutal hands of the two men who were supposed to love and protect her.

"I went mad. Lucius said I did. I wept for that child for weeks, months. Lucius put up with it for a while because he said I deserved to be miserable. I deserved to weep for letting his son die."

"Did you see the baby?" Grief-stricken herself, Beth asked, "Was it a boy?"

Yvette jerked her head back, startled.

Beth remembered that Joseph said he never talked, just let her ramble and he'd listen to whatever words she said. Beth clamped her mouth shut, afraid her question would send Yvette back to her silent watchfulness.

Shaking her head, Yvette's eyes cleared more than Beth had ever seen them.

"No, there was no way to tell. I only . . ." Yvette glanced up at Joseph and blushed. "No way to tell. But Lucius said he was sure, so he must be right."

Yvette hugged herself in such a way that Beth wondered how long it had been since anyone else had hugged her. Had anyone ever taken her in their arms in kindness. What about her mama? Where were the folks who were supposed to care about her?

"The doctor came. He asked what happened, and Lucius told him I fell down the stairs. That's where I got my black eye, too. That wasn't the way I remembered it. Lucius hit me, but I might be wrong. I'm clumsy. I do fall down. Lucius said I should stand still and take the justifiable punishment he felt I deserved. It was me dodging his blows that made me fall."

Beth had ten more questions. She didn't ask any of them. Then Yvette turned toward the stream, stretched out her legs, and began to hum. That same off-key humming.

"What is that song?"

Joseph gave her a warning look, and Beth clamped her mouth shut again.

Yvette turned to Beth again, wild and frightened. "It's . . . it's about God knowing I'm a sinner, I think. God has contempt for me. He hates me, and I can't blame Him. The words are gone. I just remember the tune only."

"God doesn't hate you, Yvette. He loves you."

She hummed again, maybe eight or ten notes. They were hard to hear because she hummed so quietly, yet they tickled something in Beth's brain.

"Can you remember any of the words, Yvette? Even a single one?"

Joseph didn't give Beth a warning glance this time. Joseph who was talented on the harmonica. He listened, leaning closer to Yvette.

The single line of music went around and around as if Yvette was stuck on one line.

Finally, Joseph, who hadn't spoken a word, said, "'When I Survey the Wondrous Cross.'"

Yvette tilted her head as if she were listening keenly.

Joseph pulled his harmonica out of his pocket and began playing. Yvette had seen Joseph play for their church service on the little mouth organ. She'd always put aside her own humming to listen to Joseph's music. He played the song through twice. The third time, Beth sang the first verse:

> "'When I survey the wondrous cross
> on which the Prince of glory died,
> my richest gain I count but loss,
> and pour contempt on all my pride.'"

The last line made Yvette's face light up. Beth hummed it again, replaying the words in her mind: *and pour contempt on all my pride*. "Yvette, there's nothing about that song that says God hates you. It's just the opposite."

"He has contempt for me." Yvette's eyes filled with tears. "Just as Papa did. Just as Lucius did. And Mama said men made the decisions, and it was a woman's lot to obey or be punished. So of course God hates me."

Joseph continued to play the song quietly while Yvette and Beth talked.

Beth pondered the song again, dwelling on the last verse—the victory-and-love verse. She sang, "'Love so amazing, so divine, demands my soul, my life, my all.'"

Yvette's expression was fiery. Her eyes blazed with the words, but Beth wasn't sure if Yvette was ready to jump for joy or jump at Beth's throat.

"That hymn is about love, Yvette. It's about Jesus dying so we can live. It's about God sacrificing His Son so we can have everlasting life. That's how much God loves you.

The line with the word *contempt* just means this earthy life is nothing without the love of God. And that love is right there for you, a gift from Him."

Yvette bit her top lip so hard that Beth was afraid she'd hurt herself, then finally she whispered, "God doesn't hold me in contempt? Lucius said He did."

Beth prayed desperately for the right words, for God to guide her. "God loves you. Your cruel husband convinced you that isn't true, but it is. Your husband was wrong. God forgives us everything and only wants to love us."

Yvette leapt to her feet and stood shaking until Beth wasn't sure how she stayed upright. Slowly Joseph, then Beth, rose.

Yvette took one step at a time, inching toward Joseph. He tucked his harmonica away and just waited. Beth approached Joseph from his left, and she looked for that knife.

As Yvette drew closer, she stretched out her hand. "He really loves me?"

Joseph whispered, "Yes, God loves you, and He has brought you here to this place where you can be safe from all the people who told you different. No one here will hurt you."

Yvette looked past Joseph to Beth, then her eyes slid to Jake, leaning against the cabin. To Mama with the two babies in her arms. She turned far enough to see Oscar by the door to the cave house. "C-can I touch you?" Her eyes beseeched Joseph.

He slowly extended his hand, palm down, and waited. He didn't touch her. Instead, he made his arm available if she wanted to touch him.

Yvette reached out and rested her open palm on the back of his hand. She then stretched out her other hand, watching Beth. "And you? Can I touch you?"

Beth did the same as Joseph. Reached out and waited.

"Yvette," Beth said quietly, "this is very much like what God does. He stays close. He invites us to reach out for Him. And if we will just turn and reach for Him, He'll come all the rest of the way to us. He doesn't ask us to be perfect. He doesn't expect that we have never sinned, never been bad. He just wants to love you and care for you."

Yvette reached out, her hand empty. If she could rest it on Beth's arm, her other hand touching Joseph, then she couldn't wield a knife.

With her hand quaking like an aspen in a windstorm, she settled it on Beth's wrist. The three of them formed a circle. They stood together, Beth still praying silently for the right words and for Yvette's broken heart to reach out just as her hand had, only for God.

"Can we g-go for a walk?" Yvette asked. "Can I put my arm through both of yours and we just walk for a while? I used to do that with gentlemen before I got married. No one hurt me when I did that."

"It would be my pleasure, Miss Yvette. You're the age my daughter would be, but she died long ago."

Yvette froze, her hand on top of Joseph's. Beth remembered how Yvette had seemed to believe she was married to Beth's father. It seemed Joseph was trying to be very clear that no such relationship existed between himself and Yvette.

Yvette smiled and nodded.

Every move Joseph made was slow and easy. Beth marveled at his wisdom and gentleness. She copied each move he made. He lowered his hand from below hers, then turned toward the far entrance of the canyon and crooked his elbow. Beth did the same.

Neither of them rushed. They waited until Yvette touched them. Without exploding.

The three of them set off on a walk past Jake, past the house. She heard Jake move behind them and knew he was watching. Then a quiet squawk told her Mama had come around the cabin with the babies.

The three of them proceeded as if she and Joseph were courtiers with a queen on their arms. She saw Oscar heading toward the cabin, watching his brother charm a madwoman. But it wasn't fear she saw on Oscar's face. It was hope.

The two strolled on. Yvette looked between her and Joseph now and then, silent but looking carefree and happy. And completely sane.

Then Beth heard a rumble that sounded like the canyon might collapse.

21

We'll meet Lloyd and Deacon by the train station. It's near the dock, right where you found me that first morning."

Seb had sent the message with a boy who hung around the telegraph office and ran such errands as this. There were several youngsters who earned coins dashing around with telegraphs and other notes.

Seb gave him a penny and knew Lloyd would give the boy a second penny when he left the note. Then Seb and Kat hurried to the train station.

Huey checked the area, then advised them where to stand so no one could get them from behind. He then faded back to watch over them. He hid where he could keep an eye on the whole situation, including if anyone else was sneaking up on either Seb or Kat.

They were barely in place when Lloyd came rushing up the sidewalk and shouted, "Sebastian! You're here!"

Seb wore his six-gun, fully loaded, in a holster. Kat had hers, too. They turned to face both men. Deacon was a few paces behind and losing ground, but he moved with a stately grace that was more proper for a lawyer, at least in his opinion.

They were in their usual dark suits. Lloyd, youthful and buzzing with energy, and Deacon, stout and calm. Both were on foot.

Seb took a few steps out from the side of the building but kept the wall at his back and waited for his lawyers to approach.

Lloyd came right up. He didn't act afraid or threatening, just his usual overactive self. "Seb, I'm so glad you sent that message. Deacon and I came up with a list for you, but it's mighty short. In fact, I think we know—"

A bullet whizzed between Seb and Lloyd. Both men froze, then wheeled to face—

"Marcus?" Seb's mouth gaped open until he had to force himself to talk. "Marcus Coleman? What are you doing here?"

"This is the man, Sebastian." Lloyd turned to stand shoulder to shoulder with Seb. Seb reached for Kat and tucked her behind him.

Deacon added, "He's been acting like he's an old and dear friend since you disappeared. We trusted him. We thought of him right away when we began a list. He was the first name we were going to tell you."

"He *is* an old and dear friend." Seb saw the still smoking muzzle of Marcus's gun. "What are you doing here?" And where was Huey?

"That was just a warning shot." Marcus was his usual polished self. He had muttonchop sideburns and a mustache that was no doubt the latest fashion. He had shining blue eyes and wore the finest clothes. He was so tidy this morning, despite the gun, it seemed clear that he still traveled with a valet, so his boots never lost their shine. His hair was neatly trimmed and combed and held in place with a pomade.

The very picture of a polished, wealthy, young American gentleman.

But his eyes blazed with hate and with death.

"You're a thief and a liar, Sebastian." Marcus raised his gun. "You made money on my work. Now I want those invention notes."

Seb reached back to keep Kat out of the line of fire. "But, Mark, we're friends. So it was you who shot me last spring? You sent that man after me in Cheyenne?"

Marcus smirked. "Don't act so surprised."

"But I am surprised. Why would you want to kill me?"

"Because you stole everything from me. My chance at fame. We created those inventions together. My name should've been on the patents."

Seb's brain usually buzzed with ideas. He was inventive in all his ways. But right now his brain felt drenched in cold molasses. He remembered when he'd thought of making himself famous. It was Marcus who'd talked of fame, and it had awakened a desire for that in Seb.

Looking at Marcus now, he saw his old friend had wanted fame in a desperate way. "We exchanged letters. You were one of the first people I wrote to from Cheyenne. I trusted you just as Lloyd did. Why would you care about patents? You're rich, Mark. You don't need more money."

"I'm brilliant. I need to show my brothers who have

taken over the family business that I'm just as good as they are."

Seb looked at his old friend and thought of his own choices—to work instead of spending time with his wife on the farm, and most important, nurturing his faith. He thought of himself and was ashamed. The gleam in Marcus's eyes made him cautious. "Yes, we worked side by side, but we worked on our own projects. I didn't expect to see my name on your patents, and you didn't ever so much as hint you'd like to see your name on mine."

"That's not true. Our work was always a partnership."

In Marcus's fevered mind, he believed that.

"I knew you'd do the right thing. I even suggested if anything happened to you, I'd take care of your work."

Seb thought back on the day, while bleeding, thinking he was dying, he'd scrawled Marcus's name and address on his packet and told Beth to send them to his friend. "I was going to do that if I thought I was dying. I had plans to write a will, leaving all of my work to you. But I got shot before I could get it done." He realized that idea was planted in his head because of a letter from Marcus. He'd suggested it, and then he'd sent a killer—twice, once in Independence, another time in Cheyenne. All Seb could think of was to keep him talking. Huey should have come out by now. Where was he?

"And now you've got a wife to put her claim to our patents."

"How did you know I got married? How did you know where I was?"

"I told him." Lloyd sounded steeped in guilt. "I thought he was your friend. He traveled to Independence a few weeks after you disappeared. He acted worried, and we told him everything—about the blood at the warehouse and how we'd broken into your home. I never even suspected anything else."

"You told him I'd married a Wadsworth? Because her name was on the note that gunman carried?"

"No. I said you were married and in Cheyenne, but I called her Kat Jones. I think." Lloyd wasn't sure. But Seb could see the man was as stunned by this as any of them.

"You said Wadsworth," Marcus sneered. "And that was all I needed to know. I'd kept up with Katherine Wadsworth. I knew Jeremy well enough to hear of his marriage and his death. I knew she'd gone mad with grief and been locked away. Later, I found out she escaped with Thaddeus Rutledge's wife."

"How in the world did you find that out?"

"I told him." An older man stepped out from behind the building where Huey Jessup had been hidden.

"Uncle Patrick?" Kat squeaked.

"And I gave him information, too. I'm Thaddeus Rutledge." Behind Uncle Patrick, a tall man, limping hard and using a cane, emerged. A third man stood behind the two newcomers.

"And Dr. Horecroft?" Kat sounded flat-out terrified.

"It's time to come home, Katherine." Patrick Wadsworth sounded severely disappointed in his niece.

"I'll help you to calm down, Mrs. Wadsworth. Or is it Mrs. Jones now?"

"They'll be calm when they're dead." Marcus's gun lowered again until it aimed right at Sebastian's gut.

Seb clawed for his gun.

"No, Coleman!" Patrick shouted. "Stop right there."

Lloyd threw himself against Seb. His arm swept Kat to the ground as shot after shot rang out, bullets flying from Marcus's gun and at least one other.

Lloyd's falling body jerked with an impact that had to be from a bullet.

Seb, Lloyd, and Kat all fell as the air filled with the smell of sulfur from exploding gunpowder.

Seb, stretched out on the ground, Lloyd on top of him, looked down at his belly expecting to see a bleeding wound. He saw none and barely realized he was unhurt.

Marcus roared, "Jones, why won't you just die!"

Thaddeus swung his cane and knocked the gun from Marcus's hand. "I need her alive."

Marcus shoved Thaddeus aside and dove on Seb, unarmed.

Marcus slammed a fist into Seb's face. Seb punched back, and the two of them tumbled to the ground. Seb had to stop this man, his old friend. He had to protect Kat.

Seb was dragged to his feet. In that brief moment, he saw Kat fighting her way out from under them, and Lloyd, bleeding on the ground, and then Deacon, flat on his back, unmoving. Patrick Wadsworth staggered, his hands clutching his belly.

Rutledge stood back, eyes blazing. "Sykes! Get out here." Rutledge turned to look behind him.

A man stormed out from behind the corner where Huey had been.

Marcus swung again, and Seb went down as the newcomer grabbed Kat and dragged her, screaming, to her feet.

Seb lunged at the man who'd put his hands on Kat.

Marcus tackled Seb and took him to the ground as Kat, fighting and screaming, was shoved at Rutledge.

"Grab Wadsworth. Let's go." Rutledge dragged Kat away.

Seb twisted free of Marcus and slammed a fist into his gut, then another and another.

Marcus, driven by jealousy, rage, and hate, only fought back harder.

22

Kat grabbed at the railing on the steps up to the train car.

She kicked Rutledge hard in the leg, and he wrenched her sideways, knocking her head against iron.

Dazed, she was barely aware of where she was until she got slammed onto the floor. Uncle Patrick landed next to her. Two men doing Thaddeus Rutledge's bidding.

She scrambled backward. "Help! Someone help me!" She screamed until her words should have peeled a man's eardrums away.

Uncle Patrick didn't move.

Thaddeus Rutledge laughed. "Sykes, tie her up."

Sykes, a thug of a man, the one who'd run around the corner where Huey was hiding, came toward her.

Uncle Patrick moaned and clutched his belly. Kat's lifelong training at her father's side roared to life, and she rolled onto her hands and knees and moved to the side of her dreadful tyrant of an uncle-in-law.

Dr. Horecroft was slower, but finally he stepped onto

the train and sat, tidy and evil, on a blue velvet couch. His hands folded. A satisfied smile on his face.

"Do you have bandages?"

Sykes, his arms outstretched to grab her, stopped. "What?"

"Bandages. Or is it your wish that Patrick Wadsworth die?" She looked at Sykes and saw him check for orders by looking at Rutledge. Her eyes riveted on Rutledge, too. A man she'd never seen before nor met, only heard about from the horror stories Beth and Ginny told. He was a man of power in Chicago who moved in the upper echelons. Jeremy should have known him, but he must not have been important enough to speak of or she'd've heard of him.

Rutledge blinked, stumped by her question it seemed.

She tried to penetrate his single-minded interest in himself. "Do you intend to let my uncle Patrick die? You won't get his money, and you'll lose a man who must be a colleague of yours. Saving him would give you a powerful connection."

Money and power, that was all Patrick and Rutledge understood.

Rutledge shook his head as if clearing it. "Sykes, get her the doctor's kit. But first give me your gun."

"Dr. Horecroft," Kat snapped as she wrestled Uncle Patrick's hands away from his belly, "get down here and help me."

"I'm not that kind of doctor."

"Surely you had to go to medical school in order to call yourself a doctor. Get over here."

Horecroft just sniffed and settled more comfortably into his cushions.

Sykes gave Kat a smirk and handed over his gun to Rutledge, who said to Sykes, "Tell the engineer to get this train moving now."

Rutledge sat down in a plush seat, put his leg up on an ottoman, rested the pistol on his thigh, and said, "So you're his mad niece, is that right?"

Sykes rushed out.

"And you're the imbecile who tried to keep your wife locked up in an asylum."

Rutledge's eyes flashed in a way that told her she'd pay for such insults later. She found she could talk and tend Uncle Patrick at the same time. He was writhing, curled up on his side, bleeding on an intricately woven Aubusson rug.

"I know your wife. She's a very sensible and rational woman. Why on earth did you decide you'd label her insane?"

"Where is she?" Though Rutledge appeared as if calm, Kat was good at reading people. Her father had taught her how important that was when treating patients. Now she saw Rutledge's hands, resting on the arms of his chair, tense up, the knuckles turning white. His eyes narrowed. Despite the cool expression, she saw that she'd struck a nerve.

She needed to stay alive. She was almost certainly headed back to Chicago, based on the direction of the train. Rutledge would stand back, unbothered, while Horecroft tortured her. But they wouldn't kill her, and if he survived, Seb would come for her.

She'd live as long as Rutledge believed she knew how to take him to Ginny. "I know exactly where she is."

Rutledge let his cold disinterest slip as he lunged forward, still seated but nearly ready to jump out of his chair. "Where? You'll tell me right now or you'll be very sorry you didn't."

"Uncle Patrick, lay back." Kat decided it was time to ignore Rutledge, and anyway, she had other things to do. "Remember, I trained at my father's side. I can help you. Rutledge's man shot you in the chaos when you tried to kidnap me."

Patrick lay back. Kat ripped open his shirt and swallowed hard at the sight of a single bullet hole right above his belt.

Sykes, Rutledge's thug, came back with a canvas bag. "Whatever medical equipment is on this train is in that bag. I told the engineer to pull out fast."

Kat opened the bag and looked inside. It was a jumble, but there were things she could use.

"Is there whiskey on this train?" She was handed a little brown bottle full of liquid. A quick sniff told her what it was. "That's laudanum. Give him that."

Rutledge's eyes darted to the bottle, his expression turning hypnotic.

Kat had seen that look before. And she'd seen Rutledge limp and had heard about Yvette fighting back against him last year when he'd hit her. Rutledge was a man who lived with pain, and it appeared he was very familiar with the milk of the poppy.

"I still need whiskey. The alcohol will sterilize the tweezers I'm going to use to get the bullet out and sterilize the needle and thread to sew him up."

Kat predicted with some confidence that Uncle Patrick

was going to die. But her medical training told her what to do and forced her to try. And anyway, she'd rather practice medicine on a doomed man than answer Rutledge's questions.

The train started moving. She tried not to panic. Help would not arrive in time to keep her from being taken to Chicago.

Seb had been pinned under that murderous so-called friend of his. Lloyd and Deacon were both down, Huey as well. Any of them would come when they could, but until they did, Kat was on her own.

Seb leapt up to go after his wife.

Marcus tackled him and slammed him to the stone street.

Twisting wildly, Seb hammered his old friend with a fist to the belly, the chin, the nose.

Marcus hung on like a leech, but he was no longer punching. Marcus had spent the last years in his parents' comfortable home, bent over a laboratory table.

Seb did that same kind of work, but he'd spent last summer on a wagon train, walking long miles, holding teams of cattle and horses steady. He'd spent the winter riding and checking cattle. Shoveling snow and chopping firewood. Building a barn.

The fight swung in Seb's direction quickly. Marcus's blows were strong but not steady, not powered by muscles hardened by work and the frontier. Marcus began to flail.

A sudden impact knocked Marcus away from Seb. Huey,

bleeding from a head wound, landed hard on top of Marcus. One, two hard blows to the chin and Marcus dropped flat to the ground, the fight gone out of him.

Seb staggered to his feet in time to see Deacon roll to his hands and knees, then crawl toward Lloyd.

Huey clamped shackles on Marcus and got to his feet. They heard a train's wheels begin to churn.

Seb's eyes met Huey's. He shouted, "He's taking Kat!"

Deacon said, "Go after her. Lloyd's wounds aren't mortal. I'll get help and have Marcus arrested."

Huey started toward the train, unsteady but game, Seb right behind him. The two of them were running flat-out before they rounded the building that blocked their view of the train station. A single engine pulling eight cars was gaining steam out of the station.

Seb shouted, "Private train! Has to be Rutledge and Wadsworth. He's taken Kat on it."

Seb dashed past Huey as the cars slipped past him, picking up more speed. He saw an open door on a baggage car, probably empty, then sprinted and leapt for the door handle and hung on as his feet swept out from under him. Dragging himself forward, he tumbled into the car. Looking back, he saw Huey catch hold of the steps on the last car, the caboose. Huey was hurt, but he clawed his way up those steps and soon vanished altogether.

Gasping for breath, Seb tried to think. Should he move forward on his own or wait for Huey? What was the best way to save Kat?

23

Kat grabbed tweezers from the medical bag, knowing it was rough medicine. But with no time to be more careful, she reached gently but much too deeply into the bullet wound.

"Who shot you, Uncle Patrick?"

"It was Sykes." Patrick's eyes flashed with pain and anger. He glared at Rutledge. "Your man, aiming for Katherine's husband, I'd guess. Was that always your plan? You knew she was married. You knew a husband put her beyond my control."

Kat's hands trembled with sickened rage as she looked away, for one brief moment, from her work. "You planned murder then. You probably hoped Marcus Colemen would do it for you."

Rutledge sniffed. "You're mistaken, Wadsworth. The bullets were all from Coleman's gun. He's a madman, much like my wife and your niece."

Kat, back working over her uncle, said, "I know you

thought I'd gone mad after Jeremy died. But his death was strange, and I thought . . . I thought . . ." Shaking her head violently, she clamped her mouth shut and drew a single blood-soaked bullet from deep in Uncle Patrick's belly. Kat set the bullet and tweezers aside and pulled a pad of bandages from the bag and pressed them hard against the wound.

Uncle Patrick groaned and held his stomach.

"I'm sorry. I know it hurts. But if I can get the bleeding stopped, then I can sew it up. You have a chance. Not all bullet wounds to the middle like this are fatal." Not all, but most. But Kat didn't say that.

"Katherine, look at me." Uncle Patrick pressed his hands down on top of hers, to help but also to draw her attention. "I need to tell you something."

"Save your strength. We can talk later."

"Hush now, there may not be a later. I sent you to the asylum because you seemed to be truly out of your mind. But you also set me to thinking, to looking closer at Jeremy's death. You were right. Not to accuse me, but his death was no accident."

With a gasp, Kat straightened and looked at Jeremy's uncle. Her grip never wavered on the bandage, but he had her full attention now.

"You checked into it? You found out what happened?"

"Yes, and you were right. I traced that carriage accident, the one on the railroad, to a . . . a cabal on my board of directors. They knew Jeremy was my heir, and he wasn't a man they wanted to take orders from." He coughed and gasped for air. "They staged that accident. I have witnesses."

"Witnesses? Uncle Patrick, are you going to get the police to charge them?"

"I already have. They've been arrested. This last year, while you've been gone, I've sat through the trial. Watched them be found guilty. Three men, all sentenced to hang."

"Jeremy was murdered." Kat's mind churned at the thought. Her heart ached. "He was a good man. He deserved better than he got from his father and from you."

Patrick patted her bloodstained hands. His eyes lost their intelligence and faded as if he were looking beyond the train car into eternity. "I was only days away from coming to get you to set you free when I found out you were gone. I set my affairs in order to make amends to you. And now, with this gunshot wound, I think you will soon be the sole heir to my properties and shares in my company. I've left it all to you, to be managed by men I trust. Good men, Katherine. It's safe to go back to Chicago now."

"Did you know I married again? My husband was the man with me, the man Mr. Rutledge's thug Sykes and that jealous Marcus Coleman were shooting at. The men who, at least one of them, shot you."

"You're married?"

"Yes, I'm Katherine Jones now, and neither you, nor anyone here, has the power to lock me in an asylum. That's my husband's prerogative. If he survives this day." Kat threw a furious look at Dr. Horecroft.

He polished his fingernails against his suit coat.

"And I can see," Uncle Patrick said through a hoarse whisper, "by your skill caring for me that you in no way belong in an asylum. I've left all the correct paperwork in Chicago to ensure that your freedom is restored."

"Uncle Patrick . . ." Kat's voice broke as she looked at the man, the tyrant who'd so utterly destroyed her life when she was in the throes of grief over Jeremy. "Th-thank you." Tears streaked down her face as she studied the man who seemed to be slipping away from her just as she might have gotten to know him.

Uncle Patrick's eyes fell shut. His chest still rose and fell, but he lapsed into unconsciousness.

Kat fumbled for more bandages and wrapped them tightly around Uncle Patrick's waist. As she fought for his life, she saw Rutledge come to stand in front of her.

"I think, Horecroft, that this very wealthy young woman might be better left locked away." Rutledge's hand clamped hard on her shoulder. "I can help her manage her newfound wealth."

"What?" She looked up at him, and he slapped her so hard that she rolled across the train car and hit the wall, leaving her stunned.

The blow to her head felt like an explosion going off.

And then she realized it wasn't the blow that was exploding.

~

Seb slammed a fist into Sykes's smug face. The blow, so unexpected, knocked him aside. Seb sprinted past him to get to Kat.

He shoved his way through the door, then across the space between the two cars, then into the next car in time to see Thaddeus Rutledge knock Kat into the wall.

Roaring, he dove across a body sprawled on the floor and tackled Rutledge.

"Sykes, get in here!"

Seb slammed him twice in the mouth, but before he could end the fight, someone shoved him aside.

Sykes, his eyes gleaming with the pleasure cruelty seemed to give him, wrapped his hands around Seb's neck.

With a twist of his body, Seb tossed Sykes over his head, then leapt to his feet in time to be grabbed from behind. A second man had been with Sykes. That man now held Seb's arms behind his back. Sykes punched Seb in the stomach with a force that showed the man had muscles of iron.

Then Sykes went over backward, and Seb saw Kat had thrown herself against his ankles.

Sykes's head hit the corner of a table just behind him. Seb jerked his arms free and turned to fight the man who'd held him from behind.

A wiry, bald man, young and vicious, threw himself at Seb and took him down on top of Sykes. The train car wasn't large. There was an unconscious man on the floor. A prim and proper man sitting, watching it all. Rutledge groaning as he tried to roll away from the chaos. And Sykes, groggy but still fighting. Now he had his hands on Kat, who was half his size. And the only thing stopping Sykes from doing terrible harm to Kat was Seb and the man attacking him being in the way.

Then a newcomer entered the fray. Huey Jessup charged into the train car, sized up the situation in a second, and grabbed the man attacking Seb, jerked him to his feet, and pounded his fists hard into the man. He grabbed his shirt, hauling him toward the door of the car, where he threw the man off the train and out onto the hard ground rushing past.

Seb hauled Sykes to his feet and pushed the man toward Jessup, who'd returned and grabbed the dazed Sykes in the same way. Soon the hired gun was tumbling on the ground after his partner.

Seb turned back to Rutledge, who backed away and shouted, "Stay away from me!"

Seb grabbed the lapels of Rutledge's fine suit, yanked him forward, passing him in the same way to Jessup. Soon the man was tumbling and sprawling on the ground. One remained. Seb rushed toward Horecroft, lifted him to his feet, and hurled him to the back of the car. Horecroft, knowing what was coming, pushed past Jessup, ran out of the car, and jumped to the ground on his own. His landing was only slightly less painful, and Seb rushed to the window to see all four men sprawled on the ground—some still, some writhing.

Beth looked around frantically for the source of the violent shaking. The entrance to their canyon was straight ahead. "Beth, Joseph, Yvette! Run!"

Jake roared at them, and Beth, instinctively trusting him, dashed straight to her right. Joseph picked left, and Beth let him go and sprinted just as a herd of mustangs stampeded into the canyon.

She screamed, waved her arms to ward them off, and ran hard. Just as she believed she'd reach the right side of the entrance and avoid the charging horses, she was hit in the shoulder and knocked to the ground by a gray stallion. A hoof grazed her shoulder again as a black mare leapt over her but didn't quite miss, and Beth glimpsed another horse bearing down on her, its eyes wild.

From the cabin she saw a flash of fur and heard barking. Their dog, the mama of the litter, bolted forward, snarling. The charging horse veered away from Beth as she and the dog slipped out of the way of the thundering herd. She stood unsteadily and pressed her back to the canyon wall, gasping for breath. She heard Jake shouting, the dog barking, Yvette screaming.

Still the thundering hooves of the mustangs rushed by—red, black, spotted, brown, every color surging past her. Looking frantically for Joseph, she saw him down in the worst depths of the stampede, with the horses leaping over him, Yvette tucked under him. A hoof kicked his shoulder and knocked him off Yvette, then he jumped back to cover her. She was screaming, clawing at him, beating him. She had her knife out, but a horse kicked it away.

Then the herd was gone, running deeper into the canyon.

Beth looked for Mama and saw her, arms full of babies, ducking behind the cabin.

Jake was sprinting straight for Beth.

"I'm not hurt. Help Joseph. Help Yvette."

Joseph rolled off Yvette, knocked aside by her lashing of him.

Oscar appeared, dropping to his knees beside his brother.

"Are you all right?" Jake tore his eyes from her to see Joseph, sprawled on his back, bleeding from his head, his arms, his legs. Kicked to pieces, stomped on. Beaten by Yvette besides.

Yvette was beyond control.

"Stop screaming!" Oscar screamed a little himself. "My brother saved you. He may have died for you!"

Yvette quieted, her chest heaving. Still on the ground, she scooted away from Joseph and Oscar on her backside. Beth pushed herself from the wall and ran toward Joseph.

"What do you need?" Though Beth's shoulder ached, she shoved past the pain to reach Oscar.

Oscar looked hard at his brother. "He's alive." Furious, he eyed Beth and snapped, "Get that knife, and don't let her have it back!"

Beth grabbed it before Yvette could react. And Yvette didn't try to get to the knife. Instead, she looked at Joseph and fought to breathe. "H-he saved me, and I attacked him."

"Has he been cut or stabbed?" Jake was on his knees beside Joseph.

"No, I don't see any cuts. It's all damage done by the stampeding herd." Oscar dragged in a deep breath. "He threw himself over Yvette to protect her."

"Beth," Oscar said, "go to the house. Reassure your ma that you're not hurt. No one but Joseph is hurt." Oscar's voice broke. "Then get hot water and bandages. Take them to the cave house. Jake and I will carry Joseph there. I'll tend him."

Beth met Oscar's eyes and saw grief and a deep fear for his brother. With one firm nod of her head, she whirled around and ran for the cabin.

A voice behind them called out, "Hey, what's going on here? Jake?" Dakota Harlan, their old wagon master, came riding into the canyon. Behind him came the O'Toole clan, including Bruce, Oscar and Joseph's brother.

Bruce's eyes went straight to Joseph. He swung down off his horse and ran to his brother's side.

"Let me help." Dakota came up to Joseph, frowning.

Maeve O'Toole dismounted and ran for Beth.

"Come to the house with me. We need bandages." They ran full out. Beth's brain crowded with questions. She asked none of them. She kept her left arm tight against her body and didn't look at it.

They got to the cabin just as Mama stepped out holding both babies. Mama's eyes were wide with shock.

"Twins!" Maeve squealed in delight.

Then Fiona was upon them, reaching for a baby.

Soon Mama's arms were empty.

Beth rapped out orders. "We need hot water, bandages. They're taking Joseph to the cave house."

"Cave house?" Little Bridget O'Toole had followed her ma. "What's a cave house?"

Conor was a pace behind her. "You have two babies?"

"Yes, Conor." Beth rushed for the water they kept warm on the stove and poured it into a bucket with her right hand.

Mama was busy with a ragbag. "Twins. Two babies born at once." She looked at Fiona. "Can you tend them while we help Joseph?"

"I can. We were riding around, watching Dakota try and track your family. Bruce refused to help, though he came along. Then we startled a herd of mustangs, and they galloped away. We were enjoying the sight of them when they seemed to run right into a stone wall and vanish. Dakota shouted, 'I think I've found Jake!' And he galloped right after those horses."

Beth hugged the basin to her body. "You've come at a good time. We need your help. Thank you."

"If Dakota hadn't come," Maeve said sharply, "he wouldn't have spooked those horses, and they wouldn't have stampeded into your canyon, and Joseph might not now be at death's door."

That reminded Beth that Maeve had taken a lot of her anger out on Dakota after her pa died. It seemed she still harbored some of it.

"Now, Maeve, hush. It was an accident. Let's pay attention to these precious little ones." Fiona smiled down at the baby in her arms. "I'm glad to get my hands on the little bairnies."

Beth rushed out of the house with her basin of hot water. It sloshed against the front of her dress, but she couldn't hold it away without using both arms.

She left Mama to fill a new pot to heat. They had water from the hot springs in the cave, too, and it was a fine warm temperature, but they always heated it more to wash clothes and do the dishes. And now to bandage wounds. Boiled was better if Joseph was to have a chance at survival.

By the time she reached the cave house, Mama was on her heels with the rags. Oscar and Bruce on either side of Joseph, with Dakota toting his legs and Jake keeping his head steady, came to the door. Mama got there just in time to swing it open for them. They moved inside, cautiously carrying Joseph.

Beth set the washbasin down, and it was only when she straightened that she gasped in pain.

Jake heard it, his head coming around fast to look at her. His eyes went wide at the sight.

24

"I'll get the train to stop and go back to Independence," Huey said. "Lloyd was going for the law—he's got some kidnappers to arrest." With that, he dashed out of the train car.

Kat scrambled to go back to caring for Uncle Patrick.

Seb came to kneel beside Kat's uncle, straight across from her.

"Did you hear what he said before Rutledge grabbed me?" she asked.

"No, Kat. I came in just in time to see Rutledge put his hands on you. Then I went berserk." Seb gave her a sheepish smile while she used a damp cloth to bathe Uncle Patrick's face.

"He found out Jeremy was murdered. He's had them arrested, and they've been convicted. He said he rewrote his will to leave me everything. He was ready to go get me from the asylum when he found out I'd escaped. Dr. Horecroft convinced him there was a thorough search going on for me, and the only reason he hadn't told Patrick of my escape was because he didn't want to worry him."

"Meanwhile, though you'd been gone nearly a year and a half, he was collecting a monthly fee for your care?" Seb didn't even bother to try to tamp down his sarcasm.

The slowly moving train screeched to a halt, shuddered, and then began inching in reverse. Back toward Independence.

Kat continued to clean her patient's face. "Patrick Wadsworth is supposed to be a very smart man. It's hard to believe he didn't have suspicions about Horecroft. Maybe he did. Maybe he thought Horecroft was going to be more help than hindrance in finding me, and he'd deal with his lies later." Kat added, "Help me sit him up. I'll try to get some water down him."

"Is he going to survive?" Seb slid an arm behind Wadsworth's back. "The bullet wound isn't that far from where mine was."

"I'm afraid it's just a few crucial inches too far in. We can only give him the best care possible, then hope and pray he lives."

Seb sat Wadsworth up with the utmost gentleness. Kat held a cup to his lips and poured in just a sip. Wadsworth swallowed, then swallowed again. His eyes fluttered open.

"Uncle Patrick, you're awake. Drink some more."

He took several good swallows before Kat set the cup aside. She grabbed a cushion off a chair and centered it behind Wadsworth's shoulder. "Let him down now, Seb."

Wadsworth groaned in pain as Seb eased him back.

"Uncle Patrick, this is my husband, Sebastian Jones. He's an inventor working on improvements to batteries.

He has several successful patents. He knew Jeremy—they went to Washington Institute together in St. Louis."

Wadsworth's eyes slid to Seb. "You knew Jeremy?"

"Yes. He was a fine man."

"Not cut out for the business world. I saw that, but Douglas demanded we bring him into the company."

"Douglas Wadsworth, Jeremy's father," Kat explained.

"I remember."

"And now the company is Kat's, and through marriage yours as well. I've got a good board of directors running it now, but you'll do with it as you see fit. Jeremy has an inheritance from his father, too. That's yours now, Katherine and Sebastian. It always has been yours, and it was Jeremy's. I thought I knew best. I didn't think you could handle the money. Jeremy would have given it to the church. And you seemed mad with grief, Katherine. I should have listened to you, but instead I had you locked away. I'm sorry. Please forgive me. I've been a man to take charge all my life, and I managed to abuse you in the worst way with my arrogant belief I knew everything."

"Uncle Patrick, are you a man of faith? Your wounds are very serious. We'll get you to a doctor as soon as we're back in Independence, but you need to think about your soul right now. Reach out in faith if you want to spend eternity with God. Your soul may not be required of you today, but it's time to get yourself right with God."

Beth cut off her gasp of pain.

The pain earned a glance at her shoulder. She saw something really wrong, but it was hard to say what. Swelling possibly, but a whole lot of it. A shocking amount, in fact. She reached for the lump on her shoulder, and just touching it was agonizing.

The horse had brushed against her was all. Or had she been hit harder than that? She'd been knocked to the ground, but somehow she'd gotten back on her feet and started running. Had she been hit a second time before she got out of the way? In all that had happened, she hadn't thought of it again. No one had.

Jake was at her side immediately. "Sit down. Oscar and Bruce and your mama will take care of Joseph. You got kicked or maybe stomped on. I wish Kat was here. She's got a good head for medicine."

Dakota said, "Kat's not here with you?"

"No." Jake positioned himself between Beth and the rest of the room.

"Ginny's Beth's ma?"

"Yes. Now stop asking questions. I need to tend Beth."

Jake carefully unbuttoned Beth's dress, and Dakota turned away to give her privacy. Both her dresses buttoned in the front to make feeding her babies easier. As Jake pulled it aside, her right arm slipped free of her loose chemise, though twisting to get her arm out sent a red-hot jolt of pain through her right shoulder. She let out a second louder gasp that she couldn't control.

Jake, his jaw tight with worry, eased the sleeve off her arm. "What happened here?"

Beth clamped her mouth shut, and still a groan of pain escaped. Once Jake had her arm free, she looked at her shoulder. Her stomach turned at the misshapen lump there. Her head swam. She had to look away before she cast up her breakfast. Staring at the wall without seeing it, her vision narrowed, and she tipped sideways.

Barely aware of a shout from Jake, she found herself lying stretched out on her back on the kitchen table, her legs bent at the knees and dangling off the small surface.

"Bruce or Oscar, one of you. Have you ever seen anything like Beth's shoulder before?"

"It's dislocated." Dakota studied her shoulder. "I helped reset a shoulder once. I think I can fix it."

Beth didn't think he sounded overly confident.

"Let me over there, Jake. You come to this side of the table."

"Dislocated? Do you mean it's broken?"

"Stop asking questions and switch sides with me." Dakota had gone into full wagon-master mode, and Jake obeyed him.

Beth's vision narrowed more, and she decided fainting was, under the circumstances, the best possible idea.

~

Uncle Patrick let Kat pray with him. The train continued its slow backward crawl toward Independence.

A brakeman came into their car. "What's going on here?" The man looked down at the bleeding patient and gasped. "Mr. Wadsworth! What happened?"

Kat thought the man was late to the crisis. "Get ready to jump off the train the moment it stops. Patrick Wadsworth needs to get to a hospital, the best one in Independence. Or the best doctor. I know very little about this town."

"I know it. I'll handle this." Seb left Kat to tend Uncle Patrick while he barked out orders to the brakeman. He'd just finished when the train pulled to a stop with squealing brakes and a blast of steam, the whistle blowing over and over.

The brakeman leapt off the car the instant it stopped and ran, shouting for a wagon to carry a wounded man.

Then Huey Jessup was back, running along the cars and coming in through the back of the private car with the engineer and the stoker at his heels.

"Be gentle with him." Kat stepped back.

"We'll get him out and transported." Seb continued to take charge. "I'll send him on his way, then get a sheriff here to pick up those men who kidnapped you."

"I'm going with my uncle to the hospital. You handle arresting Rutledge, Horecroft, Sykes, and whoever that other thug was." Kat followed closely, urging caution as all four men carried Patrick off the train. The brakeman had returned with an empty freight wagon by the time they'd gotten Uncle Patrick off the train.

Kat jumped into the wagon with her uncle, and Seb climbed in beside her.

"I'll handle the arrests, Seb," Huey shouted. "I'll find you at the hospital once things are settled here. I'll send the law there to talk to you."

"I'm just back from hauling three other men to the hospital," the wagon driver said. He slapped the reins on his team's broad backs and headed away.

No doubt Seb's lawyers and his friend Marcus.

Kat knelt beside her uncle, who'd prayed a salvation prayer with her just moments ago. She saw that he'd since passed out and was barely breathing. She looked up at Seb. "I don't think we'll get him to the hospital alive."

Seb's mouth twisted as he studied the man between them. "He fell under the gun of the madman who was after me."

"And the madman who was after me to find out information about Beth and Ginny."

"Do what you can for him. I'll pray." Seb rested both hands on Uncle Patrick's arm and bowed his head.

Kat checked the bandage. It was already tight but soaked with blood. She didn't know what else she could do, so she joined her husband in prayer for this man she'd never really known.

When the freight wagon reached the hospital, the driver leapt off the high seat and ran inside the small building, shouting for help. Two men carrying a stretcher came tearing outside, and with Seb's help they got Wadsworth into the hospital. He was still breathing.

A young doctor, whose white coat was already covered in blood, waved them into a back room. "You two wait out here. It's crowded in back."

Seb stopped.

Kat turned to look at him. "Huey is sending the law. Patrick Wadsworth is probably going to die. Thaddeus Rutledge is probably going to buy his way out of jail, then go right back to trying to grab me and force me to tell him where Ginny is hiding."

Soberly, Seb said, "And Marcus Coleman is probably going to jail if his family money doesn't get him out of it. Although he did shoot someone today."

"That ought to be enough," Kat said. Then she shook her head and added, "And yet why am I skeptical?"

"He seemed furiously mad today, and those things he

said about our patents, he cooked all that up in his head." Seb grunted. "He might just get off for reasons of insanity."

"Maybe Horecroft could recommend an asylum for men."

"Inventing is a more dangerous way to make a living than I'd ever realized. Maybe I should start helping you hunt."

"I had a man grab me and hold a gun to my head when I was hunting."

Seb shrugged. "Gather eggs?"

"I can teach you to cook. You might find yeast helping bread to rise scientific."

"Sounds safe at least."

"I may end up rich. We could hire armed guards to surround our homestead cabin."

"We'd have to build them their own cabin, but sure, we could do that." Seb reached out a hand to Kat and pulled her close, then closer. "I need to get my priorities straight because I forget what's most important when I step into my laboratory."

"What you're trying to do is important. You've already changed the world, and I'm proud of you for it."

"Yes, it's important, but it can't be first in my life. God is first. And you, Kat, you're second." He pulled her into his arms. There they stood, exhausted, frightened, bloody, and still in the midst of a cyclone. He hugged her tight. "I love you, Kathleen Pendergast Wadsworth Jones. I love you, and I'm going to make sure you know every day that you're more important than my work."

"I love you too, Sebastian Jones." Kat rested her head against his shoulder. As she let him bear her weight for a lovely moment, she wondered if she could fully trust him.

She didn't ask because the doctor came charging out and said to her, "I heard you've got doctoring skills. I need help. I've got four men who've been shot back there."

The sheriff of Independence came rushing in from outside, heading straight toward Seb. "I've got a mighty powerful rich man demanding I arrest you and take your wife into custody. You both need to answer some questions. I can't keep a man like Thaddeus Rutledge behind bars without a real good reason."

Seb said, "Let's talk about this outside. My wife will talk to you just as soon as she's done saving four men's lives." He looked at Kat, who rolled her eyes and followed the doctor into the back room.

25

Agonizing pain snapped Beth into full wakefulness before she could settle into a good solid faint.

Dakota examined her shoulder.

Jake looked like he wanted to kill his old friend.

"Appears the shoulder joint's been reseated." Dakota leaned over to get her to look right at him. "It's not broken, Beth, but it's still gonna hurt for a while. You'll need to wear a sling until it's healed up."

Mama came and looked at the shoulder a few seconds longer, then gave Jake a firm nod. "It's a nasty injury, but it looks like it's been well treated. Jake, you take care of her."

Jake leaned down and gave Ginny a kiss on the cheek. "Thanks, Mama."

Ginny gave him a weak smile, then got busy. She found another basin, divided the water between the two pans, and wrung out a rag. She turned to tend Joseph.

Oscar and Bruce, with Mama helping, crowded around Joseph. The door creaked open, and Donal O'Toole stood there looking worried. Little Conor and Bridget were beside him.

"Is there anything we can do?" Donal asked.

Beth glanced at them and shook her head. "Go see if your ma and Maeve need a hand with the babies. And there's a meaty bone simmering on the stove. Maybe Fiona could turn it into a stew."

"Keep an eye out for Yvette," Oscar said without looking away from Joseph. "But for heaven's sake, don't touch her. And don't let her get near any knives."

That sounded like plenty for Donal to do.

"Yvette ran off. I saw her run deeper into the canyon," Conor said.

"Yvette?" Bruce pulled off one of Joseph's boots. "That woman who almost killed Rutledge last year, who's now almost killed Joseph?"

"His leg is cut up," Oscar said. "Tend to it, Bruce, while I see to the cuts on his head."

"It don't look broken." Bruce frowned as he worked over Joseph. "Sorry we spooked that herd, Oscar. I knew we were close to the canyon, but I'm not sure I'd've found it. It don't look at all like I remember."

Mama washed the blood off Joseph's face, humming a single note. "It's his head that worries me."

"Did she stab him like she stabbed Rutledge?"

"He's so battered, it's hard to say." Oscar worked over his brother. "I'm afraid he may have a broken arm—it doesn't look straight. And there are bruises on his chest. He could have broken ribs or even a rib so badly shattered it might pierce his lungs or his heart."

"Does anyone know how to set a broken bone?" Beth waited, but only dead silence greeted her question.

"I'm going for the doctor," Bruce said.

Mama gasped and looked up from where she bathed Joseph's face. The fear in her eyes was terrible to behold.

"If we can't set a bone, then we need help," he said.

"Dakota, have you set broken bones?" Oscar had a frantic expression on his usually calm face.

Grimly, Dakota shook his head.

"If there's no one here to handle this"—he looked at Mama—"I could take him to the doctor. We don't want anyone knowing we're in here."

"Moving him might kill him." Jake's jaw was set in a tight line.

"Maybe. Well, we could take him south while you run for the doctor, Jake. We could meet you on the trail."

Bruce nodded. "How about we take him to the O'Tooles? If we're moving slow and Jake rides to Alton and back like the wind, it might be better than just waiting here, making Joseph wait so long."

Beth saw the concern on everyone's faces. No one wanted to make the decision before them, so she did it. "Go, Jake. We'll take the O'Tooles along as guides to find their house. Go. Quickly."

"I'll go." Dakota strode toward the door. "I've got a fast horse. You build a sledge, Jake, and bring Joseph to the O'Tooles."

Jake jerked his chin in agreement.

"Dakota!"

Bruce's shout had Dakota skidding to a stop. "What?"

"I heard the doctor there's a drunk, but as long as he don't start to sober up, he does okay. Get him even if he's sow-drunk, even if you have to hog-tie him and throw him over his horse. Bring with you a bottle of whiskey."

Dakota looked at Jake and said, "You handle the sledge, then get Beth's arm in a sling and get her settled in bed somewhere." He then ran from the room on his way to Alton.

Beth was glad to see him go, even though he did his rough medicine rather well. "Help me pull my dress back on my good arm, then get a sling fashioned. I can get back to my cabin while you help Mama and Oscar with Joseph. I'm not worth much right now."

Beth heard hooves thundering away and knew Dakota would make the ride as fast as he could.

Jake slid the dress up so gently, Beth felt tears burn her eyes. She whispered, "You really are a fine husband."

He kissed her gently on the forehead, then took the towel Dakota had draped over her when her dress had to be pulled down and got a sling arranged.

"Oscar, Ginny, I'll help Beth to the cabin. I'll be back to help with Joseph."

Bruce left to help Donal work on the sledge.

Mama came and looked over Beth, touched the sling as if to adjust it slightly. "You're going to be all right, Beth. I'll stay here and tend you while Oscar and Bruce and Jake and Donal—oh, who knows who all?—take Joseph to the O'Tooles." Mama took a solid hold of Beth's good hand. Tears flooded her eyes. "Then you and I are going to have a serious talk about what I need to do to fight my husband. We've come to a beautiful place, but I'm not going to live out the rest of my life like a gopher afraid to pop my head above ground anymore."

"Ginny, no." Oscar left his brother's side for the first time. "You know what he's like. You know we can't trust him. A judge can be bought. A jury too."

"Then we'll just have to be careful to find a judge who can't be bought."

Bruce came to the doorway. "We're ready to move him. Donal had the travois almost done before I got out there to help. Let's get moving."

They all turned to look at Joseph, who was out cold and still as death, his face pale with the crimson of blood marking his ashen skin.

Beth wondered if moving him would kill him and had to bite down hard to keep from insisting they bring the doctor all the way here. Going out to meet him would shorten the time until he got a doctor's attention, so it might balance out the danger of the move.

"We'll all talk about my troubles later." Mama stepped aside as Jake, Bruce, Donal, and Oscar, with aching gentleness, lifted Joseph and carried him out to take him on the long trip to get help.

Jake looked hard at Beth. "You stay right here. I'll be back once we get Joseph settled."

Since Beth was afraid she'd collapse if she sat up, she didn't even consider disobeying him. Mama stood at her side, tears flowing down her face, taking all the blame for the danger on her own shoulders.

Jake returned then and lifted Beth into his arms. He carried her to the house. "I'm going along to take Joseph to the O'Tooles. Fiona, Maeve, and the youngsters are staying here with you to help tend the babies while the men are gone. Fiona is asking questions. I think it's time we took them into our confidence."

26

Kat and Seb returned to the boardinghouse to sleep that night, with plans to accompany Patrick Wadsworth's body back to Chicago.

She'd had a long day doctoring; he'd had a long day talking with the sheriff.

They'd brought Huey Jessup along and rented him his own room for the night. The sheriff said he wanted to talk to all of them again.

Thaddeus Rutledge was in jail for kidnapping, as was Dr. Horecroft. Horecroft protested that he'd never touched Kat, but the sheriff told him that standing by, following along, with full knowledge of a kidnapping and doing nothing made him part of the crime. The sheriff said he had plans to hang both of them, along with Sykes and his partner.

But Kat knew how rich and well-connected Thaddeus Rutledge was. She believed he'd find a way to go free.

Marcus Coleman was in a jail cell along with everyone

else. His family had been informed, and they were sending the top lawyer in St. Louis to straighten things out.

"Marcus ranted and raved to the sheriff," said Seb, "about how I'd promised him a partnership in my inventions. The sheriff saw the way he was acting. I expect when his family comes for him, they'll make promises about getting him help, and the sheriff will let him go." Seb frowned. "I don't believe Thaddeus Rutledge will end up in jail. Their story about getting you out of the line of gunfire is weak, but Rutledge has a lawyer coming in from Chicago, and I expect a lot of money will change hands. The man will go free, and Dr. Horecroft along with him most likely."

"At least he has a broken arm." Kat had refused to help set it. That should slow him down some.

They hadn't told Aunt Vivian about their day. Maybe they would over supper in an hour.

Kat looked down at her bloodstained dress. "I need to wash up and change clothes before Aunt Vivian gets a look at me."

Seb went to the pitcher on the dressing table and poured water into a basin. "I'll get you a new dress. I'm afraid that one is finished."

The pretty green calico they'd bought together in Omaha. Ruined. With both hands, she gripped the collar and ripped the dress apart. Half out of her wits, she tore at the dress and tore and tore until it was in shreds on the floor by her feet. Then she saw her chemise, bloodstained like her dress. As she reached for the neckline, Seb came and gathered her into his arms.

She broke down and sobbed.

"I'm sorry about today," Seb murmured as she buried her face against his chest and wept. "It was Marcus who brought all this down on us. It was my past that drove me out west, that caught up with us so soon after we emerged and brought us to the gunfight. I'm sorry about it all."

He held her, his heart aching as she wept, as any reasonable person would do after being shot at, kidnapped, and watching her uncle die just as she found he wasn't quite the awful man she'd always thought. She'd spent the entire afternoon surrounded by wounds and blood and pain, focusing first on her uncle, then both of Seb's lawyers. Even Rutledge needing a cast had kept the doctors busy, leaving more for her to do. Huey needed stitches, as did Sykes. Dr. Horecroft looked bruised, but no one bothered much with him. Sykes's partner had been knocked out cold, although he'd eventually regained consciousness and shuffled out with Sykes in the sheriff's shackles.

A deputy had come back to fetch Rutledge and Horecroft, both men highly indignant.

She cried for all of that, and he held her. Finally, the tears ebbed and changed to sniffles. Seb dragged a handkerchief out of his pocket and pressed it into her hand.

When she finally wiped her eyes and blew her nose, she looked up at him. Her eyes were awash in exhaustion and worries.

"Maybe tomorrow on our train ride to Chicago with your uncle Patrick's remains, we can discuss the fact that you're now one of the wealthiest women in Chicago."

"There's nothing to discuss, Seb. I'm going to sell everything, turn it into gold, and donate a chunk of it to every church in Chicago and Cheyenne. Then we're moving back into our homestead cabin."

"Can we save a few dollars of it so I can buy chemicals?"

Kat nodded. "We probably don't need Patrick's money for that, but you can keep as much money as you want."

"I'll sell my house and warehouse here, and we can stop at churches along the way to Cheyenne and drop a nice chunk of the money in their offering boxes. I like that idea. And you're right—I'll probably be able to pay for the chemicals with my own money."

"I'd like to buy some chickens and a milk cow in Omaha. They're hard to come by in Cheyenne no matter the price."

"Sounds like our whole life is nicely planned. When we get to Cheyenne, let's ride on past to Idaho and get that package back we mailed to the O'Tooles and see about visiting Hidden Canyon."

Kat reached out and snagged Seb's wrist, shaking her head almost violently. "What if we get snowed in for another winter?"

She felt him shudder at the very idea.

"Can we get changed for supper now?" Seb leaned forward and kissed her on her very shiny nose. Then she looked down on the rags she'd made of her dress. "Without destroying the rest of our clothes?" Then he shrugged one shoulder. "Unless it makes you feel better. In which case . . ." He stepped well back as if to give her plenty of room to do her shredding.

Kat gave a weak smile, then changed into a new chemise and dress in a completely civilized manner.

27

Joseph survived, but he didn't return home with Jake and Oscar and Dakota. Instead, he stayed at the O'Tooles' place and might well be there all winter. The doctor declared that he had a broken arm and possibly a fractured skull. Definitely some broken ribs, as he fought for most every breath he took.

All in all, he was definitely too fragile to move. Beth's arm and shoulder healed slowly. Jake had talked to the doctor about her but hadn't brought him back to Hidden Canyon. The doctor advised having her move it as usual despite the pain to promote a full healing. She was improving daily.

Dakota asked if he could live in the cave house for the winter and gentle the herd of mustangs. Oscar agreed and let him have Seb's room.

No one had seen Yvette, and no one had gone looking. She hadn't come back to take her meals on her boulder. But it was getting colder, and she might have wanted to give that up anyway. Beth, on Mama's orders, had left a few things in her cave, including warmer clothes, yet no one had seen her, and no one checked to see if she was staying there.

They didn't know how she'd taken Joseph's injuries, but she was definitely avoiding them, and Joseph, who'd connected most closely to her, wasn't there to try to renew the connection.

Over the days of tumult following the stampede, Beth noticed Mama was particularly quiet and contemplative. She guessed what was on her mind.

They'd told the O'Tooles everything and asked them to keep it a secret, and before they returned to their homestead, Mama announced she was going to fight Father so they didn't have to hide in the canyon for the rest of their lives. If they did stay, it would be their choice, not a necessity.

"I don't even know the law. Beth, you've tried to talk to me about it, but I've always been too afraid to listen. No more. What have you learned?"

"Well, a woman named Elizabeth Packard was locked in an asylum and only released after years of confinement. When she got out, her husband locked her in a room in his house and had plans to move her to another asylum. She dropped a note out a small window to a passerby. The note was delivered to a friend, who got a judge to demand that Mrs. Packard appear before him. It ended up in a trial to prove her sanity, and the jury found in her favor. Since then she's traveled the country fighting for changes in the laws. Last I heard, she's helped five states update their laws, making it illegal for a husband to simply declare his wife insane and have her locked up. A woman must be given a chance to prove her sanity."

"Insane until proven sane?" Oscar scowled. "Sounds too much like guilty until proven innocent."

"That's what it sounds like to me, too. I know it's a risk, but if one woman can stand up for herself like that, then I can."

Beth said, "Elizabeth Packard, who spent years in an insane asylum, changed the world, Mama. Working alone, she made it safer for women like you. It might be hard and possibly dangerous, although I can't imagine any reasonable jury in the world finding you insane. You can do it."

"Joseph was badly harmed, and a lot of that is because we are so far from help out here. Even when Dakota went for a doctor, I was too afraid to let the doctor come here, so we moved Joseph and possibly did more harm to him because of my situation. I can do it. I can, and I will." Mama would have sounded much more convincing if she wasn't trembling when she spoke. But fearful or not, Mama was determined to face her husband and defy his cruel efforts to declare her insane.

Mama nodded and said, "Come spring, or whenever this canyon thaws open, I am leaving Hidden Canyon to find a lawyer to discuss how to handle my case. We will go to court and slap my husband down hard for what he did to me. And what he continues to do by chasing after me."

Oscar was planning to accompany her so he could steal her away again in the event she lost her case. They wouldn't risk Rutledge getting his hands on her.

The days passed, and they settled into what might be their last winter in Hidden Canyon. It was a shame because it really was a beautiful place.

They spent the winter with a more reckless kind of

man. Dakota was a different man, more on edge than on the wagon train. Of course, she'd mostly been paying attention to Jake.

Dakota was determined to capture and tame the herd of mustangs. Considering how far they were from a doctor, Beth thought it was a poor excuse for an idea. But Dakota wouldn't be deterred and spent time each day busting broncs.

It made the winter livelier with him around.

Oscar found Yvette living back in the cave where she'd spent last winter. This winter she had a straw tick for a mattress, changes of clothes, and plenty of blankets. Mama took Yvette her meals once a day, but Yvette hid until Mama, with Oscar always at hand, set down the fresh plate of food, took plates from the day before, and left. Whatever progress she'd made in calming her mind seemed to have been lost.

Beth watched it all as the canyon was closed in by snow. Dakota survived being thrown over and over by the mustangs, and Yvette skulked around the edges of their lives.

And her babies grew into toddlers.

She loved her life in the canyon and feared what would happen when Mama emerged in the spring to fight for her right to walk around free.

Kat endured the most elaborate funeral a man ever had. It was a parade, for heaven's sake. A glass caisson drawn by four black horses with black feathers in their manes and shining brass livery, with a marching band playing mournful tunes.

The next day she called a meeting of the board of directors for her uncle's business and announced it was for sale.

She walked out of the meeting with a fortune because the board had bought her out. In fact, they'd done it eagerly and with much excitement, almost like they were glad Uncle Patrick was dead and a weak-minded woman had inherited everything.

Her uncle had owned property besides his company: a mansion, carriages, horses, fine clothing, gold watches and cuff links, and much more. Kat also discovered a generous trust fund due to Jeremy's widow. It made her angry to think how they'd watched their pennies, how she'd gone back to work at her pa's side to make ends meet, and they'd been denied the chance to buy a home because they couldn't afford it, all when there'd been so much money available.

She and Seb left for Cheyenne bearing trunks full of gold, afraid with every step that they'd be robbed, even though they'd left thousands behind in every church offering box they could find in Chicago.

The train crossing Iowa was a chance to donate generously, followed by churches in Omaha that received their gold, and on across the state of Nebraska—leaving money in every town as they traveled on toward Cheyenne and home. Seb had also ordered a huge number of supplies to do his experiments. And animals for the farm to be shipped west.

Despite using a very generous hand, they arrived in Cheyenne and donated to every church there and still had a fortune. Very odd how hard it was to give away so much money.

Between the funeral and Kat's business dealings, it was late enough in the year that they decided to postpone their trip to Idaho. They wrote to the O'Tooles and asked them to mail Seb's packet back, which was waiting for them in Cheyenne along with the supplies Seb had ordered. And a few things for the farm. Two milk cows. A flock of chickens. A small herd of pigs. A pair of hound dogs. A cat. A cookstove. Honestly, they'd gotten whatever they could think of, but they really didn't need much, and their brush with greed back east had given them even less interest in wealth.

Seb had directed his lawyers to sell his house and laboratory in Independence. He'd invited Mrs. Gundersen to move to Cheyenne and live near them, but she'd declined.

They had wired ahead, and Mr. Walther had built them a chicken coop, a pigsty, a bigger barn, and corrals large enough for their cows and for the horses they'd left behind being boarded in Cheyenne.

Mr. Walther was done and gone from their property by the time they arrived.

They'd also ordered a plow, which they couldn't use for a while because winter was closing in.

With everything done and in place, finally they were home. Kat fully expected, once they were home, Seb would disappear into his laboratory, and she'd again need to face a lonely life.

This time she was determined to get more involved in the church in Cheyenne and any other groups she found interesting. She'd no longer suffer loneliness because of her lunkhead of a husband.

Seb moved all his supplies into the laboratory while

Kat got the chickens and pigs and cows and dogs and cat settled. She was surprised to find him in the house when she was done with working in the barn.

"Why aren't you working?" she asked.

Seb came to her and drew her into his arms. "I'm not working because, from this day forward, I promise you most sincerely that you're never going to regret marrying me."

Kat let herself be held for long moments. Then she said quietly against his chest, "I love you, Sebastian Jones, and I will never regret marrying you."

He pulled away, but just a few inches, and held on to her. "I've told you I love you. Just as you've told me. But my love is going to be more than words. After all that we've been through. After seeing how smart you are and how much better our lives are when we work together . . . things are going to be different around here."

Kat narrowed her eyes. "Does that mean you're going to make me help you in the laboratory?"

Seb chuckled, then laughed out loud and kissed her soundly. "No, that is not what I mean. I'm not doing my experiments until the chores are done around here. I'm going to pay attention to life outside the laboratory. What I'm working on is fascinating, though, and I think it'll make the world a better place. But seeing how excited Marcus became over inventions because he wanted the attention and fame made me realize I harbored some of the same things inside me that he did."

"But you would never steal another man's work to make yourself famous," Kat said.

"No, I would not. And I wouldn't hire someone to shoot

a man, nor do it myself. Even so, I had that same sinful wish to be important in the world, to make a name for myself. The Good Book says, 'For what shall it profit a man, if he shall gain the whole world, and lose his own soul?'"

"Your work wouldn't cost you your soul, Seb."

"I believe my faith is solid, but my work could cost me my wife's happiness. It could cost me a place of service in church and the chance to be a good neighbor and a good friend. Those are real losses, and they make me a poor Christian and a poor husband. I don't want that to be my legacy." He pulled her close and kissed her. "Now, it's time for supper, and the cookstove is in place. Oscar taught me how to do some simple cooking. I want you to sit down at the dinner table and let me take care of you. I'll fry up a steak from the beef we bought in town, and I'll serve you supper."

Kat couldn't quite believe it, but oh she wanted to.

"How about instead we make supper together and you tell me about your experiments? And then we can plot out how best to hide our gold and how to spend it wisely in a way that will further God's work here on earth."

Seb kissed her again and whispered, as if there were others around who might overhear him, "Thank you. I'm not sure I can make this meal without burning down the house."

Epilogue

Kat came back from town with a letter.

"Who's it from?" After two weeks back in Cheyenne, Seb was doing better at balancing his life. And he felt right about it. His head was clearer, his heart purer, his faith stronger. The balance even made his work go better because getting away from his chemicals and implements brought him back to his work with new ideas.

"It's from Beth. She got a letter to the O'Tooles, and they took it to town. She wants me to look into finding a lawyer for Ginny who will represent her in a trial to prove she's sane. They also want me to find a doctor who will test Ginny for sanity and testify for her in the trial."

"You can ask Mr. Etherton if he knows anyone in Idaho. You're out of danger with your uncle, and if Thaddeus Rutledge comes after you, it won't have anything to do with the law. It'd only be to force you to tell him where Ginny is. But Etherton has probably looked into the laws concerning all this by now. He might be able to recommend a doctor, too." Seb read through the letter as he spoke.

They had discussed hiring security and had even offered the job to Huey Jessup. He'd declined, deciding instead to travel to Montana to ranch with his younger brothers.

"They're hoping to come out of hiding next summer, so I've got time to figure it out."

"*We've* got time, you mean." Seb looked up and saw Kat flash her bright smile at him.

"Yes, that *is* what I meant."

"We can help Ginny to face life without fear. And maybe her courage in challenging an unfair law can change the world. That's as good as anything I'd ever invent."

Read on
for a *sneak peek* at

INTO THE SUNSET

by Mary Connealy

Book 3 of

A WESTERN LIGHT

Available in the fall of 2024

September 1873

A bullet smashed into a boulder, ricocheted off, and burned Dakota Harlan's cheek. He threw himself backward, landed hard, flipped over, and was crawling on his elbows, shoving forward on his belly as another shot fired, then fired again. He moved without thinking.

A Winchester 73. Dakota recognized the rifle because he had one of his own. He gripped his Winchester now, always keeping it close to hand, and he was relentless about that since the day he'd survived an earlier attack.

Judging by where the shooter was located, and Dakota knew this land well, he crawled farther, keeping himself low. He slithered more like, not wanting to give the shooter anything to aim at.

At last he reached a row of sheltering stones, each of them half the height of a man. These boulders hadn't found their way here by accident. He'd ringed the edge of the pasture with them. It was months of brutally hard work in the hot sun. In fact, two years of Dakota's life had been spent getting the boulders dragged around into this shelter. He had many such shelters all through his valley.

He'd analyzed the entrances to this meadow, the lookouts where a sneaking gunman might set up, the likely places—and a couple less likely—where a man might open up on him from cover. He'd hoped to never need them, but right now he was grateful for every hard hour he'd spent, every blister he'd earned.

The rifle stopped firing. That fool out there had emptied his weapon, even one that held as many bullets as the Winchester 73. He was probably reloading now. Dakota had counted the shots. Thirteen rounds, the number of bullets in a fully loaded Winchester with the longest barrel and the smallest caliber.

Dakota crawled on, angling, keeping in mind his assailant's position. He wondered if the fool would decide to move. Probably not. Most likely he thought he had Dakota pinned down. But Dakota knew exactly where the would-be killer was hiding.

His breathing slowed as he crawled, circling the meadow, closing the distance between them. He needed to leave this meadow, get to higher ground. He headed toward a fall of rocks that were perfectly placed, also there by the sweat of his brow. He'd use the rocks to conceal himself while he climbed into position.

His pulse slowed. His mind focused on something so sharp, so vivid, it was nearly painful. Dakota drew from all his years of accumulated knowledge, from his time spent on the wagon train, the miserable year homesteading, the wandering he'd done. And finally the decision to find a quiet, safe place near a good friend and start a ranch.

The rifle picked up firing again. The shots shattered rock and ricocheted all over with ugly pings, but they were one hundred feet behind him and fifty feet below.

It was a harsh reminder that he hadn't managed the quiet, and he sure as all get-out hadn't managed the safe.

For this wasn't the first killer to come calling.

Inching along with his Winchester, he made it to the rocks that would shelter him as he moved upward while that fool unloaded his gun again into the place where Dakota had vanished from.

The man must dearly love the sound of gunfire. Or maybe he loved buying bullets because he was wasting a lot of lead.

Climbing, shielded by the massive stones, Dakota went up and up until he knew he'd gotten high enough. Surely the gunman wouldn't unload his rifle again, would he? Maybe he figured he'd winged Dakota with one of his shots.

A trickle on his chin had him swiping his face with his shirtsleeve. Sure enough, his hand came away red. The sidewinder *had* grazed him! He thought of the bullet earlier that struck the boulder near him and ricocheted. Thankfully it hadn't done much damage.

A few moments later, Dakota reached the spot he was aiming for and stopped. Lying on his back, his rifle clutched in both hands across his chest, Dakota listened, waited, and then, sure as the sunrise, the shooter opened up again. He'd be focused on those same rocks, now far away from Dakota.

Dakota could have gone higher and come up behind the varmint shooting, but he wasn't about to shoot anyone in the back. Instead, he leaned forward to a perfectly located crack between two rocks, where he saw the reckless, bullet-wasting fool emptying his gun again. He'd climbed out of a decent hiding place and was now in plain sight.

Slowly, Dakota closed the space between them until he

was only about twenty feet away. He'd circled a good portion of the meadow, closed in on his assailant, and could finally get a good look at him. He didn't want this. He didn't want a life of always being on edge.

A life of fight or die.

The gunfire ceased when the rifle was empty once again. Gathering himself, Dakota sprang to his feet and leveled his rifle on the man. "Drop your gun! Get your hands in the air now."

Dakota's eyes stayed locked on the man. Something about him hit a nerve, but Dakota didn't allow himself to be distracted by whatever was buzzing around in his head.

The man lowered his rifle, taking his time with dropping it. Rage glinted in the varmint's eyes, and it seemed like more than just fury that Dakota had gotten the drop on him. The rage was personal. Yet Dakota didn't know this man with the silver-gray hair and black eyes. He had a weathered face and a strange hawklike nose. Something about him, though, niggled Dakota's memory.

The rifle clattered when it hit the stony ledge the man stood on. Dakota had him under his control now. He'd tie him up, then haul the man to the sheriff nearly a full day's ride away.

After the man let go of the rifle, his right hand swept up lightning fast. In the hand was a pistol he'd pulled from a holster under his coat.

"No!" Dakota howled, then pulled the trigger of his Winchester.

Bright red bloomed on the man's chest.

The pistol fired into the ground over and over, the gunfire echoing off the walls of Dakota's canyon.

His eyes met those black ones. "Why? You had no chance. Why would you want me dead?"

Then the eyes and the beak nose clicked in his memory. Two memories, in fact. Dakota had faced off with two men very much like this one. It could just be chance, but with a sinking stomach Dakota knew it wasn't.

The man pitched forward and fell. He'd been high up on a rocky ledge, and now he plunged forward.

With a cold feeling in his gut, Dakota noticed he hadn't fallen far from another grave. Sickened, he realized he had his own cemetery now. Or he would once this man was buried.

The smell of gunpowder faded. The breeze wafted with the scent of pine. A cow mooed down on the grasslands of his meadow. This beautiful place Dakota had found and now owned. Heavily wooded in spots, a rich piece of land full of belly-high grass. A stream nearby ran with cold water teeming with trout. Mountains stood all around, arranged in such a way that they cut the wind even in the bitter-cold Idaho winters.

It was the perfect place to make a home. But not if killers came calling.

Sighing, Dakota went over and stared down at the dead man, a grizzled old-timer. He wished he'd had a chance to reason with him.

The ice he felt in his chest was hard enough, and cold enough, he wasn't sure how his heart went on beating. The way this man had shot at him from cover was too much like the other one. And he held a strong resemblance to the man who'd attacked before.

Dakota knelt beside the man, wondering if he could

find anything to learn who he was. Who were *they*? He searched the body and came up with a letter, folded and still inside an envelope.

Slumping to the ground to sit, Dakota opened the letter and read the name Darnell. Closing his eyes, he didn't read on. Not yet.

Darnell told him enough.

The bank robber he'd run afoul of during his year of wandering was called Vic Darnell. And he'd been a dark-haired man with a hawkish nose and black eyes.

And this letter was a call to kinfolk. A blood feud. With Dakota's name in it and precious little else. Which might explain why it had taken this man so long to find him.

Of course, Dakota hadn't known where he was headed when he'd stopped Vic Darnell and a few other townsfolk from a wild killing spree when Vic had been cornered after a murderous bank robbery gone bad.

Dakota had been wandering. Who would have known to find him here? It'd taken a lot of work and some skill to track Dakota to this meadow. He hadn't even bought it yet, though he intended to. He'd found the spot, knew it was near his friend Jake, and had moved in and set up ranching.

He looked down at the letter again. Crude handwriting, full of misspelled words, from a man who barely knew how to write.

Mort,

Yer boy Vic's bin kilt by a man name'a Dakota Harlan. I'm writin t'others and coming west to put this right. No one kills my grandson, your son, and lives. See if you can pick up the scent. It hapend in Oregone, but the vermin what kilt our kin is runnin' skeered, or he had oughta be. A blood feud. I'm callin' fer it.

If'n you find him first, it's yer right to settle this on yer own. If'n you don't find him, help's a-comin'.

Pa

Dakota flipped the envelope over and saw *Ezra Darnell* scrawled in one corner and the letter addressed to Mort Darnell.

How many of these letters had been sent? How many more Darnells were out there searching for him?

He'd have to live his life on a razor's edge from now to the end of his days to survive because, judging by the two who'd come here, these weren't face-to-face kind of men. They didn't stand before you and challenge you. They were back-shooting coyotes. And that kind wasn't much on talking.

Dakota was a man of faith. He hadn't wanted a life that was surrounded by the need to kill. He had no idea how to end this feud. It seemed he was trapped in a cycle of danger and death. He had no hope he could convince one of these Darnells to reconsider the back-shooting and live a peaceable kind of life.

He went and got a shovel and, half an hour later, had a hole dug. Dakota dropped the man in the hole and buried him. He left a small heap of dirt on the grave. The other grave had nearly disappeared back to meadow grass.

By the time he was done, the day had worn down. The

sun slanted steeply in the west over the jagged tops of the mountains that guarded the west side of his ranch.

Those mountaintops reached for him like claws, sent toward Dakota by God to grab ahold of him and crush him before he could hurt anyone else.

His chest ached as he stood and let himself be cast in shadows, just as his whole life had been cast in shadows. He stood staring at the pair of graves, unmarked because it seemed blasphemous to put a cross on the graves, and unwise to risk drawing attention by posting the Darnell name on them.

He stood there alone. And because he was alone, because he would always be alone, he thought of a pretty redheaded Irish girl who might have joined her life to his at one time in the past.

Before her father had died and before Dakota had treated her wrong. Before he'd told her the unhappy truth that they had to roll on and leave her father far behind on the lonely prairie. His grave by now was as vanished from the world as these would soon be.

He'd had no choice, and yet she hadn't seen it that way.

And all the anger that so often followed death got landed straight on Dakota. His shoulders were strong enough to take it, but that didn't mean he wasn't sorry he had to do it. And that was before Dakota's life had become something he could never dare let anyone share.

She'd seen him as a heartless brute.

He wondered if maybe she was right. If Maeve O'Toole could see this crude little graveyard of his, she'd know she was right and would set her heart even more against him.

Dakota sat down hard on the ground and studied the

final resting place of the ones who'd come with intent to kill. His cold heart thawed a bit, and he felt the pain. His throat hurt. His soul ached with loneliness and the utter belief that God couldn't want Dakota to kill like this.

But he had no notion of how to stop it.

Mary Connealy writes romantic comedies about cowboys. She's the author of the Brothers in Arms, Brides of Hope Mountain, High Sierra Sweethearts, Kincaid Brides, Trouble in Texas, Wild at Heart, and Cimarron Legacy series, as well as several other acclaimed series. Mary has been nominated for a Christy Award, was a finalist for a RITA Award, and is a two-time winner of the Carol Award. She lives in eastern Nebraska with her very own romantic cowboy hero. They have four grown daughters—Joslyn, married to Matt; Wendy; Shelly, married to Aaron; and Katy, married to Max—and seven precious grandchildren. Learn more about Mary and her books at

MaryConnealy.com
facebook.com/maryconnealy
petticoatsandpistols.com